BUGHOUSE

volume 2

by Steve Lafler

Baja, February 2002. Story and art © 2002 by Steve Lafler. Edited by Chris Staros.
Published by Top Shelf Productions Inc., Brett Warnock and Chris Staros, Po Box 1282,
Marietta GA., 30061-1282. Top Shelf Productions and the Top Shelf logo are TM & ©
2000 Top Shelf Productions Inc. The stories, characters and incidents featured in this
publication are entirely fictional. No Part of this book may be reproduced without
permission, except small excerpts for purposes of review. Check out our website at
www.topshelfcomix.com. Printed in Canada.

Baja/ Steve Lafler
ISBN 1-891830-27-9
1. Music, Jazz, Music History
2. Graphic Novels
3. Cartoons

for little Max, with all my love

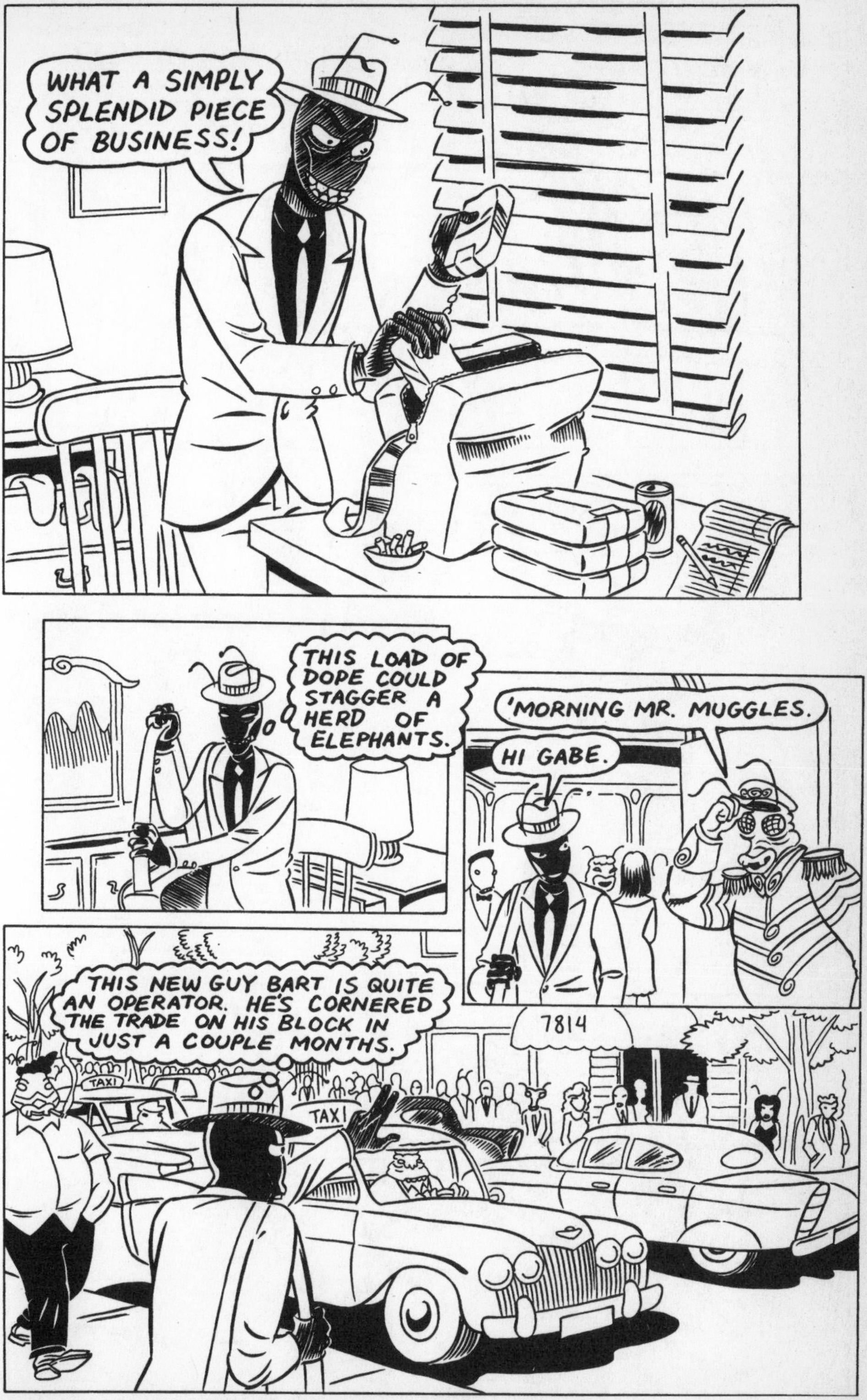
WHAT A SIMPLY SPLENDID PIECE OF BUSINESS!
THIS LOAD OF DOPE COULD STAGGER A HERD OF ELEPHANTS.
'MORNING MR. MUGGLES.
HI GABE.
THIS NEW GUY BART IS QUITE AN OPERATOR. HE'S CORNERED THE TRADE ON HIS BLOCK IN JUST A COUPLE MONTHS.
7814
TAXI
TAXI

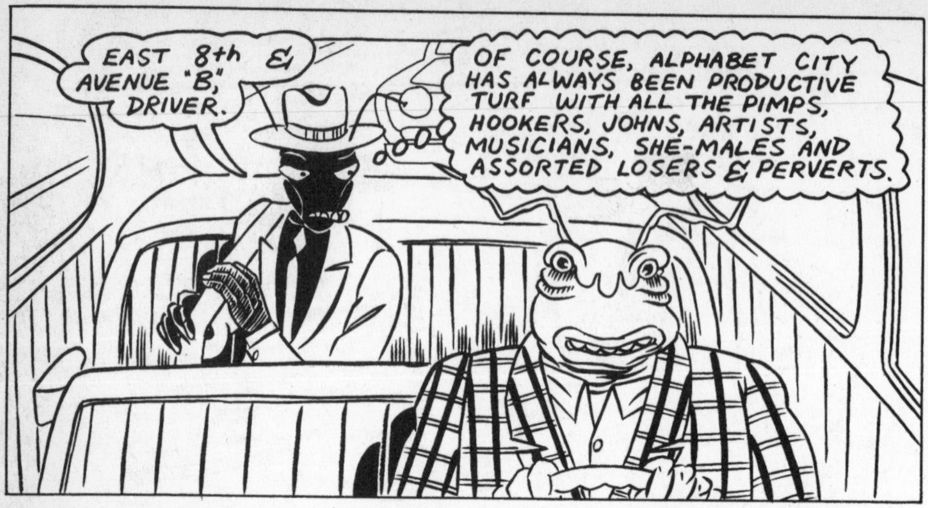
EAST 8th & AVENUE "B," DRIVER.
OF COURSE, ALPHABET CITY HAS ALWAYS BEEN PRODUCTIVE TURF WITH ALL THE PIMPS, HOOKERS, JOHNS, ARTISTS, MUSICIANS, SHE-MALES AND ASSORTED LOSERS & PERVERTS.

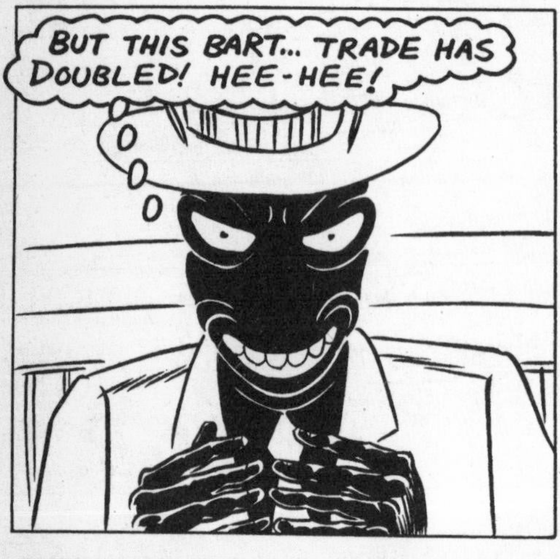
BUT THIS BART... TRADE HAS DOUBLED! HEE-HEE!

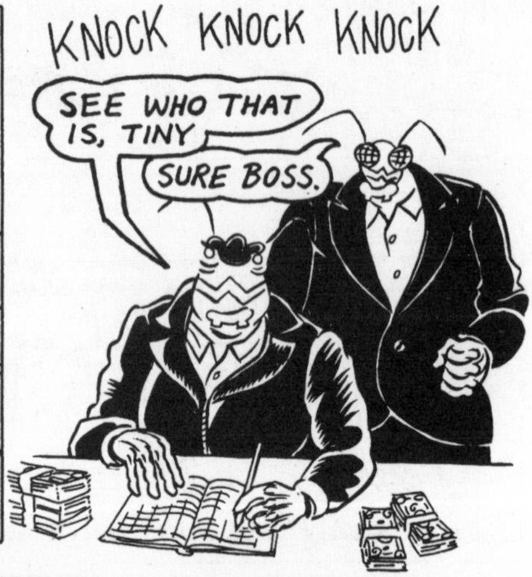
KNOCK KNOCK KNOCK
SEE WHO THAT IS, TINY
SURE BOSS.

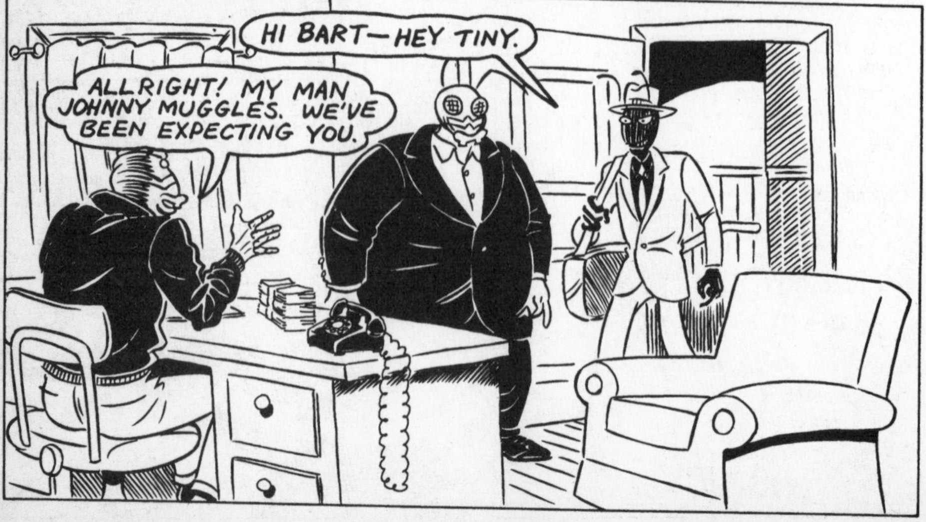
HI BART—HEY TINY.
ALLRIGHT! MY MAN JOHNNY MUGGLES. WE'VE BEEN EXPECTING YOU.

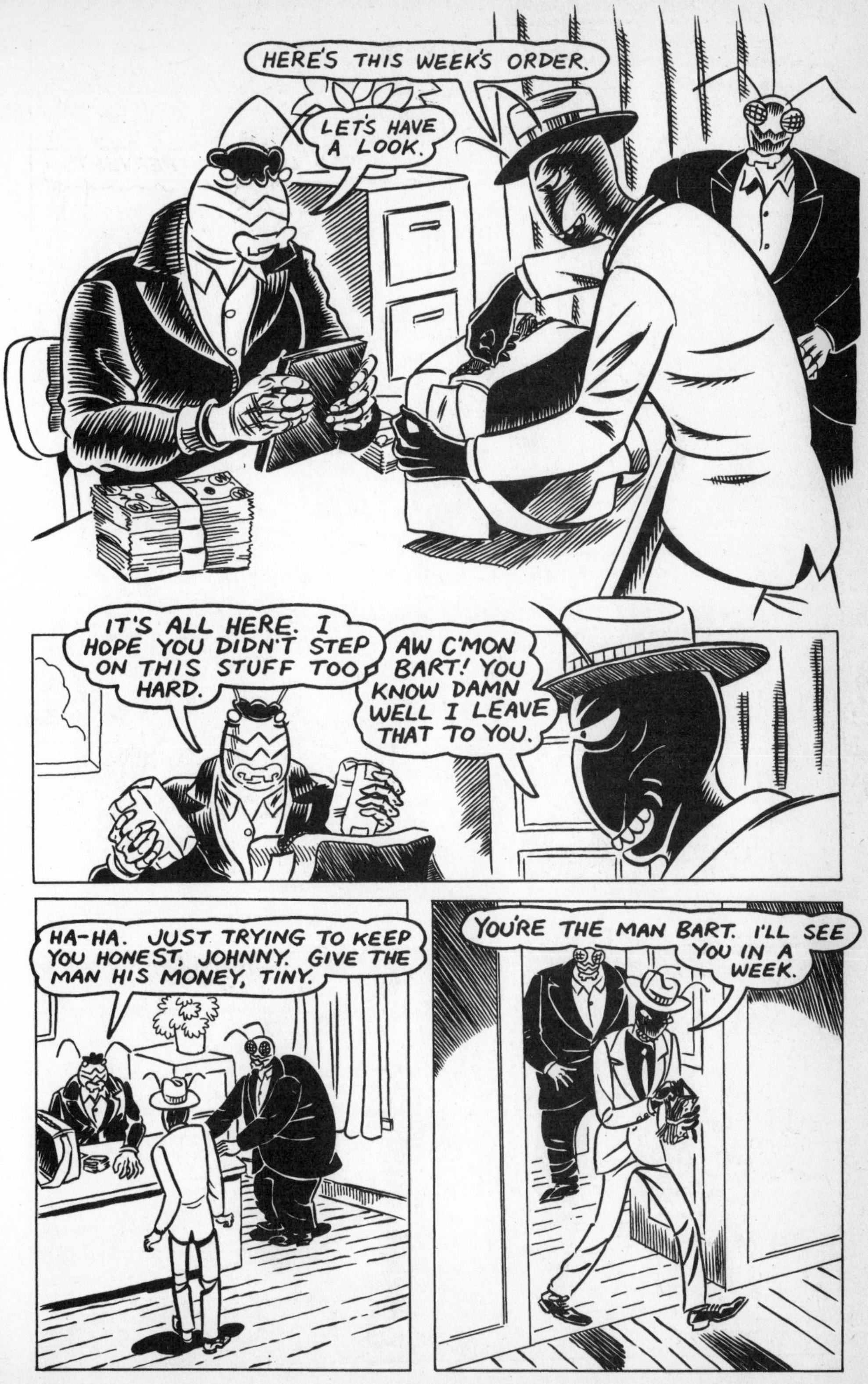
HERE'S THIS WEEK'S ORDER.
LET'S HAVE A LOOK.
IT'S ALL HERE. I HOPE YOU DIDN'T STEP ON THIS STUFF TOO HARD.
AW C'MON BART! YOU KNOW DAMN WELL I LEAVE THAT TO YOU.
HA-HA. JUST TRYING TO KEEP YOU HONEST, JOHNNY. GIVE THE MAN HIS MONEY, TINY.
YOU'RE THE MAN BART. I'LL SEE YOU IN A WEEK.

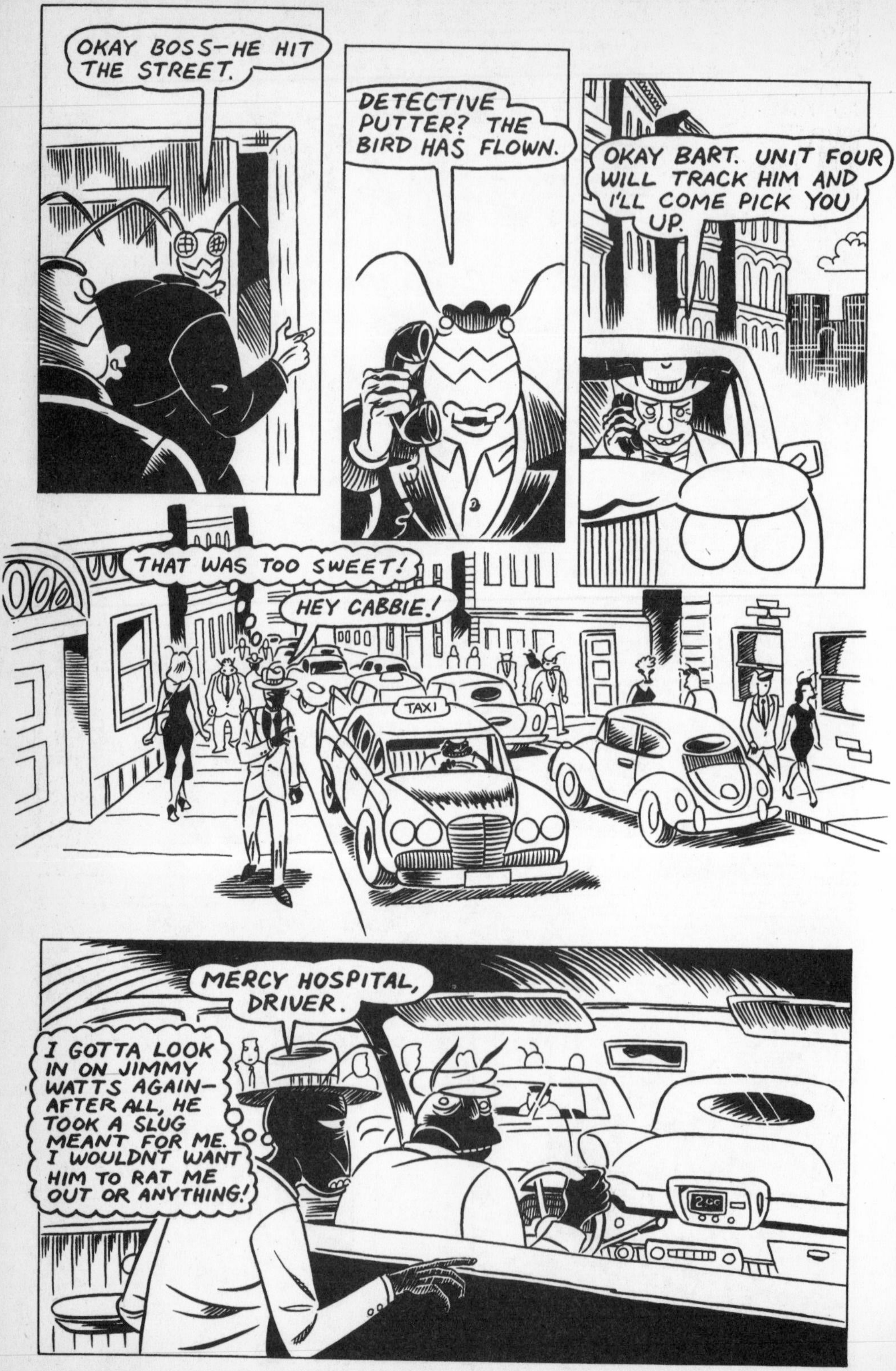
OKAY BOSS—HE HIT THE STREET.
DETECTIVE PUTTER? THE BIRD HAS FLOWN.
OKAY BART. UNIT FOUR WILL TRACK HIM AND I'LL COME PICK YOU UP.
THAT WAS TOO SWEET!
HEY CABBIE!
TAXI
MERCY HOSPITAL, DRIVER.
I GOTTA LOOK IN ON JIMMY WATTS AGAIN—AFTER ALL, HE TOOK A SLUG MEANT FOR ME. I WOULDN'T WANT HIM TO RAT ME OUT OR ANYTHING!

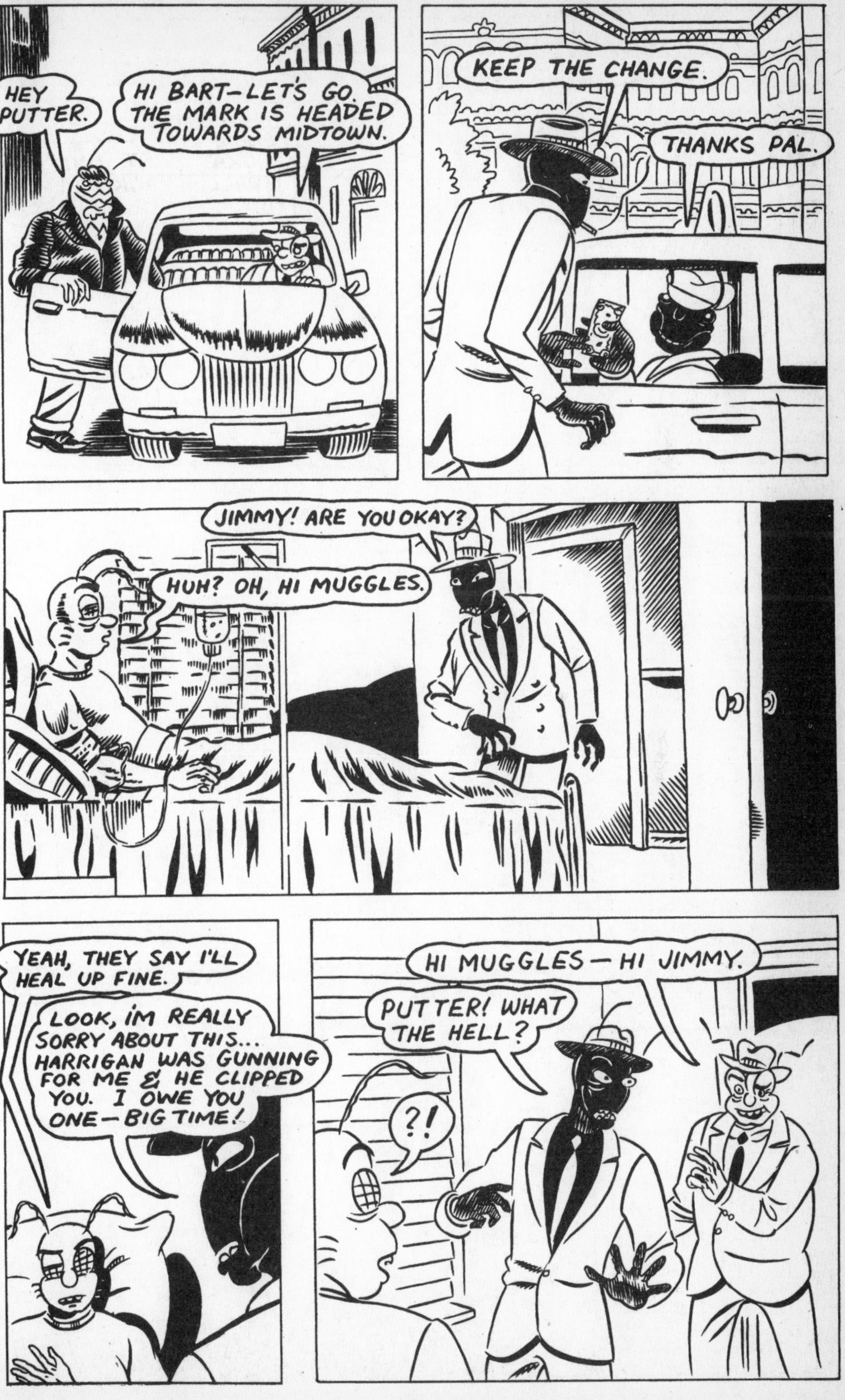
HEY PUTTER.
HI BART—LET'S GO. THE MARK IS HEADED TOWARDS MIDTOWN.
KEEP THE CHANGE.
THANKS PAL.
JIMMY! ARE YOU OKAY?
HUH? OH, HI MUGGLES.
YEAH, THEY SAY I'LL HEAL UP FINE.
LOOK, IM REALLY SORRY ABOUT THIS... HARRIGAN WAS GUNNING FOR ME & HE CLIPPED YOU. I OWE YOU ONE—BIG TIME!
HI MUGGLES—HI JIMMY.
PUTTER! WHAT THE HELL?
?!

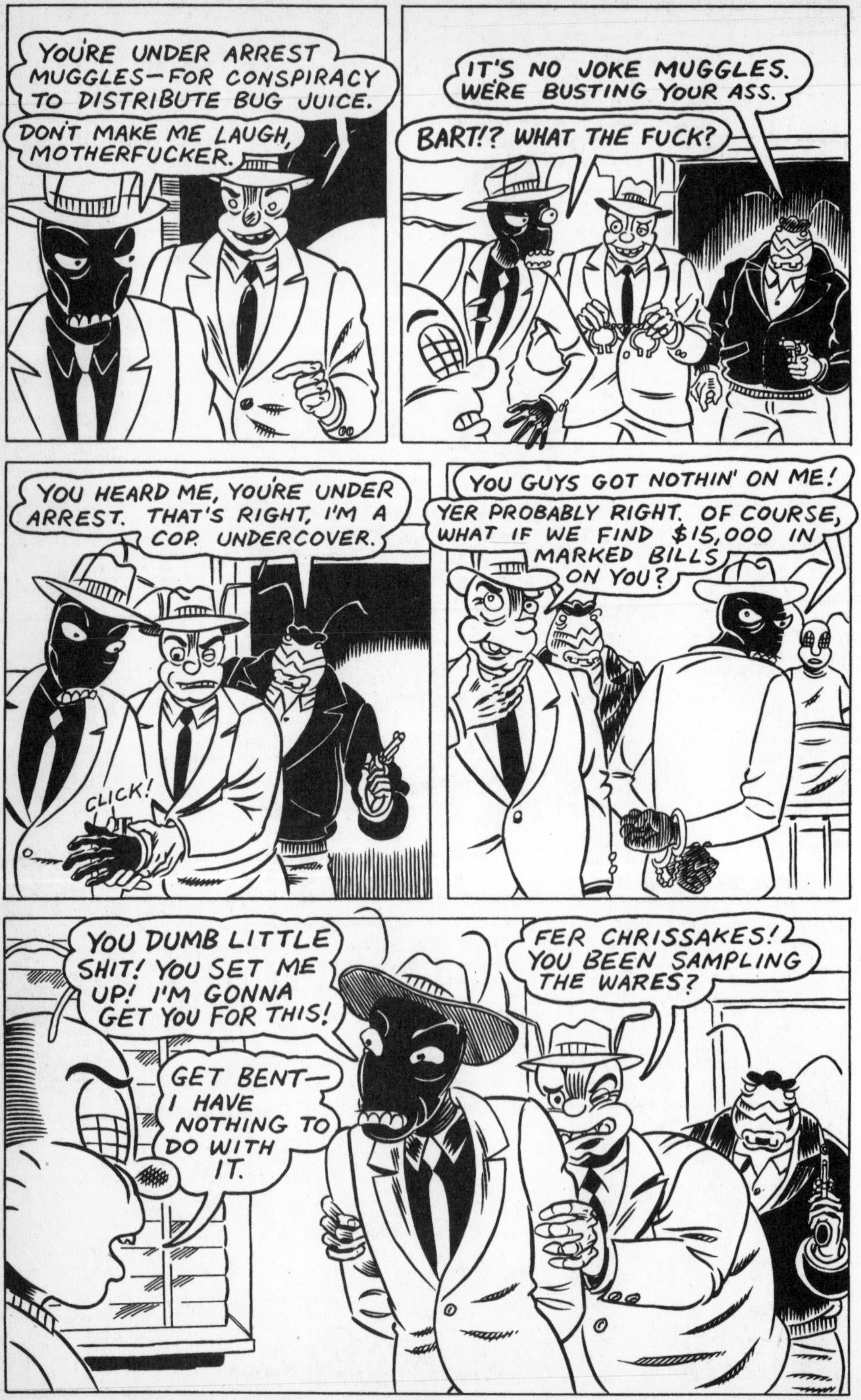
YOU'RE UNDER ARREST MUGGLES—FOR CONSPIRACY TO DISTRIBUTE BUG JUICE.
DON'T MAKE ME LAUGH, MOTHERFUCKER.
IT'S NO JOKE MUGGLES. WE'RE BUSTING YOUR ASS.
BART!? WHAT THE FUCK?
YOU HEARD ME, YOU'RE UNDER ARREST. THAT'S RIGHT, I'M A COP. UNDERCOVER.
CLICK!
YOU GUYS GOT NOTHIN' ON ME!
YER PROBABLY RIGHT. OF COURSE, WHAT IF WE FIND $15,000 IN MARKED BILLS ON YOU?
YOU DUMB LITTLE SHIT! YOU SET ME UP! I'M GONNA GET YOU FOR THIS!
GET BENT— I HAVE NOTHING TO DO WITH IT.
FER CHRISSAKES! YOU BEEN SAMPLING THE WARES?

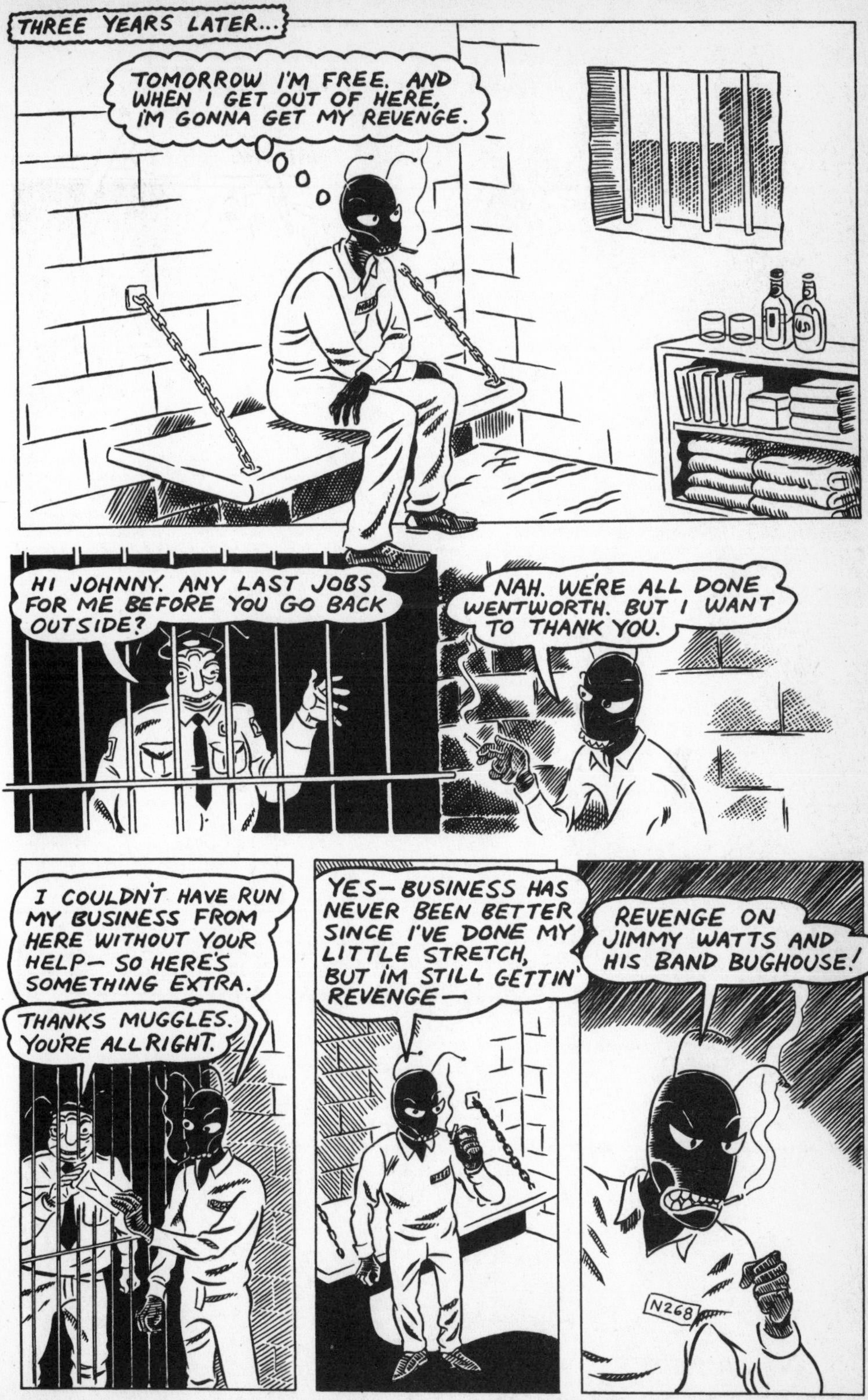
THREE YEARS LATER...
TOMORROW I'M FREE. AND WHEN I GET OUT OF HERE, I'M GONNA GET MY REVENGE.
HI JOHNNY. ANY LAST JOBS FOR ME BEFORE YOU GO BACK OUTSIDE?
NAH. WE'RE ALL DONE WENTWORTH. BUT I WANT TO THANK YOU.
I COULDN'T HAVE RUN MY BUSINESS FROM HERE WITHOUT YOUR HELP— SO HERE'S SOMETHING EXTRA.
THANKS MUGGLES. YOU'RE ALLRIGHT.
YES— BUSINESS HAS NEVER BEEN BETTER SINCE I'VE DONE MY LITTLE STRETCH, BUT I'M STILL GETTIN' REVENGE—
REVENGE ON JIMMY WATTS AND HIS BAND BUGHOUSE!
N268

Baja

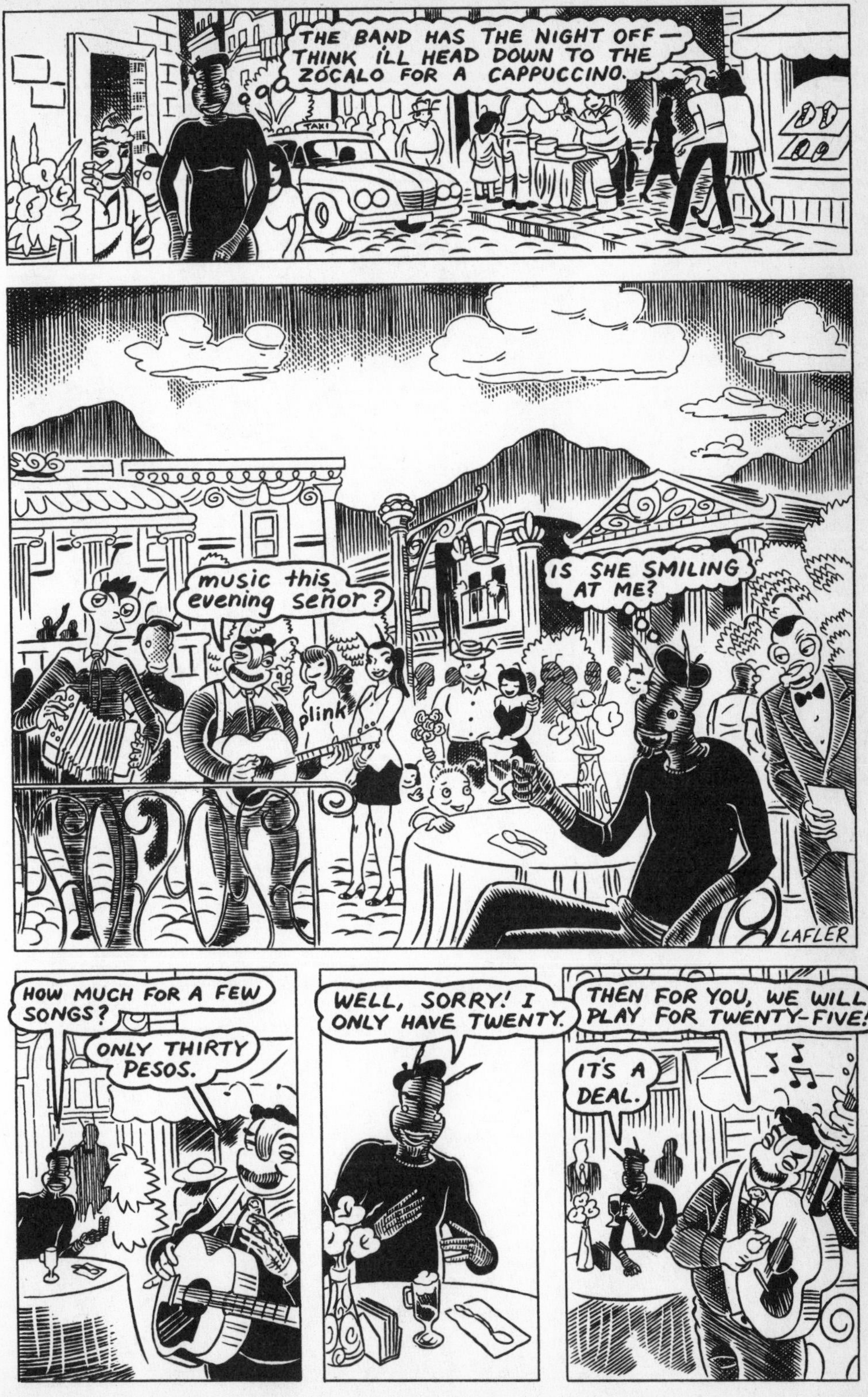
THE BAND HAS THE NIGHT OFF— THINK I'LL HEAD DOWN TO THE ZÓCALO FOR A CAPPUCCINO.
TAXI
music this evening señor?
plink
IS SHE SMILING AT ME?
LAFLER
HOW MUCH FOR A FEW SONGS?
ONLY THIRTY PESOS.
WELL, SORRY! I ONLY HAVE TWENTY.
THEN FOR YOU, WE WILL PLAY FOR TWENTY-FIVE!
IT'S A DEAL.

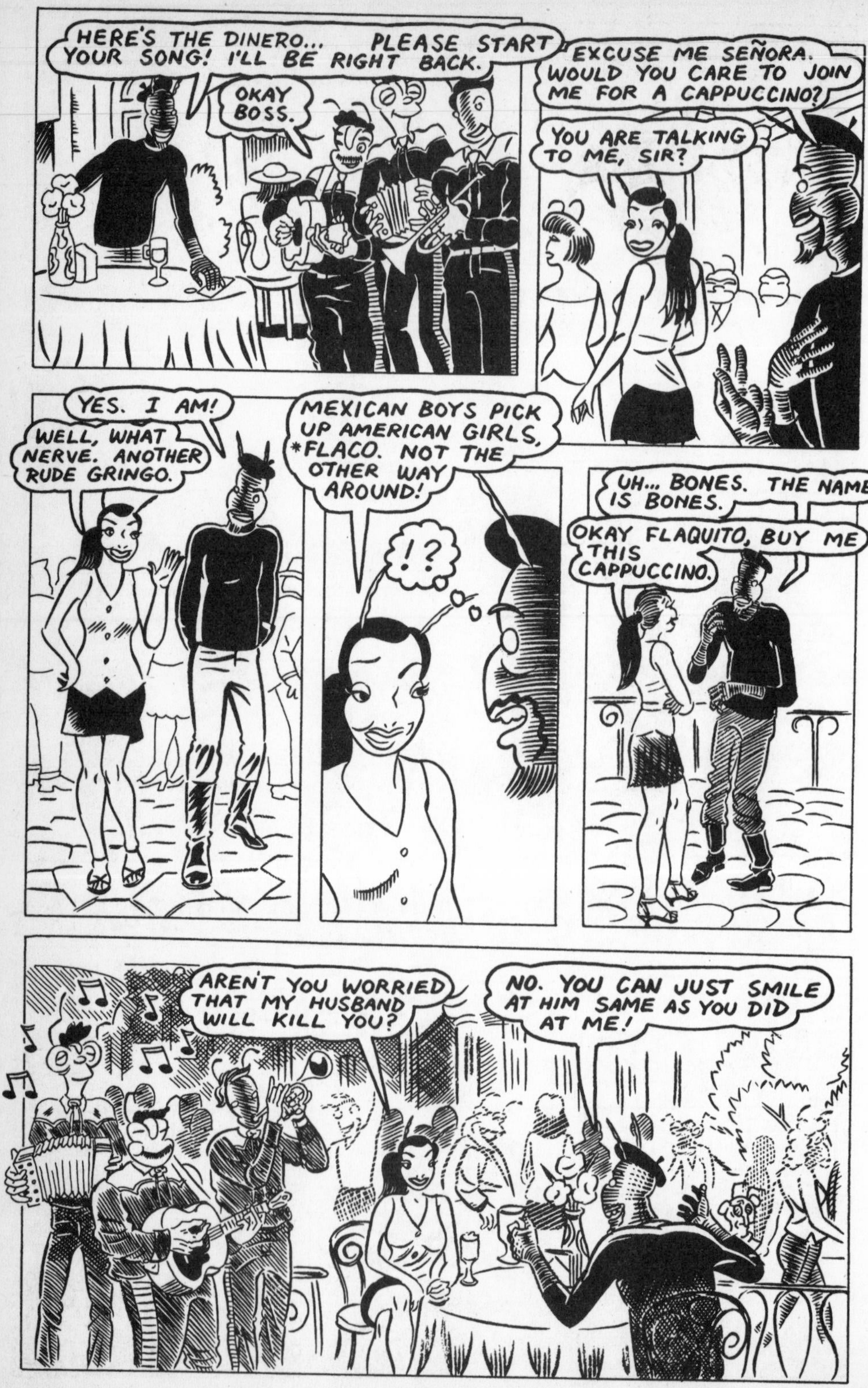
HERE'S THE DINERO... PLEASE START YOUR SONG! I'LL BE RIGHT BACK.
OKAY BOSS.
EXCUSE ME SEÑORA. WOULD YOU CARE TO JOIN ME FOR A CAPPUCCINO?
YOU ARE TALKING TO ME, SIR?
YES. I AM!
WELL, WHAT NERVE. ANOTHER RUDE GRINGO.
MEXICAN BOYS PICK UP AMERICAN GIRLS, *FLACO. NOT THE OTHER WAY AROUND!
!?
UH... BONES. THE NAME IS BONES.
OKAY FLAQUITO, BUY ME THIS CAPPUCCINO.
AREN'T YOU WORRIED THAT MY HUSBAND WILL KILL YOU?
NO. YOU CAN JUST SMILE AT HIM SAME AS YOU DID AT ME!

*SKINNY

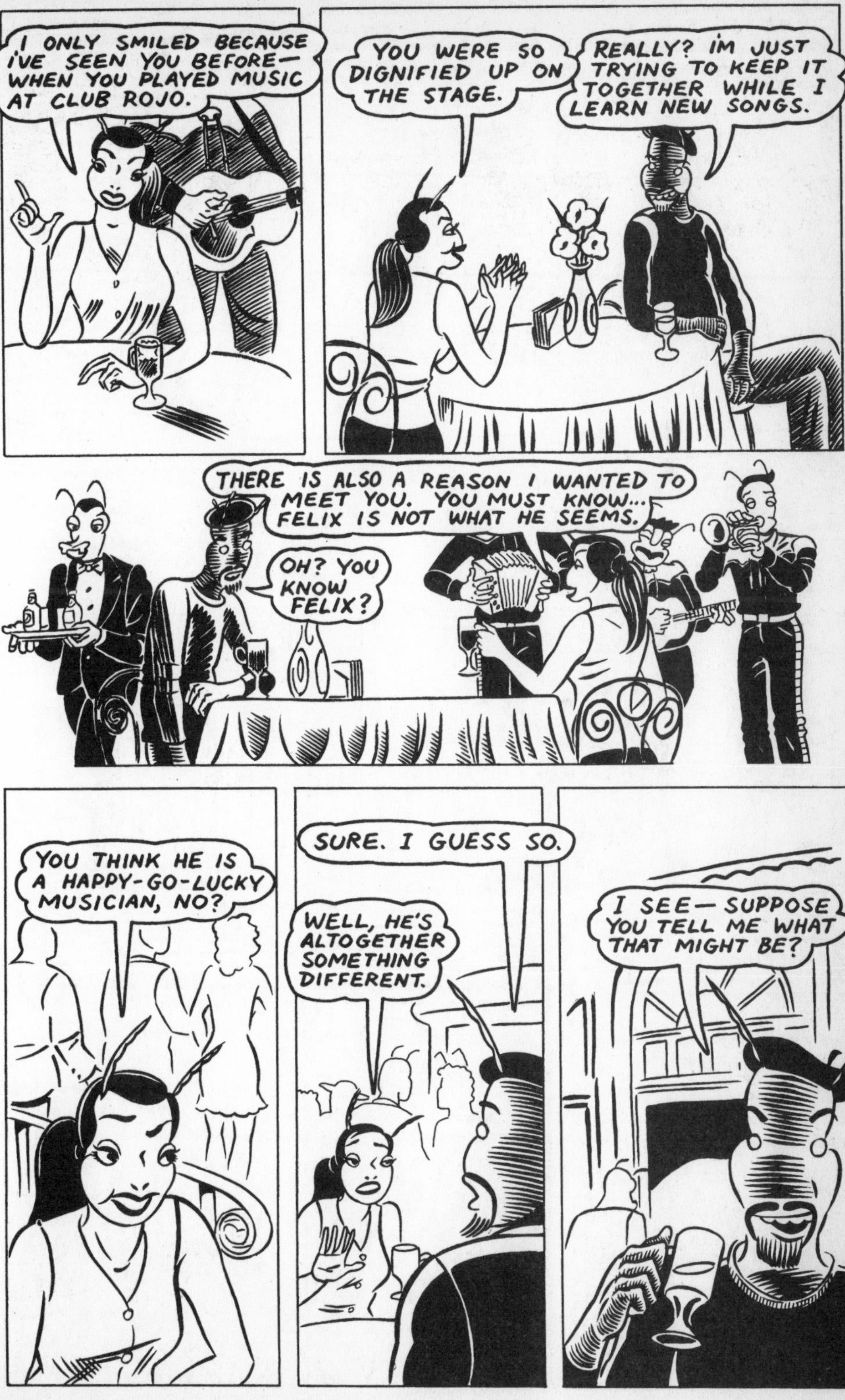
I ONLY SMILED BECAUSE I'VE SEEN YOU BEFORE— WHEN YOU PLAYED MUSIC AT CLUB ROJO.
YOU WERE SO DIGNIFIED UP ON THE STAGE.
REALLY? I'M JUST TRYING TO KEEP IT TOGETHER WHILE I LEARN NEW SONGS.
THERE IS ALSO A REASON I WANTED TO MEET YOU. YOU MUST KNOW... FELIX IS NOT WHAT HE SEEMS.
OH? YOU KNOW FELIX?
YOU THINK HE IS A HAPPY-GO-LUCKY MUSICIAN, NO?
SURE. I GUESS SO.
WELL, HE'S ALTOGETHER SOMETHING DIFFERENT.
I SEE— SUPPOSE YOU TELL ME WHAT THAT MIGHT BE?

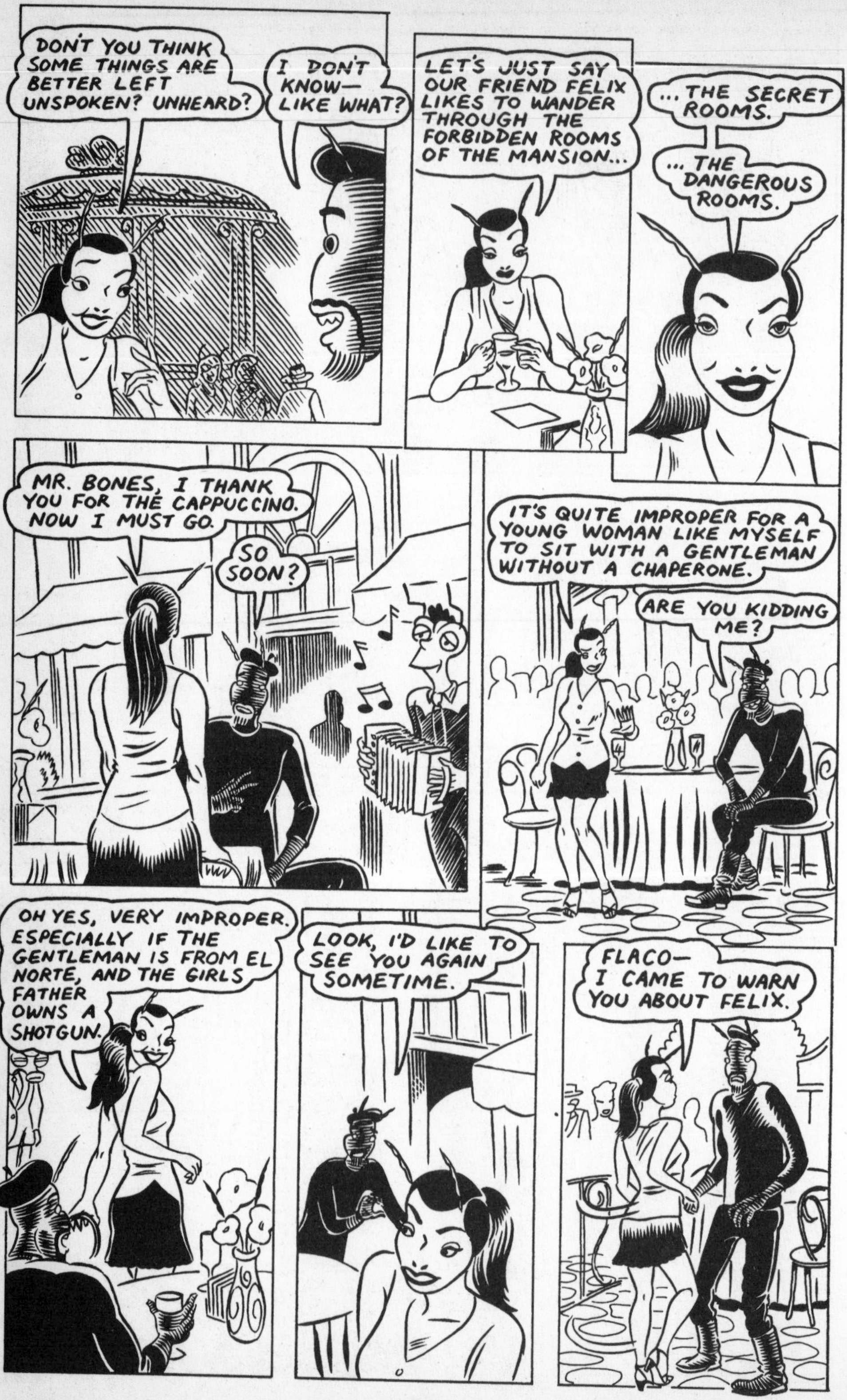
DON'T YOU THINK SOME THINGS ARE BETTER LEFT UNSPOKEN? UNHEARD?
I DON'T KNOW— LIKE WHAT?
LET'S JUST SAY OUR FRIEND FELIX LIKES TO WANDER THROUGH THE FORBIDDEN ROOMS OF THE MANSION...
...THE SECRET ROOMS.
...THE DANGEROUS ROOMS.
MR. BONES, I THANK YOU FOR THE CAPPUCCINO. NOW I MUST GO.
SO SOON?
IT'S QUITE IMPROPER FOR A YOUNG WOMAN LIKE MYSELF TO SIT WITH A GENTLEMAN WITHOUT A CHAPERONE.
ARE YOU KIDDING ME?
OH YES, VERY IMPROPER. ESPECIALLY IF THE GENTLEMAN IS FROM EL NORTE, AND THE GIRLS FATHER OWNS A SHOTGUN.
LOOK, I'D LIKE TO SEE YOU AGAIN SOMETIME.
FLACO— I CAME TO WARN YOU ABOUT FELIX.

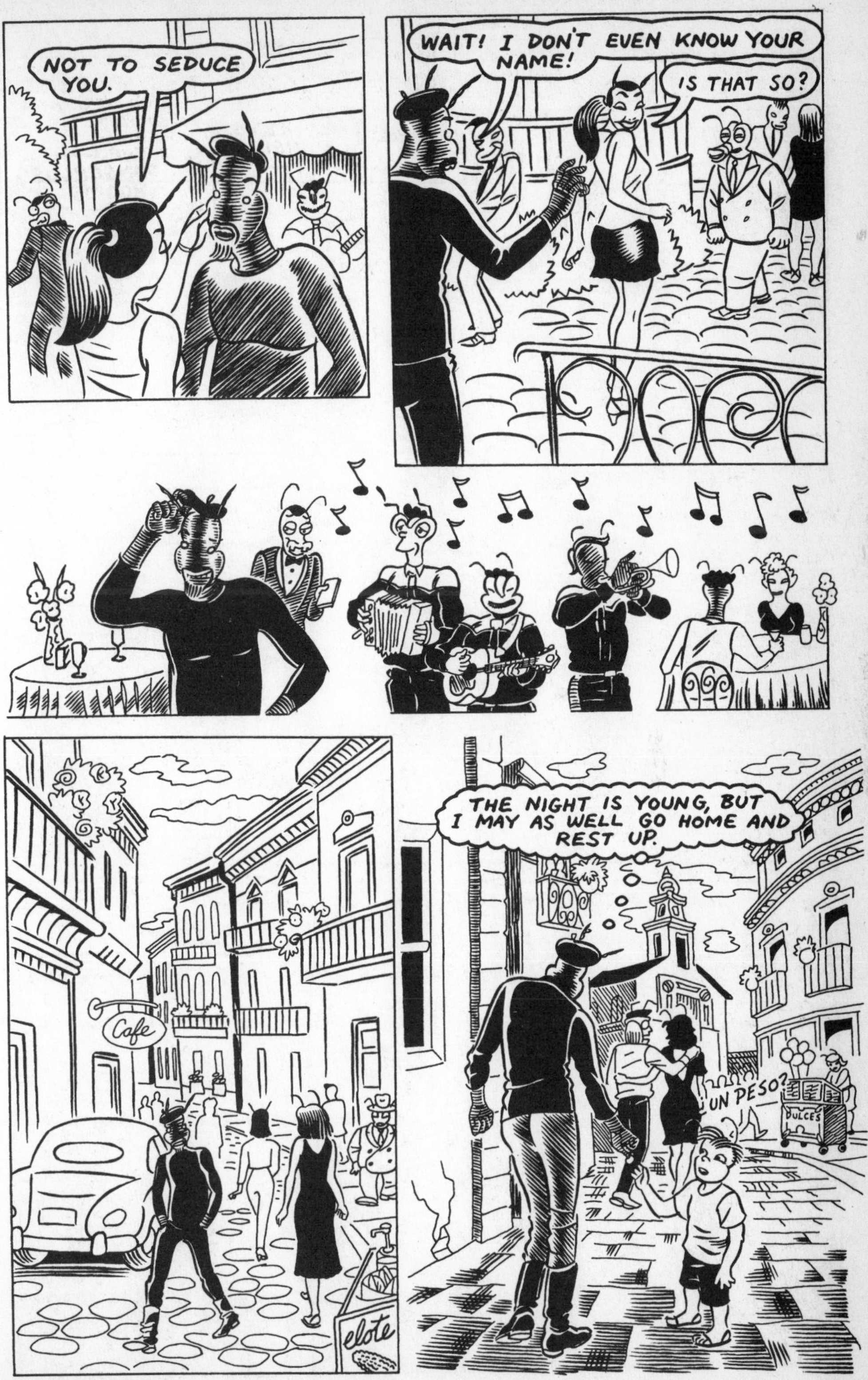
NOT TO SEDUCE YOU.
WAIT! I DON'T EVEN KNOW YOUR NAME!
IS THAT SO?
Cafe
elote
THE NIGHT IS YOUNG, BUT I MAY AS WELL GO HOME AND REST UP.
UN PESO?
DULCES

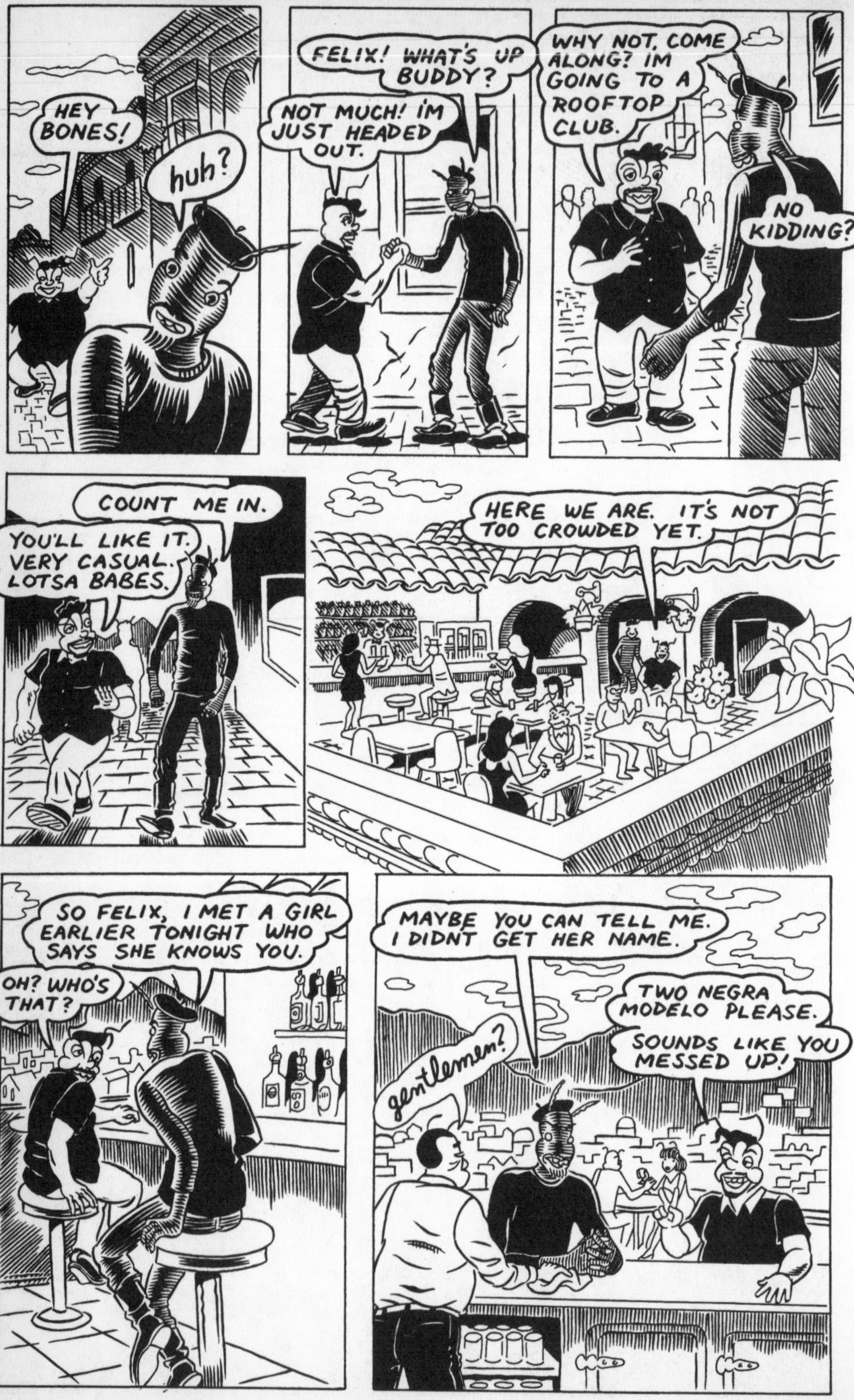
HEY BONES!
huh?
FELIX! WHAT'S UP BUDDY?
NOT MUCH! I'M JUST HEADED OUT.
WHY NOT, COME ALONG? I'M GOING TO A ROOFTOP CLUB.
NO KIDDING?
COUNT ME IN.
YOU'LL LIKE IT. VERY CASUAL. LOTSA BABES.
HERE WE ARE. IT'S NOT TOO CROWDED YET.
SO FELIX, I MET A GIRL EARLIER TONIGHT WHO SAYS SHE KNOWS YOU.
OH? WHO'S THAT?
MAYBE YOU CAN TELL ME. I DIDN'T GET HER NAME.
gentlemen?
TWO NEGRA MODELO PLEASE.
SOUNDS LIKE YOU MESSED UP!

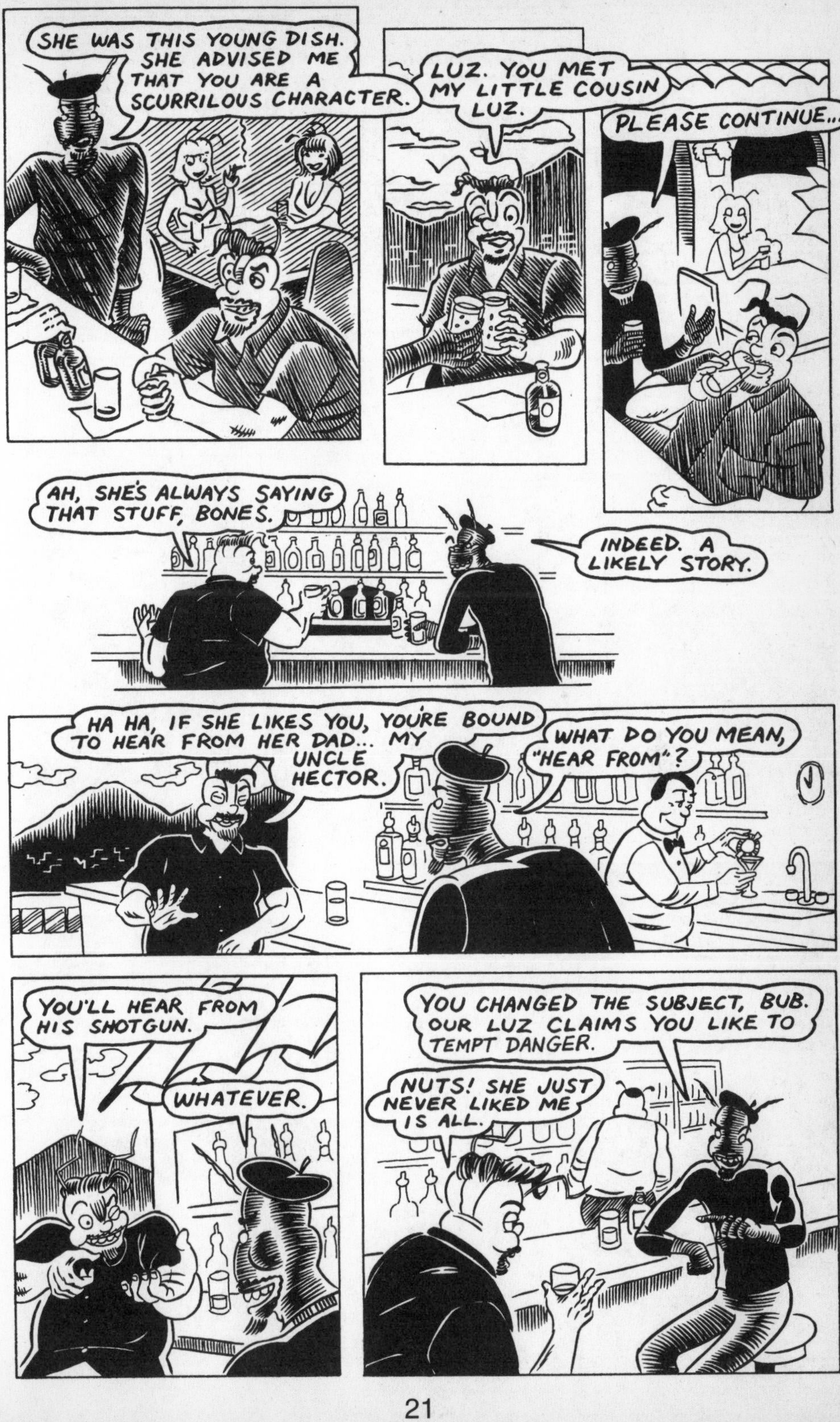
SHE WAS THIS YOUNG DISH. SHE ADVISED ME THAT YOU ARE A SCURRILOUS CHARACTER.
LUZ. YOU MET MY LITTLE COUSIN LUZ.
PLEASE CONTINUE...
AH, SHE'S ALWAYS SAYING THAT STUFF, BONES.
INDEED. A LIKELY STORY.
HA HA, IF SHE LIKES YOU, YOU'RE BOUND TO HEAR FROM HER DAD... MY UNCLE HECTOR.
WHAT DO YOU MEAN, "HEAR FROM"?
YOU'LL HEAR FROM HIS SHOTGUN.
WHATEVER.
YOU CHANGED THE SUBJECT, BUB. OUR LUZ CLAIMS YOU LIKE TO TEMPT DANGER.
NUTS! SHE JUST NEVER LIKED ME IS ALL.

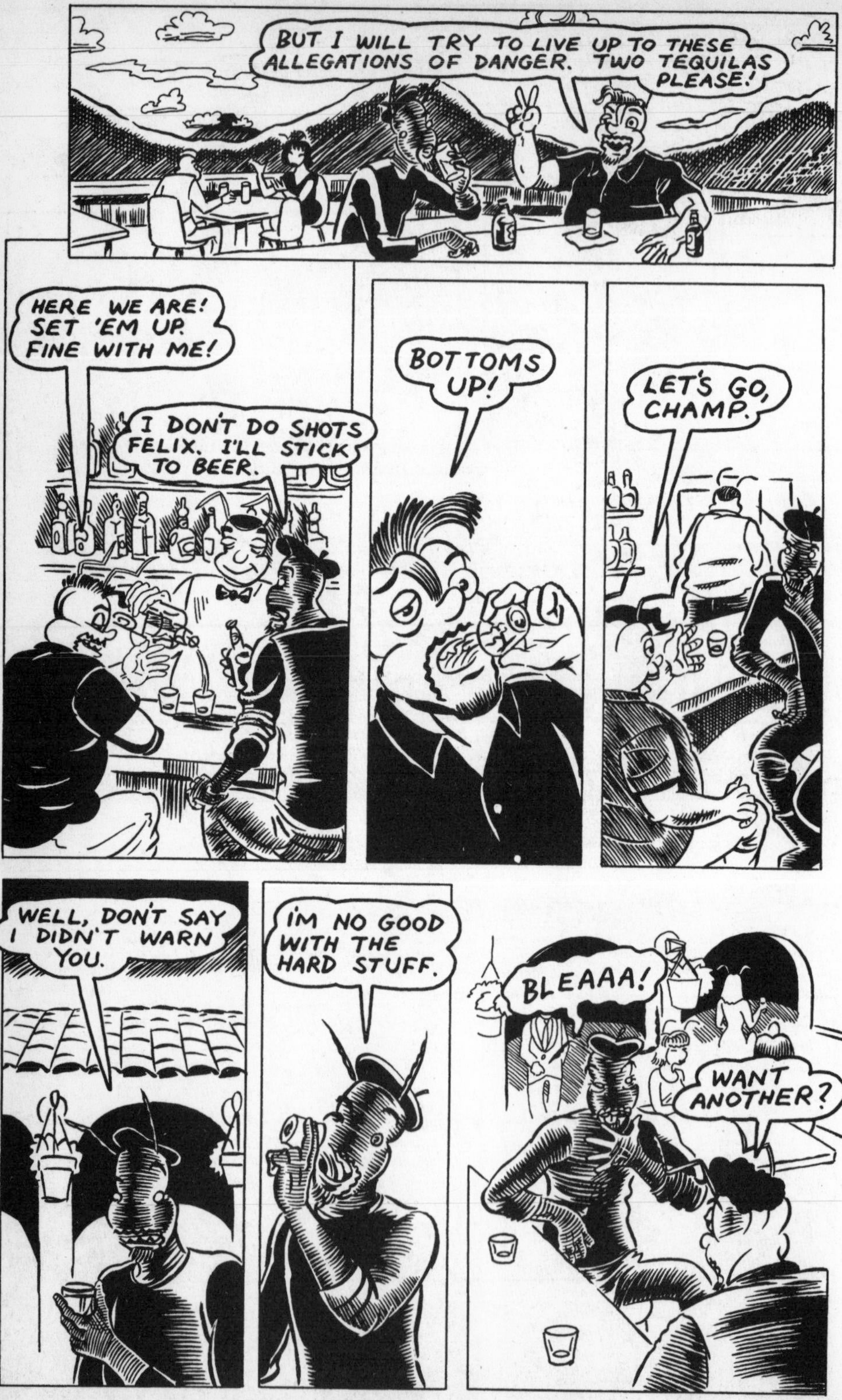
BUT I WILL TRY TO LIVE UP TO THESE ALLEGATIONS OF DANGER. TWO TEQUILAS PLEASE!
HERE WE ARE! SET 'EM UP. FINE WITH ME!
I DON'T DO SHOTS FELIX. I'LL STICK TO BEER.
BOTTOMS UP!
LET'S GO, CHAMP.
WELL, DON'T SAY I DIDN'T WARN YOU.
I'M NO GOOD WITH THE HARD STUFF.
BLEAAA!
WANT ANOTHER?

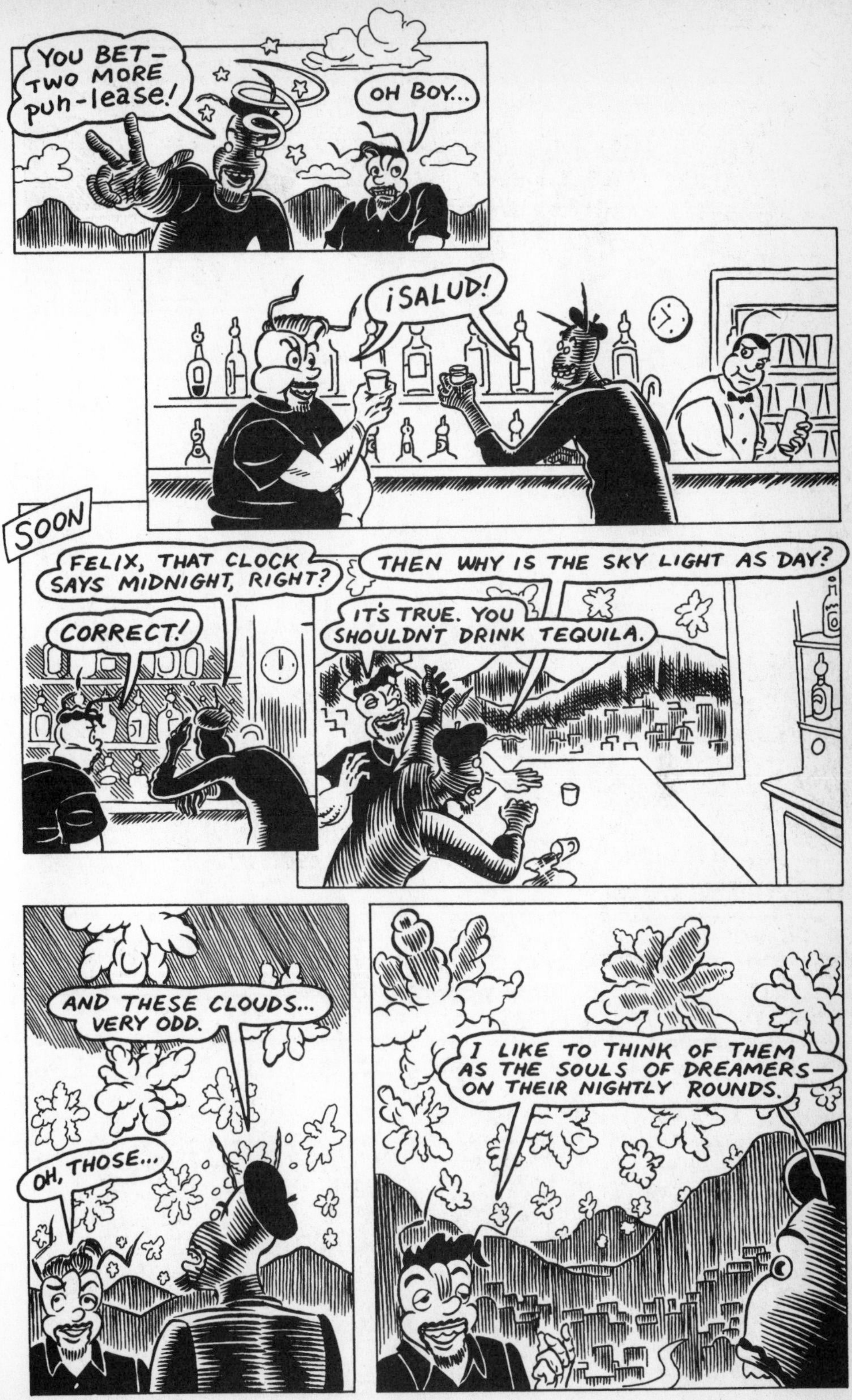

YOU BET— TWO MORE puh-lease!
OH BOY...
¡SALUD!
SOON
FELIX, THAT CLOCK SAYS MIDNIGHT, RIGHT?
CORRECT!
THEN WHY IS THE SKY LIGHT AS DAY?
IT'S TRUE. YOU SHOULDN'T DRINK TEQUILA.
AND THESE CLOUDS... VERY ODD.
OH, THOSE...
I LIKE TO THINK OF THEM AS THE SOULS OF DREAMERS— ON THEIR NIGHTLY ROUNDS.

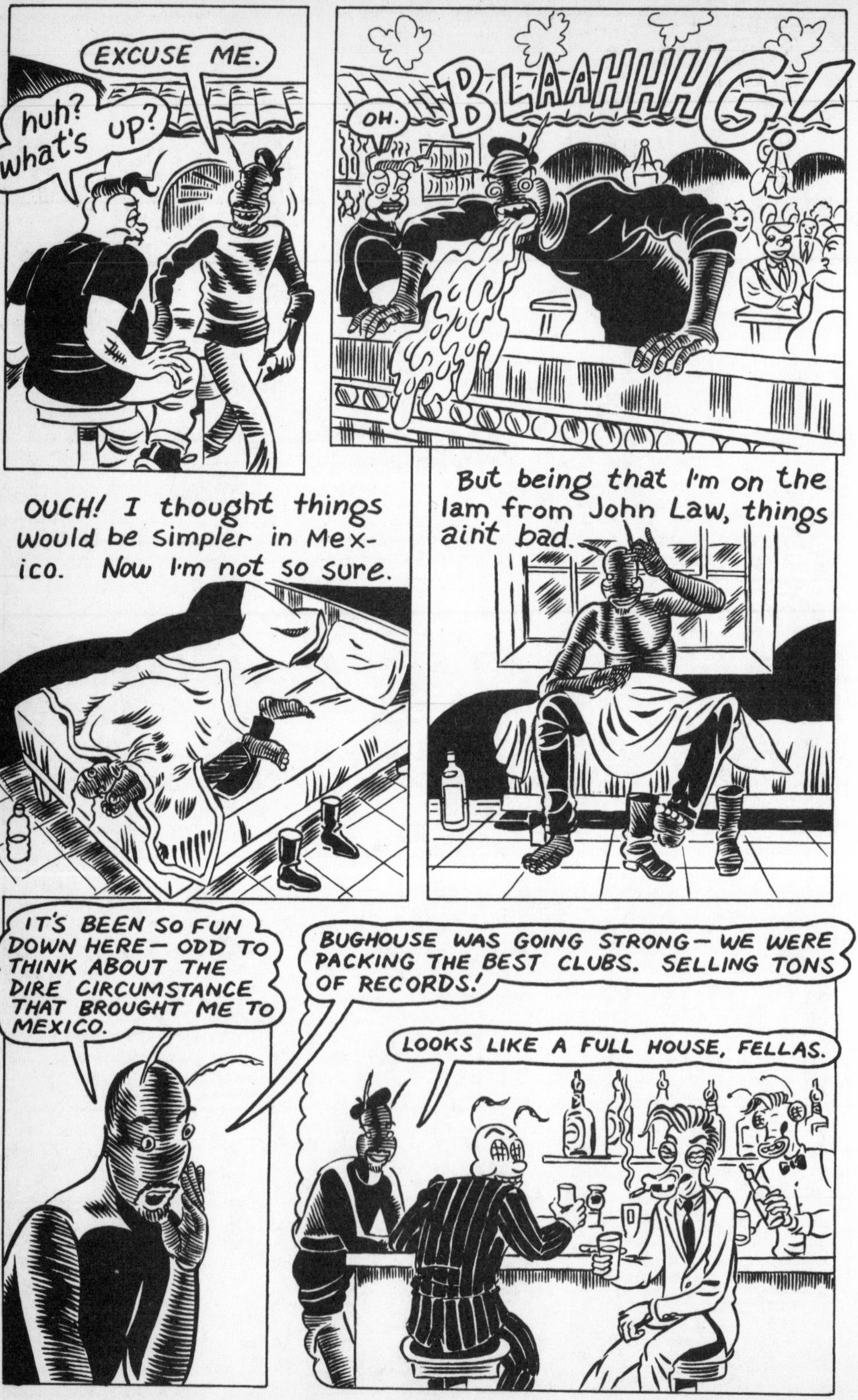
EXCUSE ME.
huh? what's up?
OH.
BLAAHHHG!
OUCH! I thought things would be simpler in Mex-ico. Now I'm not so sure.
But being that I'm on the lam from John Law, things ain't bad.
IT'S BEEN SO FUN DOWN HERE— ODD TO THINK ABOUT THE DIRE CIRCUMSTANCE THAT BROUGHT ME TO MEXICO.
BUGHOUSE WAS GOING STRONG— WE WERE PACKING THE BEST CLUBS. SELLING TONS OF RECORDS!
LOOKS LIKE A FULL HOUSE, FELLAS.

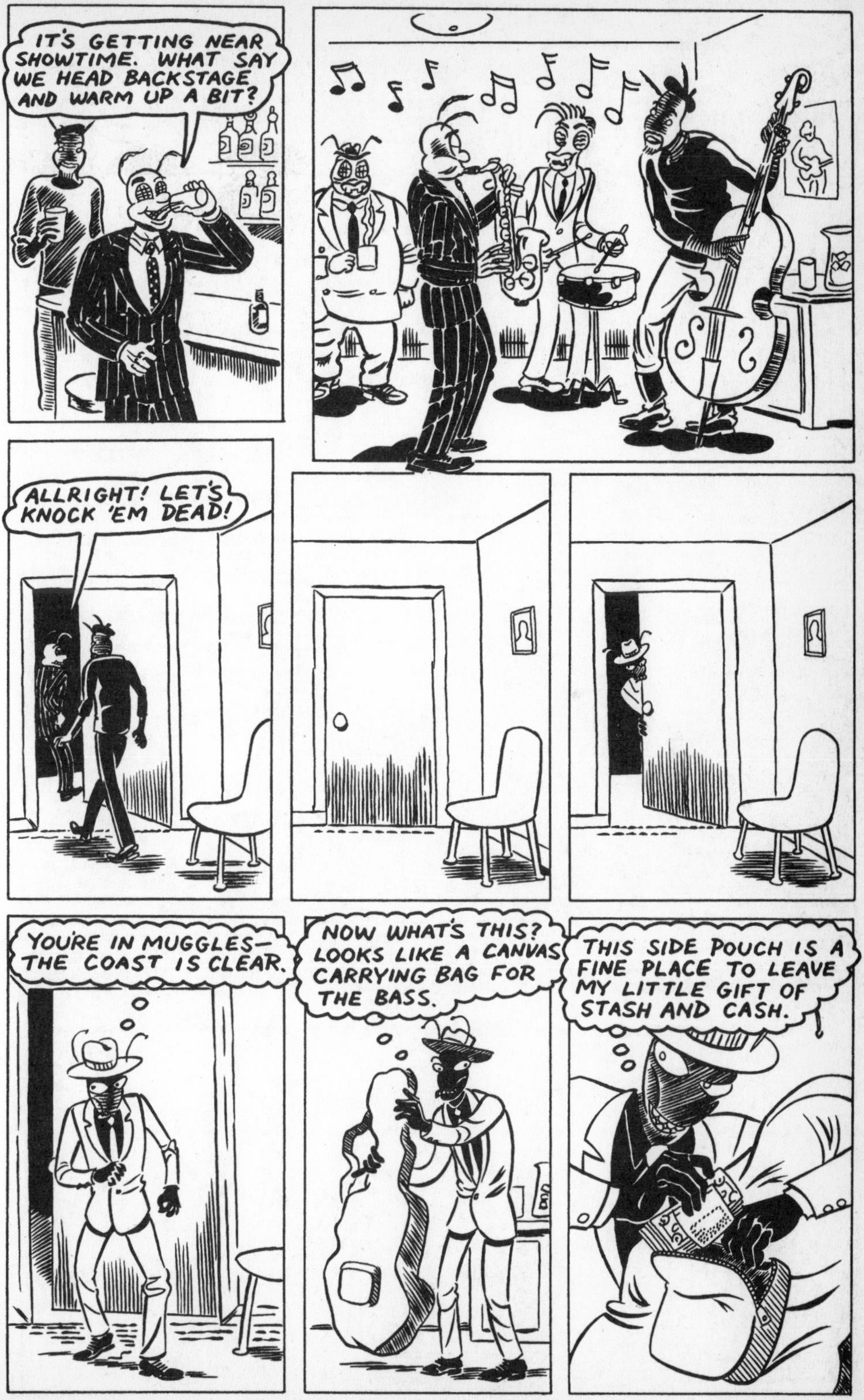
IT'S GETTING NEAR SHOWTIME. WHAT SAY WE HEAD BACKSTAGE AND WARM UP A BIT?
ALLRIGHT! LET'S KNOCK 'EM DEAD!
YOU'RE IN MUGGLES-THE COAST IS CLEAR.
NOW WHAT'S THIS? LOOKS LIKE A CANVAS CARRYING BAG FOR THE BASS.
THIS SIDE POUCH IS A FINE PLACE TO LEAVE MY LITTLE GIFT OF STASH AND CASH.

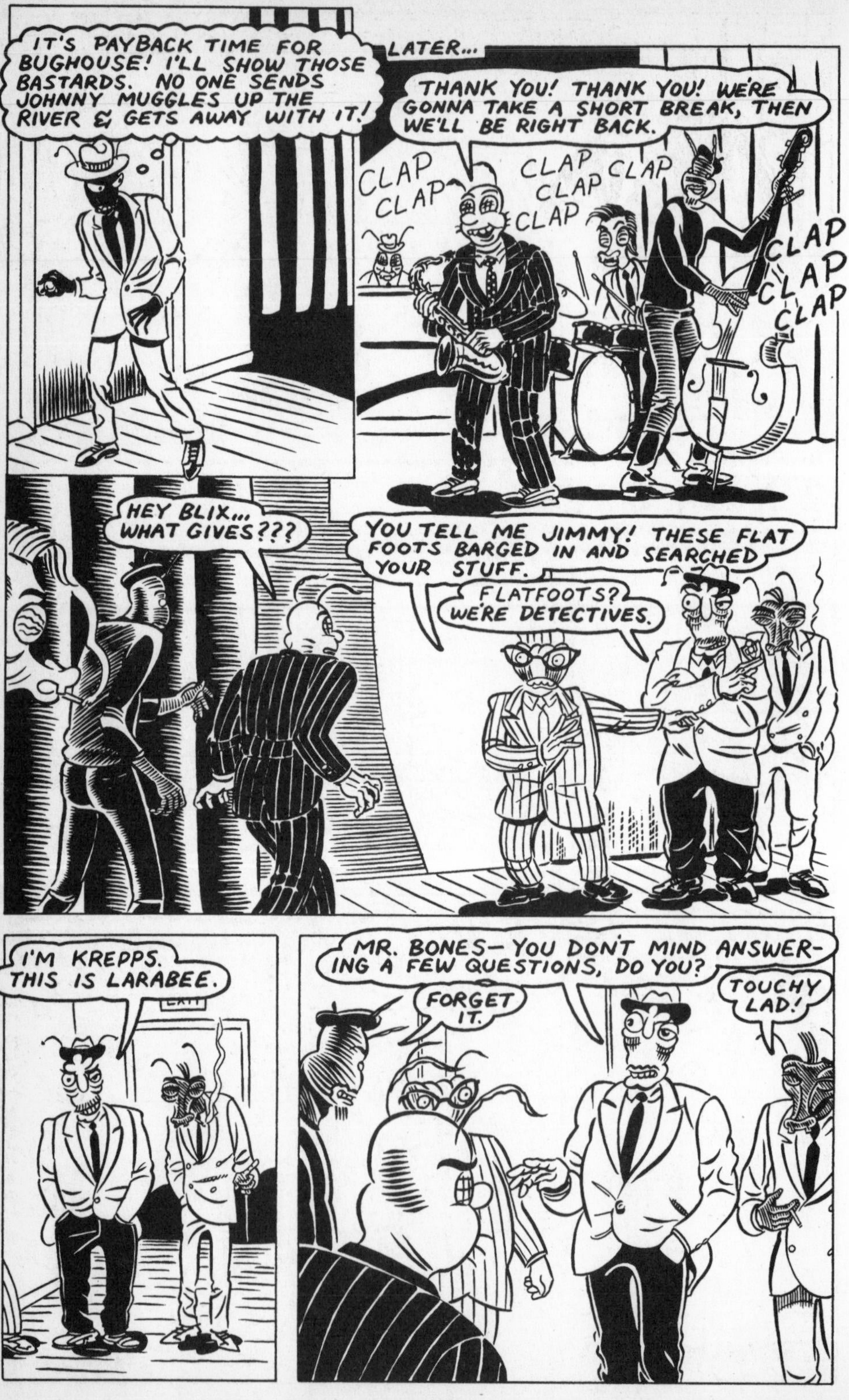
IT'S PAYBACK TIME FOR BUGHOUSE! I'LL SHOW THOSE BASTARDS. NO ONE SENDS JOHNNY MUGGLES UP THE RIVER & GETS AWAY WITH IT!
LATER...
THANK YOU! THANK YOU! WE'RE GONNA TAKE A SHORT BREAK, THEN WE'LL BE RIGHT BACK.
CLAP CLAP
CLAP CLAP CLAP CLAP
CLAP CLAP CLAP
HEY BLIX... WHAT GIVES???
YOU TELL ME JIMMY! THESE FLAT FOOTS BARGED IN AND SEARCHED YOUR STUFF.
FLATFOOTS? WE'RE DETECTIVES.
I'M KREPPS. THIS IS LARABEE.
EXIT
MR. BONES— YOU DON'T MIND ANSWERING A FEW QUESTIONS, DO YOU?
FORGET IT.
TOUCHY LAD!

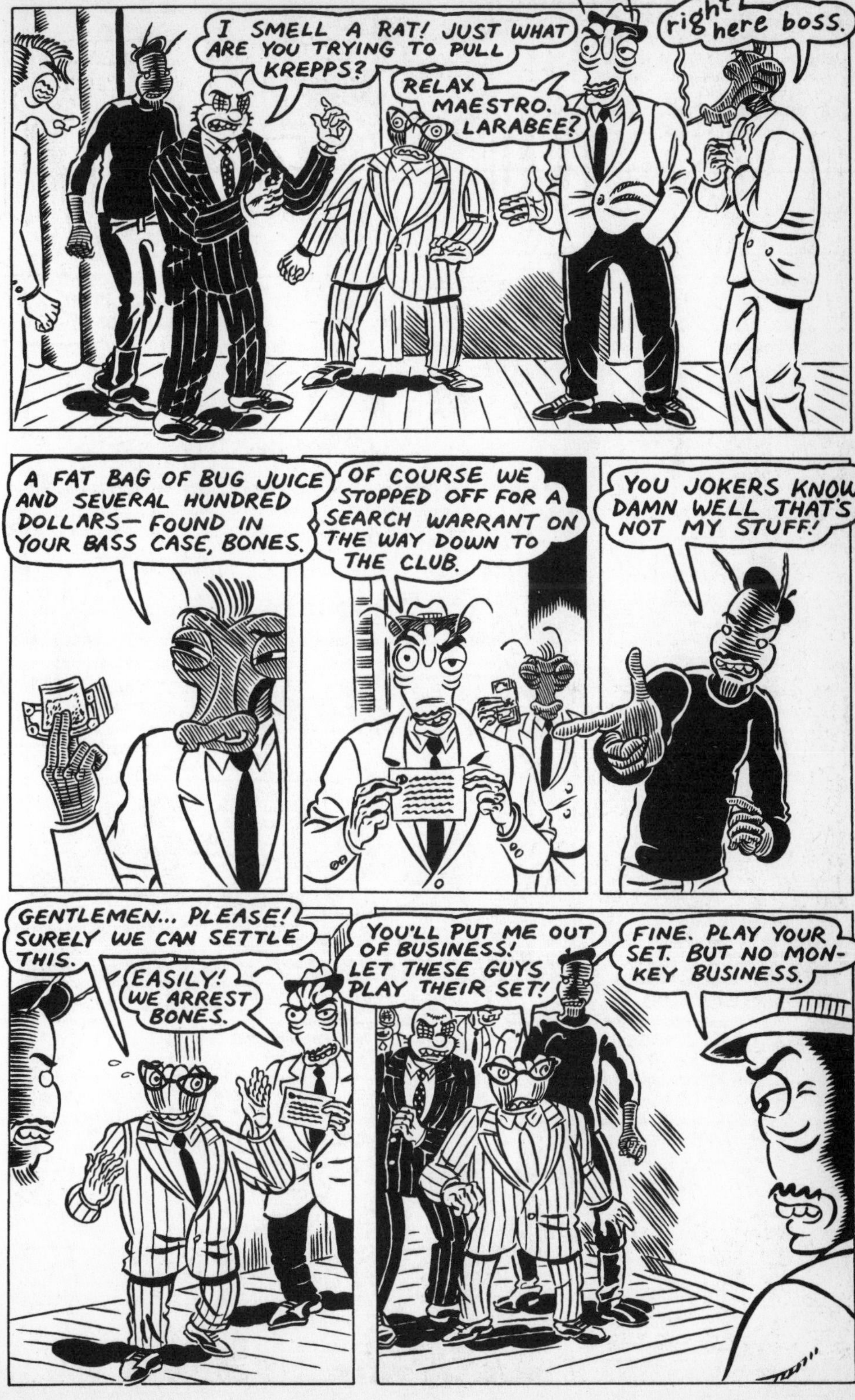
I SMELL A RAT! JUST WHAT ARE YOU TRYING TO PULL KREPPS?
RELAX MAESTRO. LARABEE?
right here boss.
A FAT BAG OF BUG JUICE AND SEVERAL HUNDRED DOLLARS— FOUND IN YOUR BASS CASE, BONES.
OF COURSE WE STOPPED OFF FOR A SEARCH WARRANT ON THE WAY DOWN TO THE CLUB.
YOU JOKERS KNOW DAMN WELL THAT'S NOT MY STUFF!
GENTLEMEN... PLEASE! SURELY WE CAN SETTLE THIS.
EASILY! WE ARREST BONES.
YOU'LL PUT ME OUT OF BUSINESS! LET THESE GUYS PLAY THEIR SET!
FINE. PLAY YOUR SET. BUT NO MON-KEY BUSINESS.

HOW MUCH DO YOU FIGURE IT'S WORTH TO STAY OPEN TONIGHT, BLIX?

LET'S GET OUT OF HERE FOR A MINUTE, YOU GUYS.

I'VE BEEN SET UP!

I'D WAGER SOMEONE'S TRYING TO EVEN A SCORE WITH ME BY TAKING YOU DOWN.

YOUR CHECKERED PAST HAS COME CALL-ING, JIMMY.

THOSE COPS WILL BE FRONT AND CENTER WATCHING US. THERE WILL BE NO SLIPPING AWAY.

UNLESS WE GET GEORGE THE BAR-TENDER TO SLIP 'EM A MICKEY.

YEAH, BUT THEN WHAT? THEY'LL JUST GET A WARRANT AND COME AFTER ME TOMORROW.

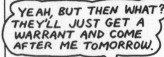

BUT WHAT, IF THEY CAN'T FIND YOU? THEY HAVEN'T OFFICIALLY ARRESTED YOU YET!

WHAT THE HELL ARE YOU GETTIN' AT?

HEY BONES—YOU BEEN KEEPING UP ON YOUR SPANISH?

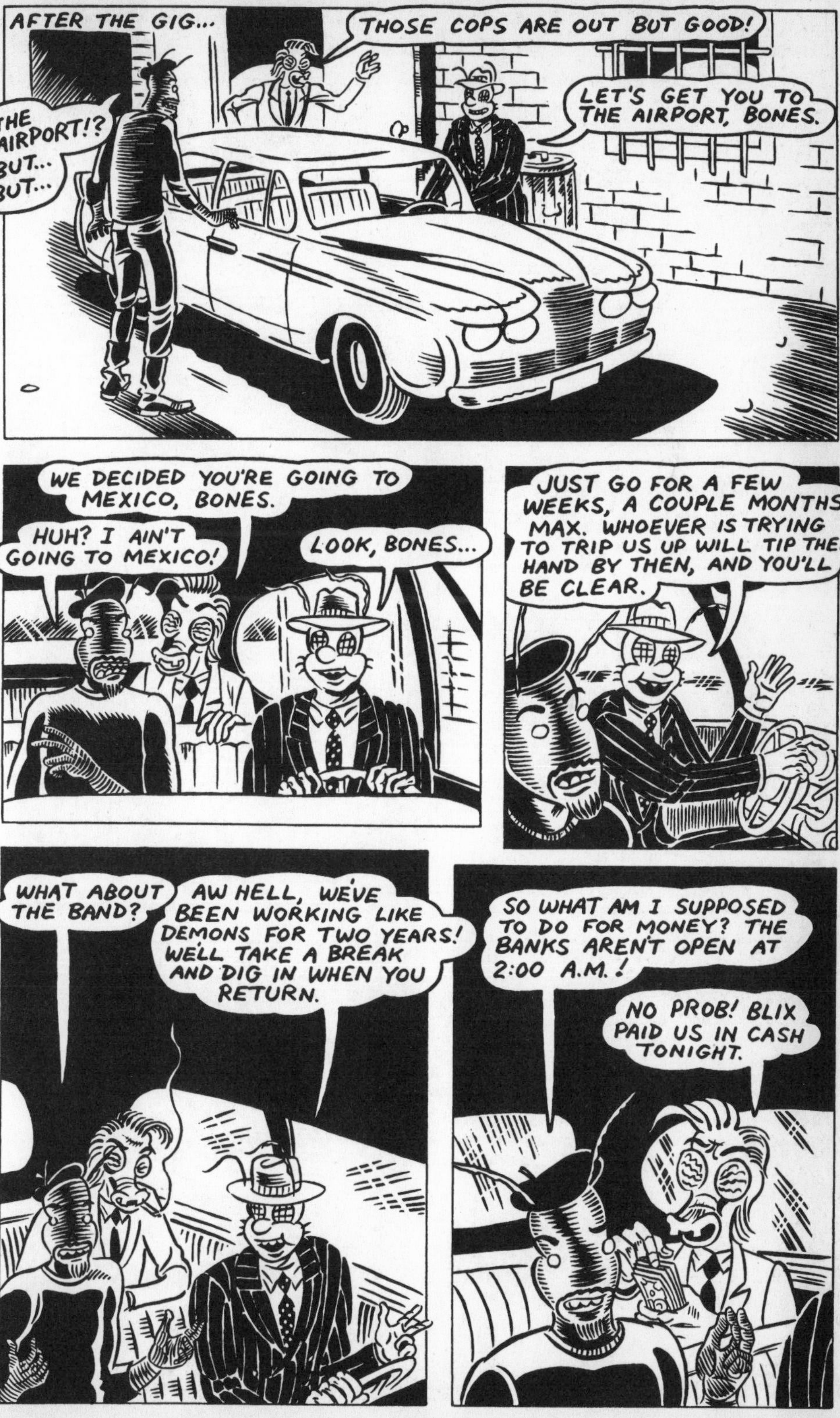
AFTER THE GIG...
THOSE COPS ARE OUT BUT GOOD!
LET'S GET YOU TO THE AIRPORT, BONES.
THE AIRPORT!? BUT... BUT...
WE DECIDED YOU'RE GOING TO MEXICO, BONES.
HUH? I AIN'T GOING TO MEXICO!
LOOK, BONES...
JUST GO FOR A FEW WEEKS, A COUPLE MONTHS MAX. WHOEVER IS TRYING TO TRIP US UP WILL TIP THEIR HAND BY THEN, AND YOU'LL BE CLEAR.
WHAT ABOUT THE BAND?
AW HELL, WE'VE BEEN WORKING LIKE DEMONS FOR TWO YEARS! WE'LL TAKE A BREAK AND DIG IN WHEN YOU RETURN.
SO WHAT AM I SUPPOSED TO DO FOR MONEY? THE BANKS AREN'T OPEN AT 2:00 A.M.!
NO PROB! BLIX PAID US IN CASH TONIGHT.

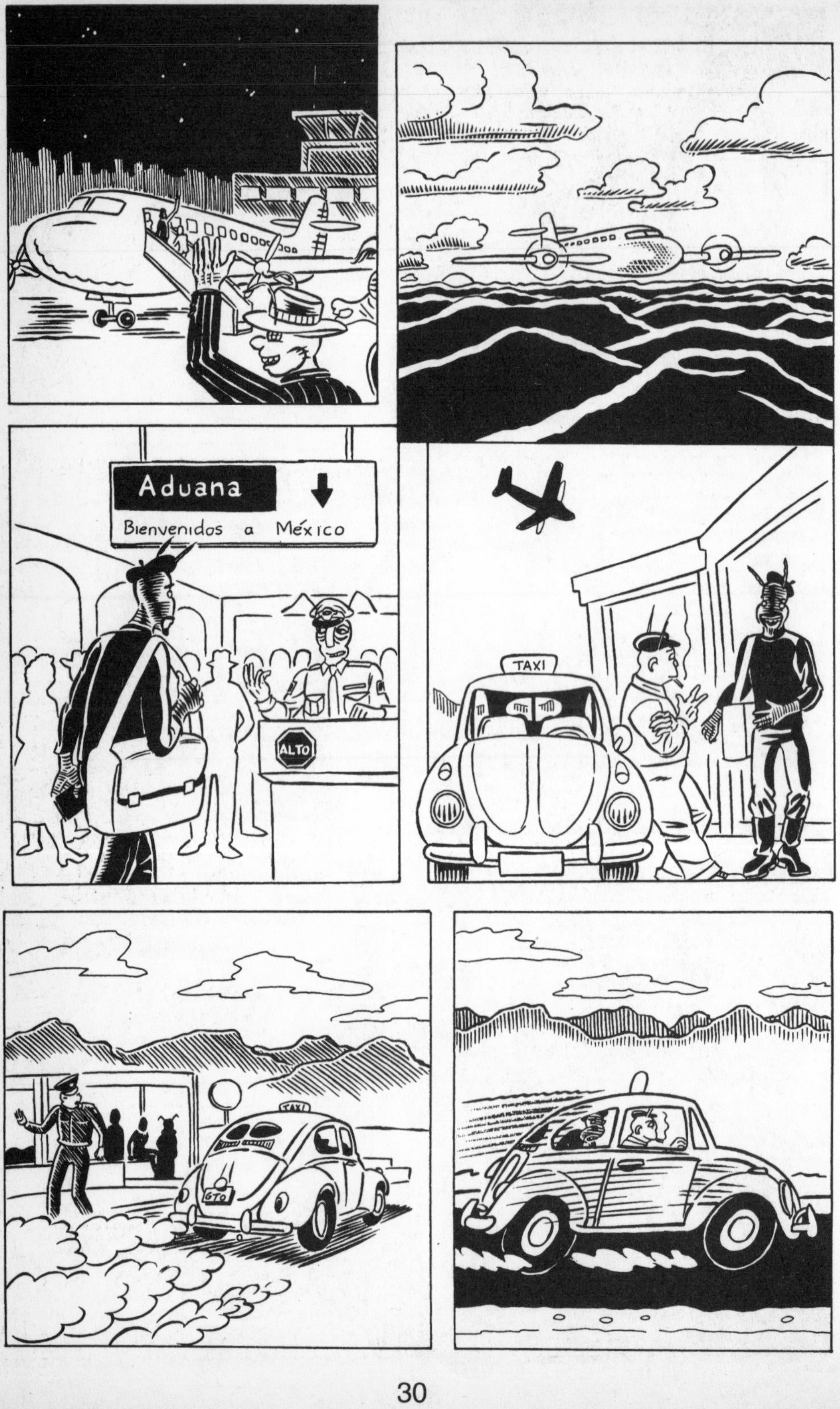
Aduana
Bienvenidos a México
ALTO
TAXI
TAXI
GTO

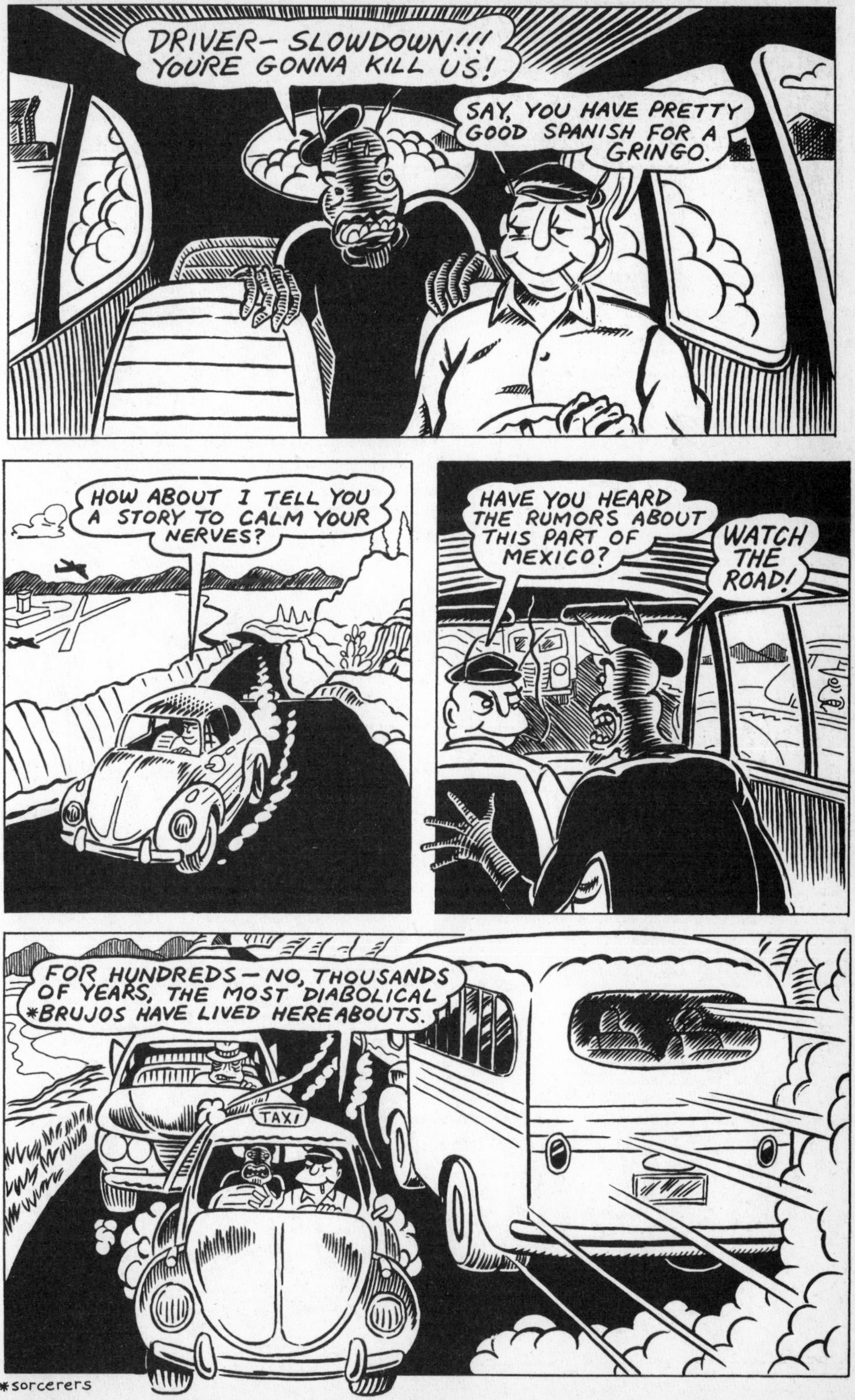
DRIVER- SLOWDOWN!!! YOU'RE GONNA KILL US!
SAY, YOU HAVE PRETTY GOOD SPANISH FOR A GRINGO.
HOW ABOUT I TELL YOU A STORY TO CALM YOUR NERVES?
HAVE YOU HEARD THE RUMORS ABOUT THIS PART OF MEXICO?
WATCH THE ROAD!
FOR HUNDREDS—NO, THOUSANDS OF YEARS, THE MOST DIABOLICAL *BRUJOS HAVE LIVED HEREABOUTS.
TAXI

*sorcerers

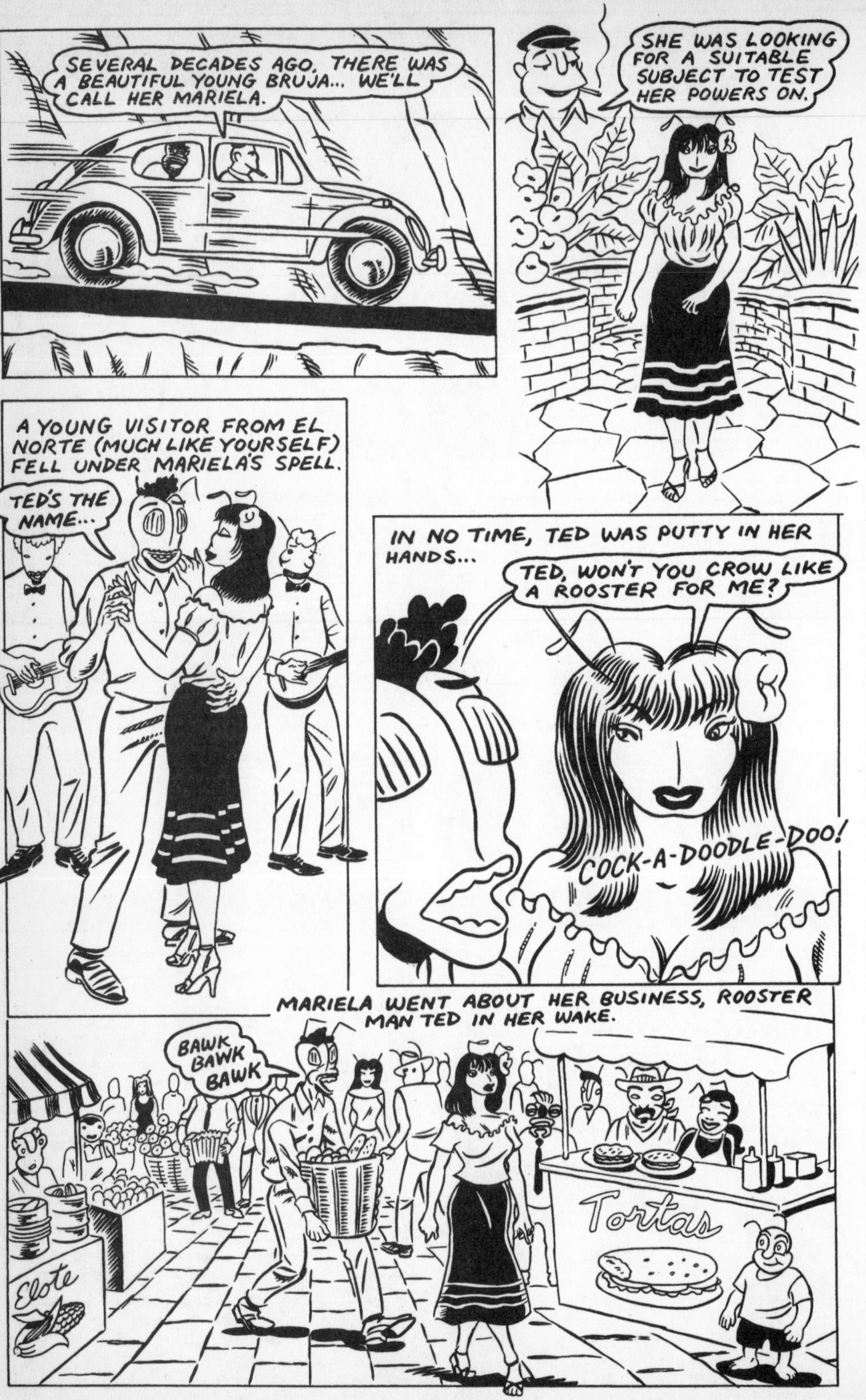
SEVERAL DECADES AGO, THERE WAS A BEAUTIFUL YOUNG BRUJA... WE'LL CALL HER MARIELA.
SHE WAS LOOKING FOR A SUITABLE SUBJECT TO TEST HER POWERS ON.
A YOUNG VISITOR FROM EL NORTE (MUCH LIKE YOURSELF) FELL UNDER MARIELA'S SPELL.
TED'S THE NAME...
IN NO TIME, TED WAS PUTTY IN HER HANDS...
TED, WON'T YOU CROW LIKE A ROOSTER FOR ME?
COCK-A-DOODLE-DOO!
MARIELA WENT ABOUT HER BUSINESS, ROOSTER MAN TED IN HER WAKE.
BAWK BAWK BAWK
Elote
Tortas

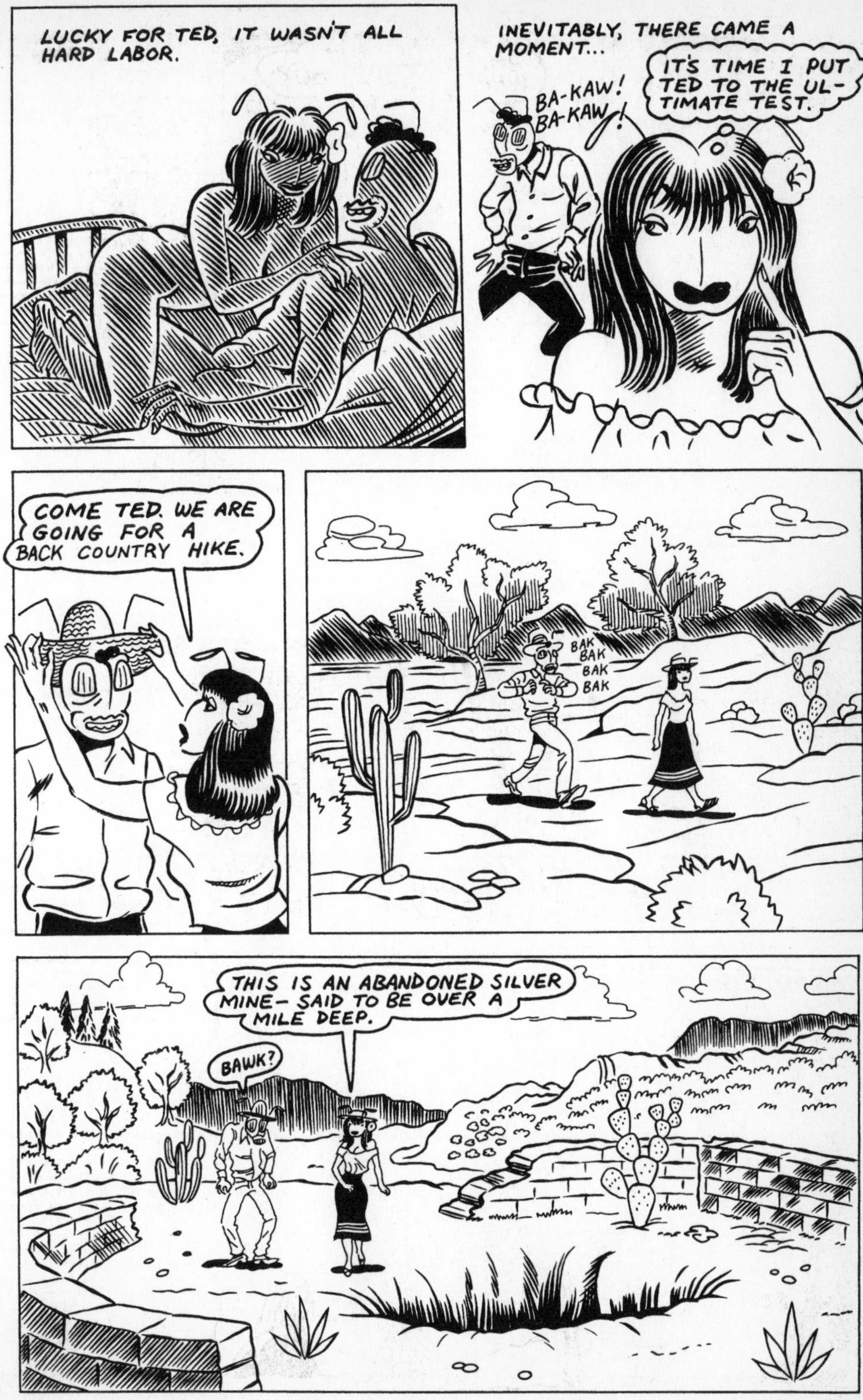
LUCKY FOR TED, IT WASN'T ALL HARD LABOR.
INEVITABLY, THERE CAME A MOMENT...
BA-KAW! BA-KAW!
IT'S TIME I PUT TED TO THE ULTIMATE TEST.
COME TED. WE ARE GOING FOR A BACK COUNTRY HIKE.
BAK BAK BAK BAK
THIS IS AN ABANDONED SILVER MINE- SAID TO BE OVER A MILE DEEP.
BAWK?

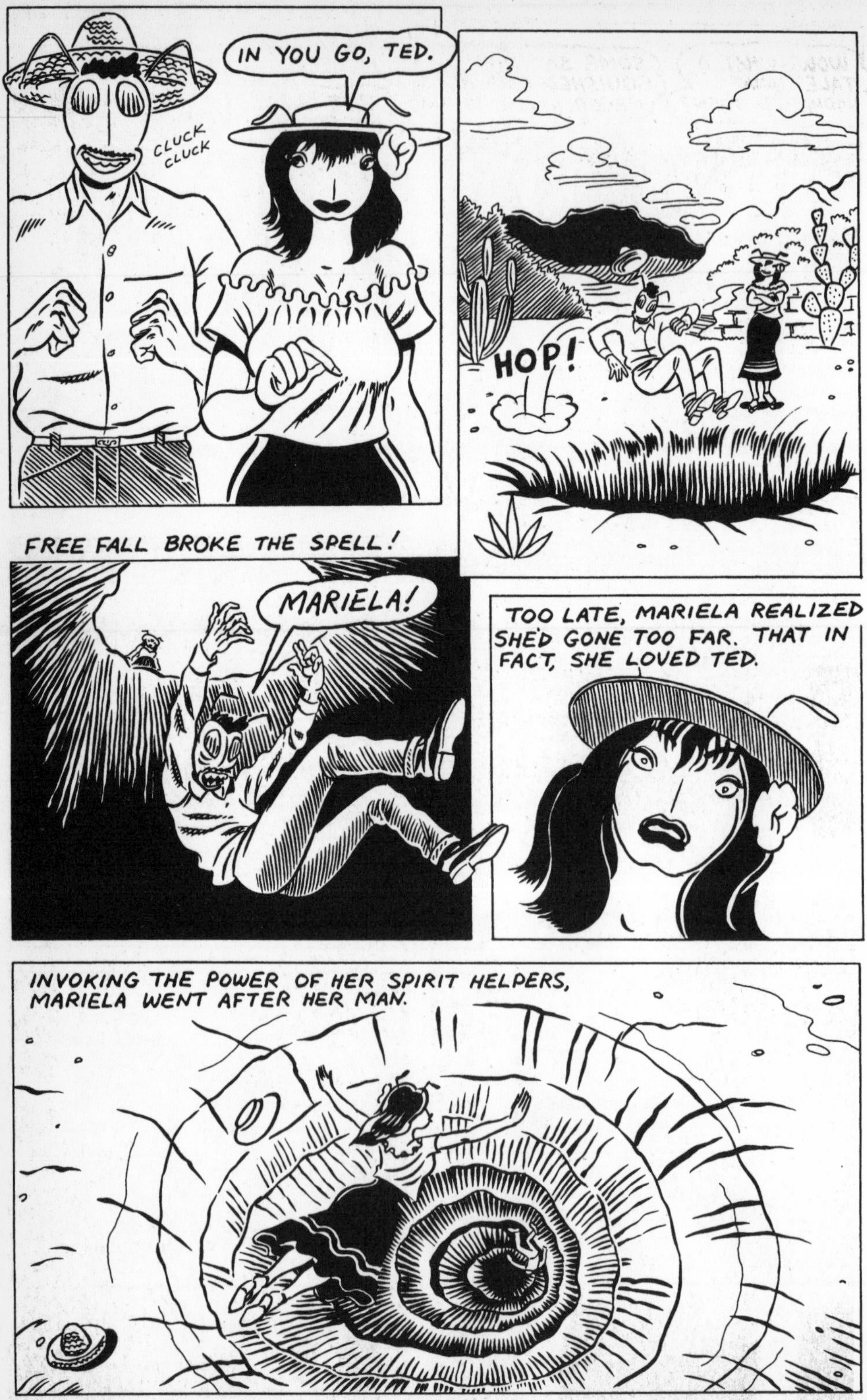

IN YOU GO, TED.
CLUCK CLUCK
HOP!
FREE FALL BROKE THE SPELL!
MARIELA!
TOO LATE, MARIELA REALIZED SHE'D GONE TOO FAR. THAT IN FACT, SHE LOVED TED.
INVOKING THE POWER OF HER SPIRIT HELPERS, MARIELA WENT AFTER HER MAN.

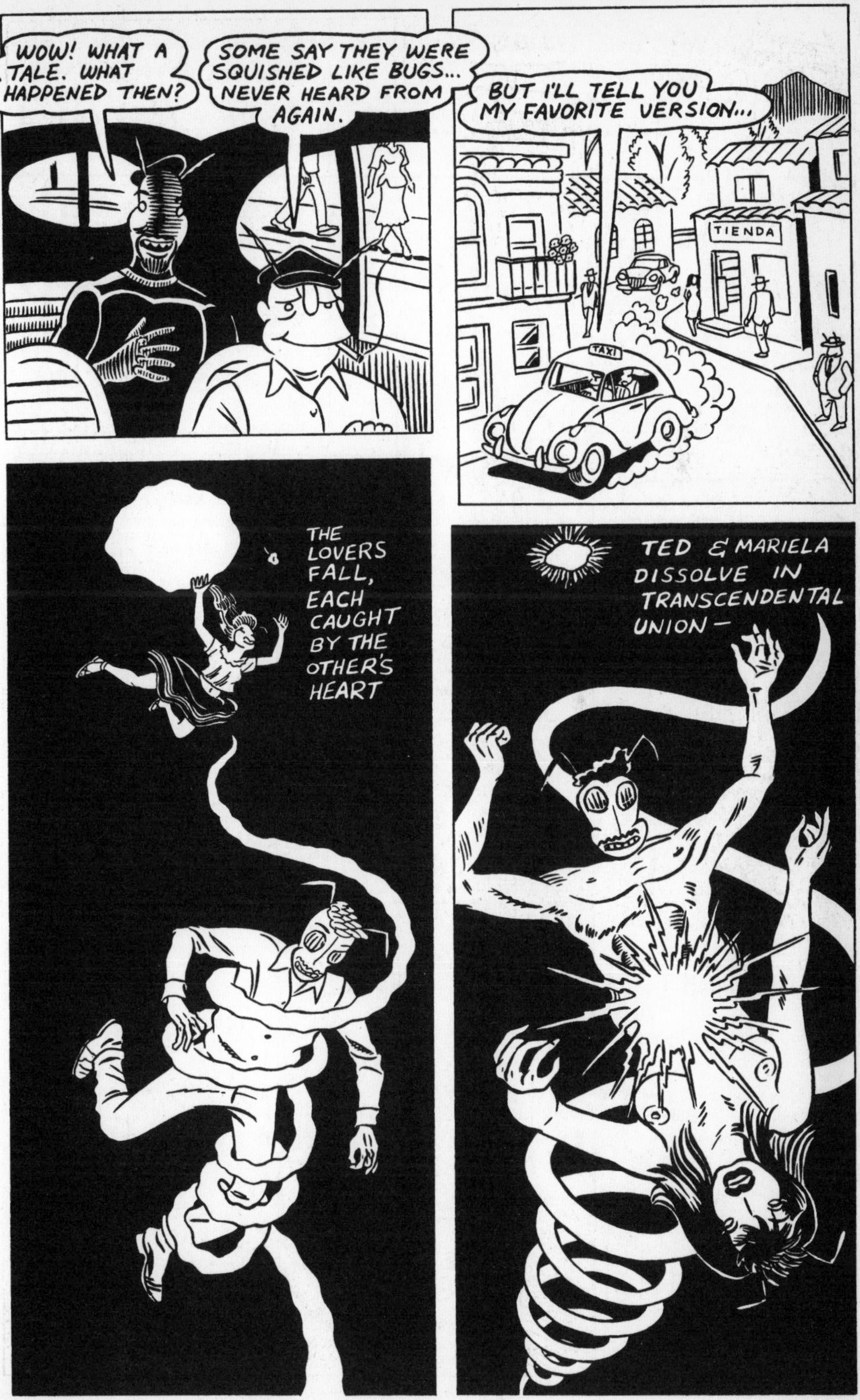
WOW! WHAT A TALE. WHAT HAPPENED THEN?
SOME SAY THEY WERE SQUISHED LIKE BUGS... NEVER HEARD FROM AGAIN.
BUT I'LL TELL YOU MY FAVORITE VERSION...
TIENDA
TAXI
THE LOVERS FALL, EACH CAUGHT BY THE OTHER'S HEART
TED & MARIELA DISSOLVE IN TRANSCENDENTAL UNION —

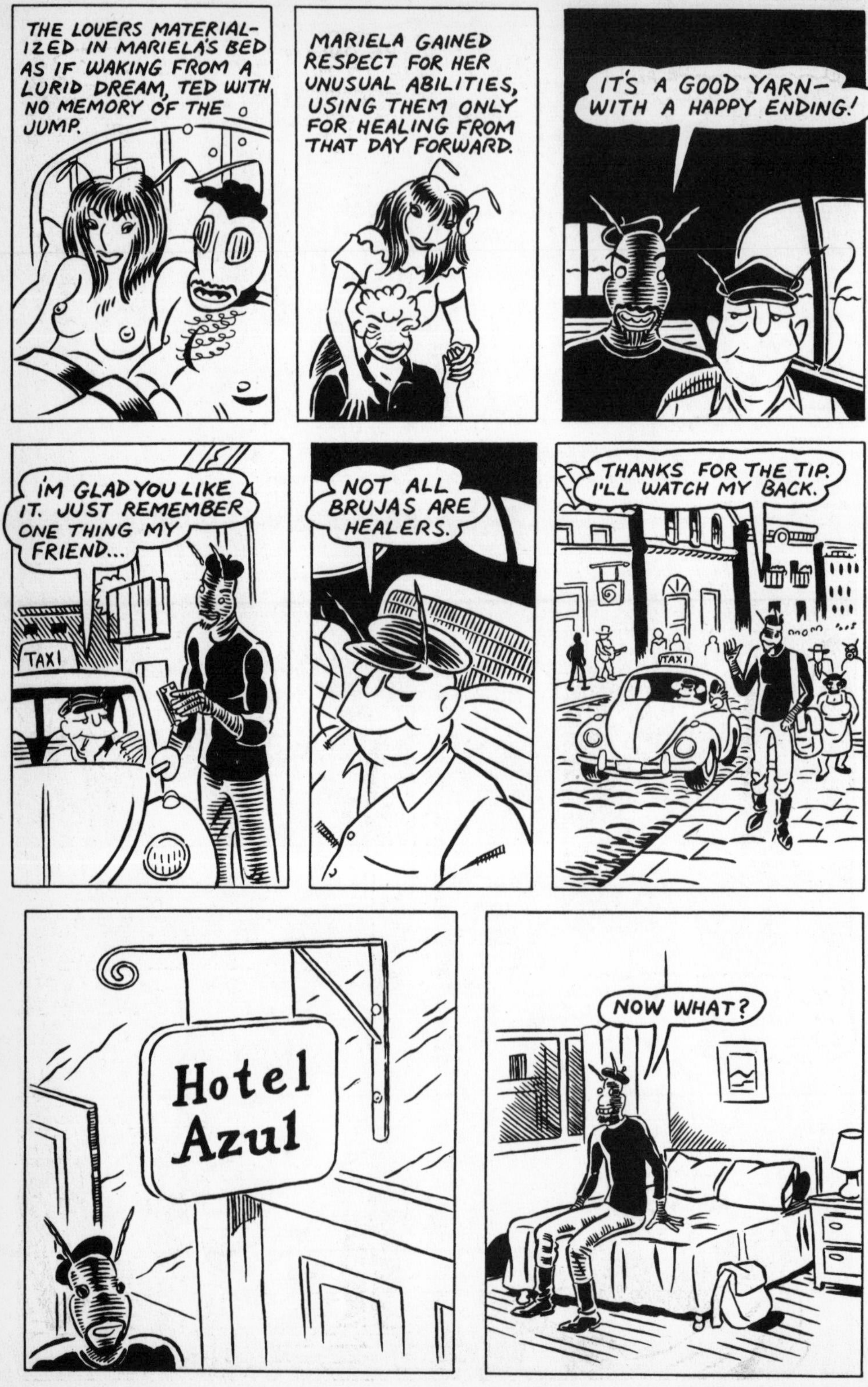
THE LOVERS MATERIALIZED IN MARIELA'S BED AS IF WAKING FROM A LURID DREAM, TED WITH NO MEMORY OF THE JUMP.
MARIELA GAINED RESPECT FOR HER UNUSUAL ABILITIES, USING THEM ONLY FOR HEALING FROM THAT DAY FORWARD.
IT'S A GOOD YARN— WITH A HAPPY ENDING!
I'M GLAD YOU LIKE IT. JUST REMEMBER ONE THING MY FRIEND...
TAXI
NOT ALL BRUJAS ARE HEALERS.
THANKS FOR THE TIP. I'LL WATCH MY BACK.
TAXI
Hotel Azul
NOW WHAT?

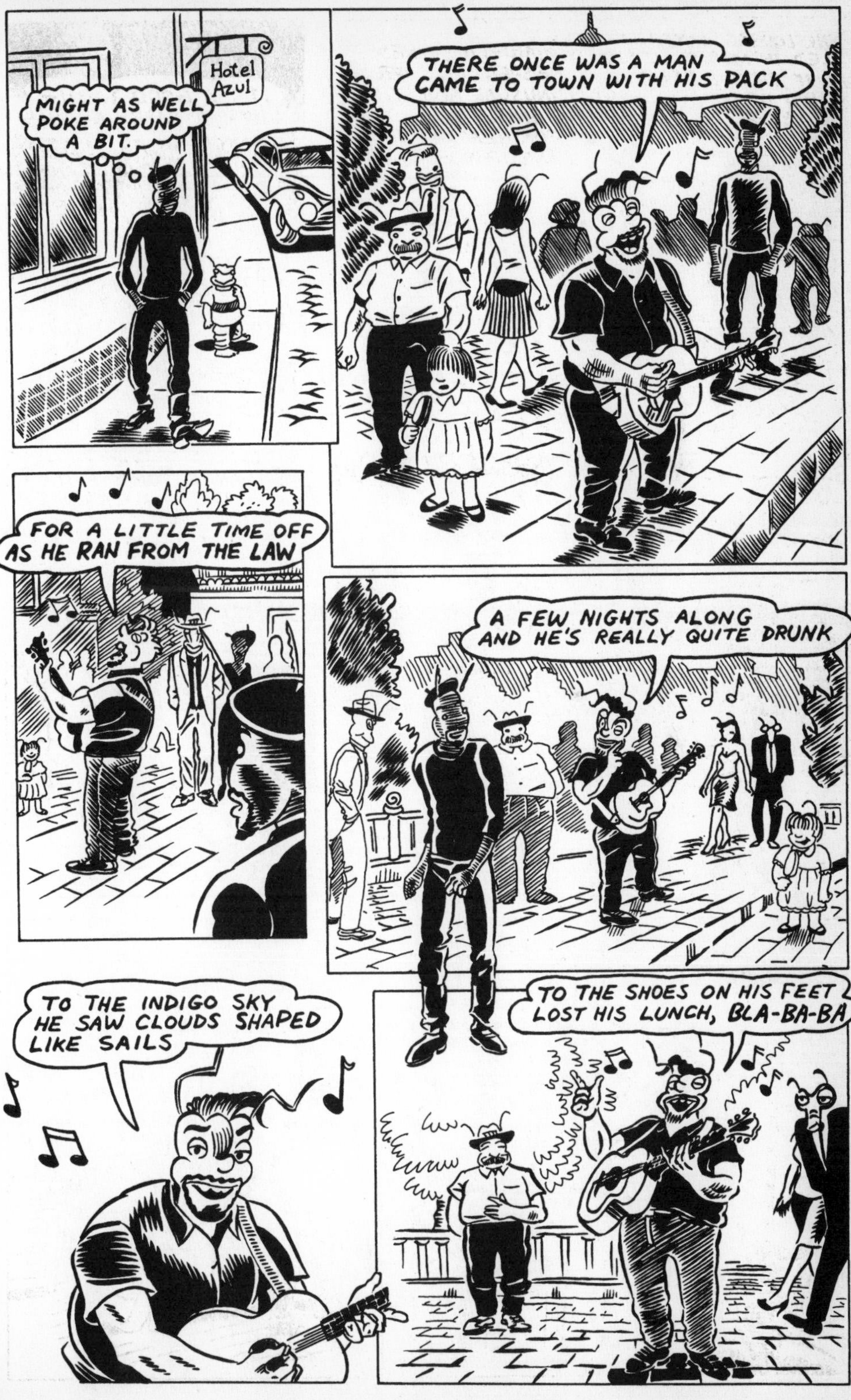
Hotel Azul
MIGHT AS WELL POKE AROUND A BIT.
THERE ONCE WAS A MAN CAME TO TOWN WITH HIS PACK
FOR A LITTLE TIME OFF AS HE RAN FROM THE LAW
A FEW NIGHTS ALONG AND HE'S REALLY QUITE DRUNK
TO THE INDIGO SKY HE SAW CLOUDS SHAPED LIKE SAILS
TO THE SHOES ON HIS FEET LOST HIS LUNCH, BLA-BA-BA

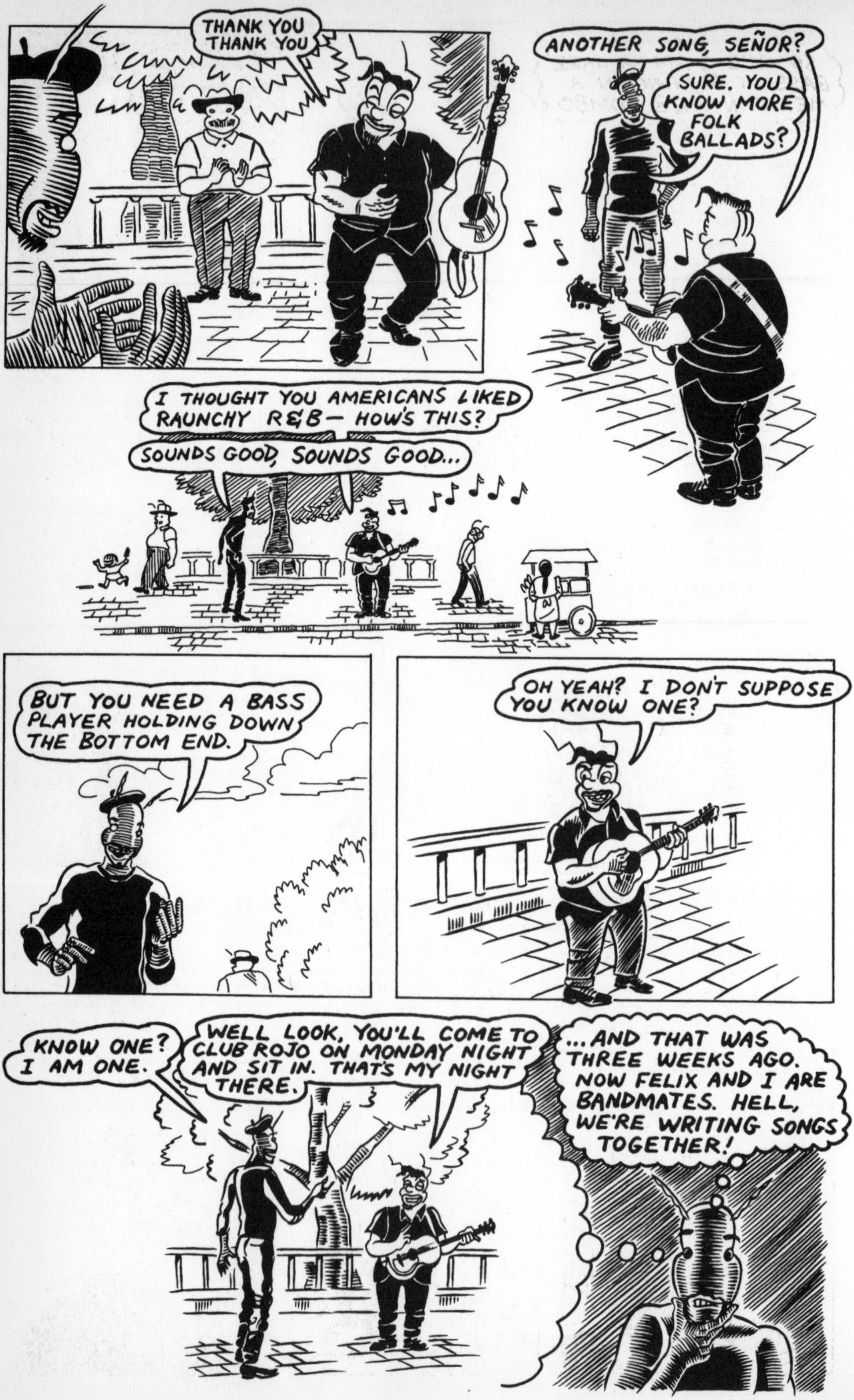
THANK YOU THANK YOU
ANOTHER SONG, SEÑOR?
SURE. YOU KNOW MORE FOLK BALLADS?
I THOUGHT YOU AMERICANS LIKED RAUNCHY R&B— HOW'S THIS?
SOUNDS GOOD, SOUNDS GOOD...
BUT YOU NEED A BASS PLAYER HOLDING DOWN THE BOTTOM END.
OH YEAH? I DON'T SUPPOSE YOU KNOW ONE?
KNOW ONE? I AM ONE.
WELL LOOK, YOU'LL COME TO CLUB ROJO ON MONDAY NIGHT AND SIT IN. THAT'S MY NIGHT THERE.
...AND THAT WAS THREE WEEKS AGO. NOW FELIX AND I ARE BANDMATES. HELL, WE'RE WRITING SONGS TOGETHER!

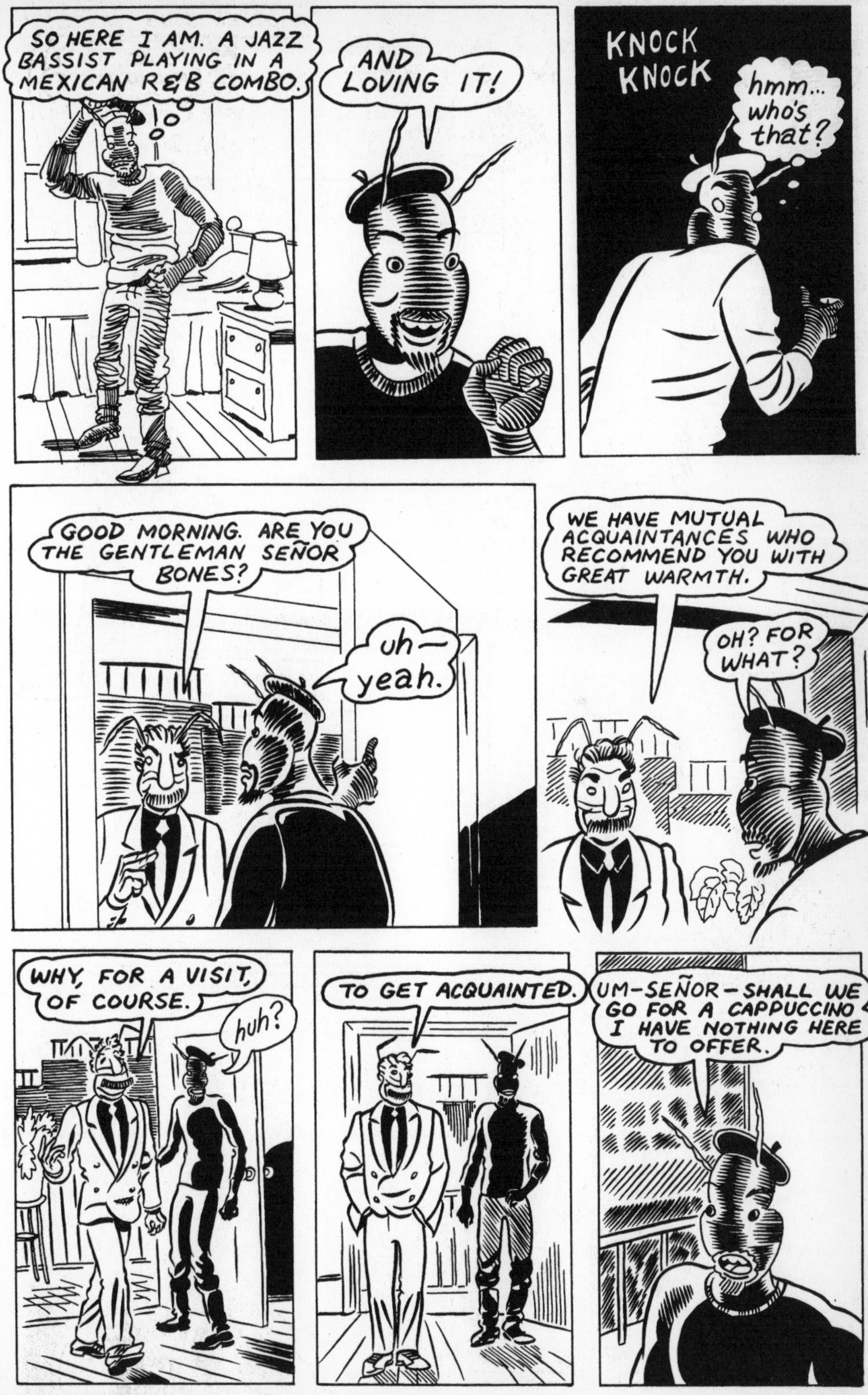
SO HERE I AM. A JAZZ BASSIST PLAYING IN A MEXICAN R&B COMBO.
AND LOVING IT!
KNOCK KNOCK
hmm... who's that?
GOOD MORNING. ARE YOU THE GENTLEMAN SEÑOR BONES?
uh— yeah.
WE HAVE MUTUAL ACQUAINTANCES WHO RECOMMEND YOU WITH GREAT WARMTH.
OH? FOR WHAT?
WHY, FOR A VISIT, OF COURSE.
huh?
TO GET ACQUAINTED.
UM-SEÑOR-SHALL WE GO FOR A CAPPUCCINO I HAVE NOTHING HERE TO OFFER.

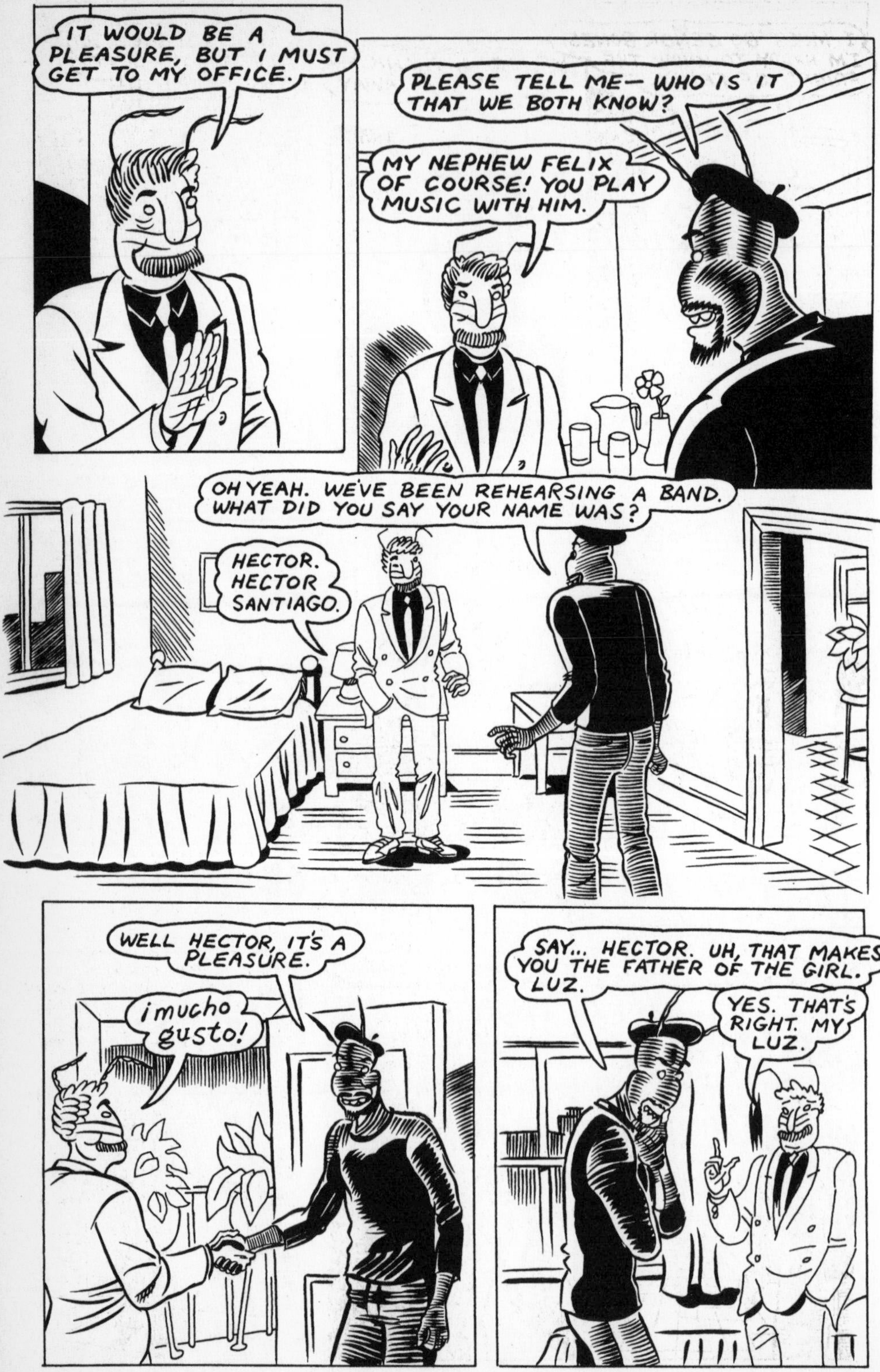
IT WOULD BE A PLEASURE, BUT I MUST GET TO MY OFFICE.
PLEASE TELL ME— WHO IS IT THAT WE BOTH KNOW?
MY NEPHEW FELIX OF COURSE! YOU PLAY MUSIC WITH HIM.
OH YEAH. WE'VE BEEN REHEARSING A BAND. WHAT DID YOU SAY YOUR NAME WAS?
HECTOR. HECTOR SANTIAGO.
WELL HECTOR, IT'S A PLEASURE.
¡mucho gusto!
SAY... HECTOR. UH, THAT MAKES YOU THE FATHER OF THE GIRL. LUZ.
YES. THAT'S RIGHT. MY LUZ.

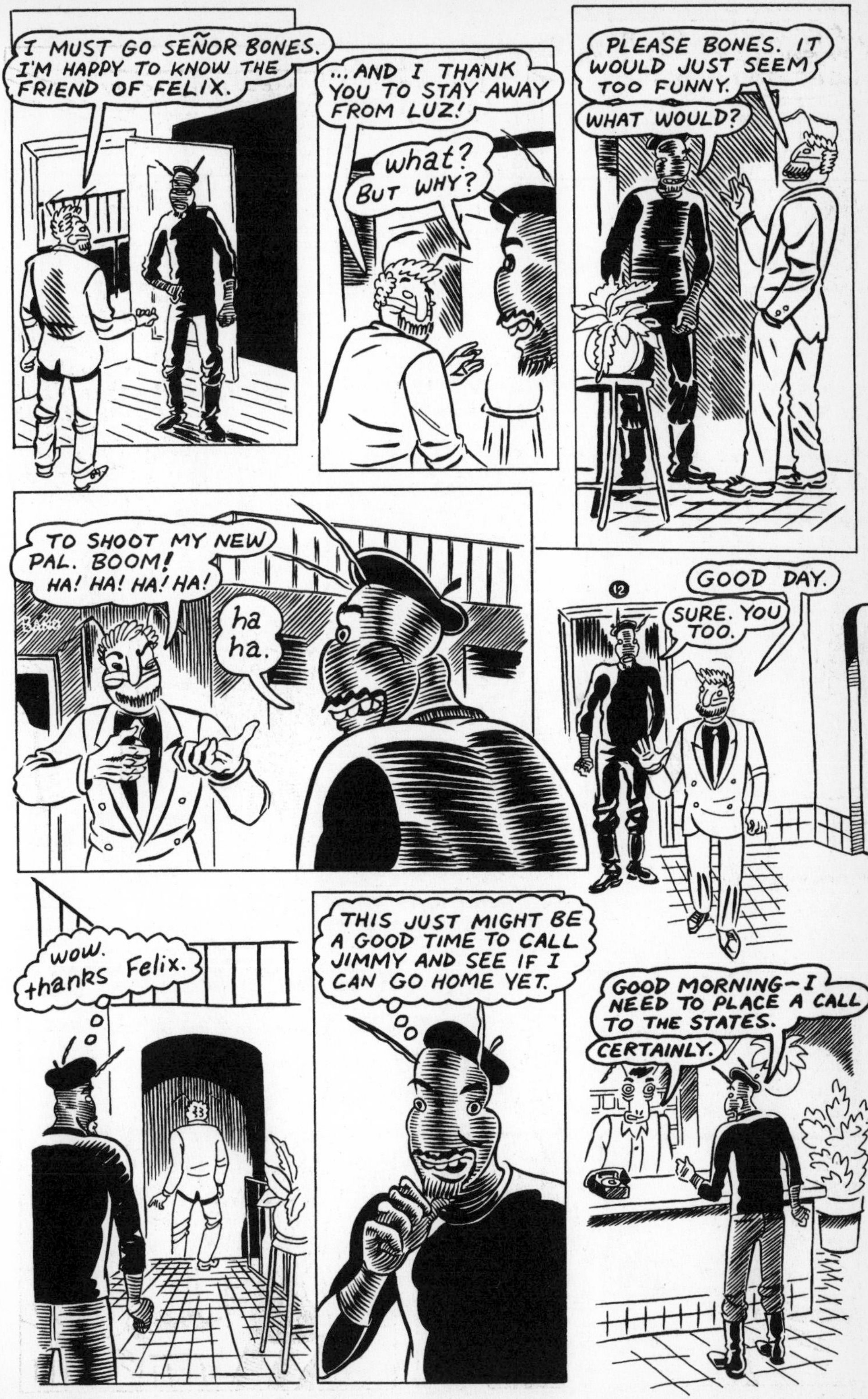
I MUST GO SEÑOR BONES. I'M HAPPY TO KNOW THE FRIEND OF FELIX.
...AND I THANK YOU TO STAY AWAY FROM LUZ!
what? BUT WHY?
PLEASE BONES. IT WOULD JUST SEEM TOO FUNNY.
WHAT WOULD?
TO SHOOT MY NEW PAL. BOOM! HA! HA! HA! HA!
ha ha.
GOOD DAY.
SURE. YOU TOO.
wow. thanks Felix.
THIS JUST MIGHT BE A GOOD TIME TO CALL JIMMY AND SEE IF I CAN GO HOME YET.
GOOD MORNING—I NEED TO PLACE A CALL TO THE STATES.
CERTAINLY.

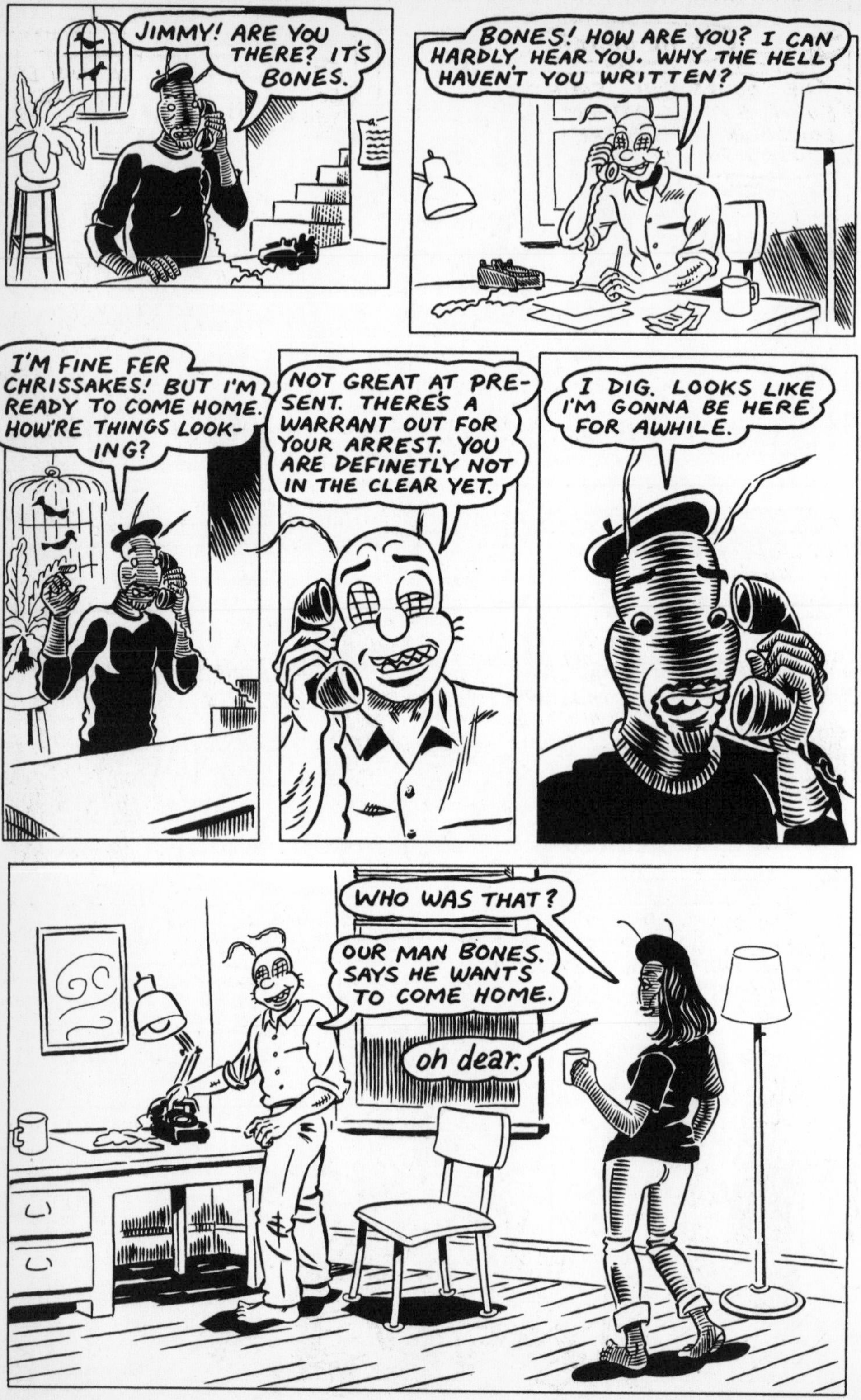
JIMMY! ARE YOU THERE? IT'S BONES.
BONES! HOW ARE YOU? I CAN HARDLY HEAR YOU. WHY THE HELL HAVEN'T YOU WRITTEN?
I'M FINE FER CHRISSAKES! BUT I'M READY TO COME HOME. HOW'RE THINGS LOOKING?
NOT GREAT AT PRESENT. THERE'S A WARRANT OUT FOR YOUR ARREST. YOU ARE DEFINETLY NOT IN THE CLEAR YET.
I DIG. LOOKS LIKE I'M GONNA BE HERE FOR AWHILE.
WHO WAS THAT?
OUR MAN BONES. SAYS HE WANTS TO COME HOME.
oh dear.

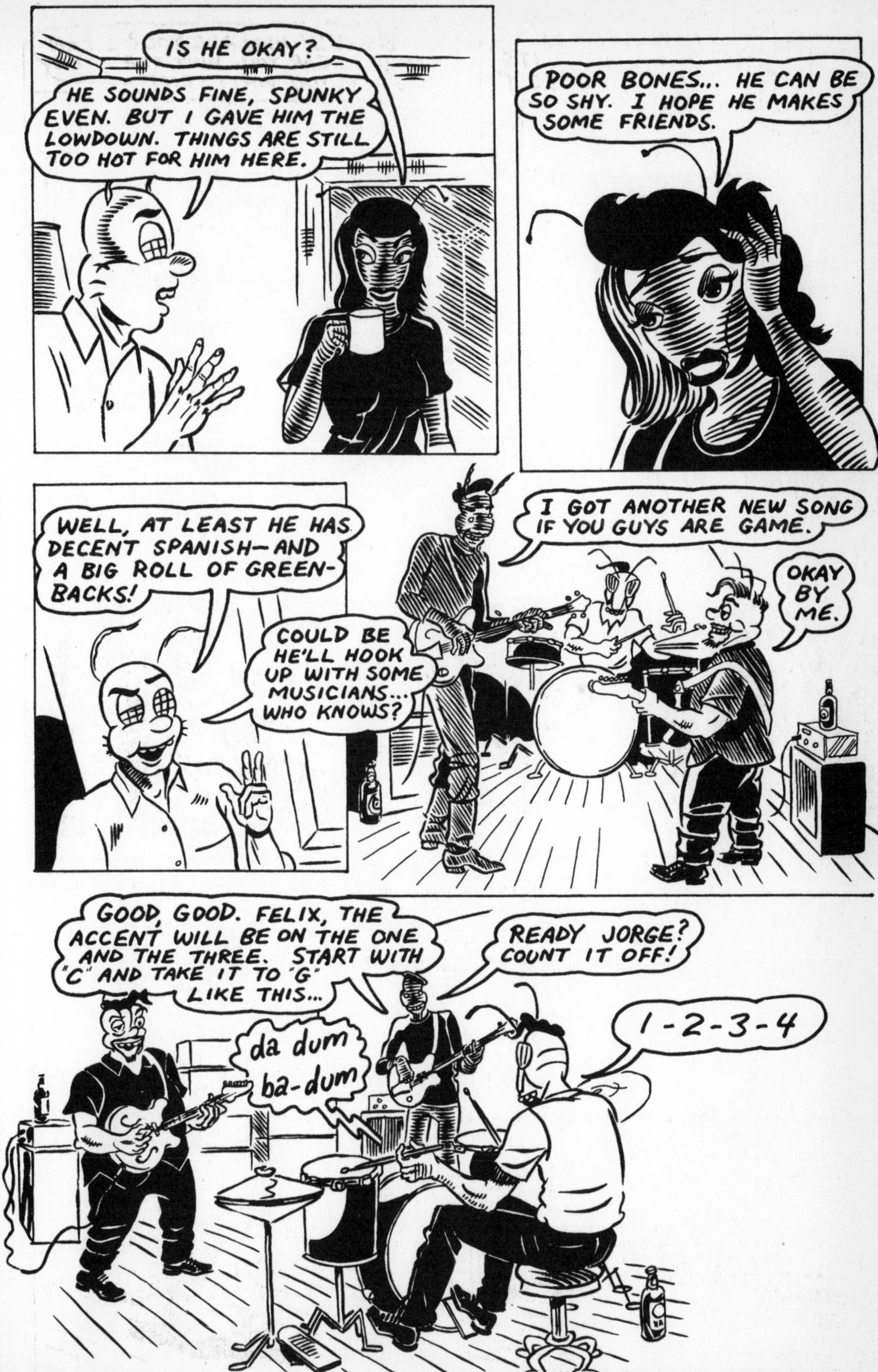
IS HE OKAY?
HE SOUNDS FINE, SPUNKY EVEN. BUT I GAVE HIM THE LOWDOWN. THINGS ARE STILL TOO HOT FOR HIM HERE.
POOR BONES... HE CAN BE SO SHY. I HOPE HE MAKES SOME FRIENDS.
WELL, AT LEAST HE HAS DECENT SPANISH— AND A BIG ROLL OF GREEN-BACKS!
COULD BE HE'LL HOOK UP WITH SOME MUSICIANS... WHO KNOWS?
I GOT ANOTHER NEW SONG IF YOU GUYS ARE GAME.
OKAY BY ME.
GOOD, GOOD. FELIX, THE ACCENT WILL BE ON THE ONE AND THE THREE. START WITH "C" AND TAKE IT TO "G" LIKE THIS...
READY JORGE? COUNT IT OFF!
da dum ba-dum
1-2-3-4

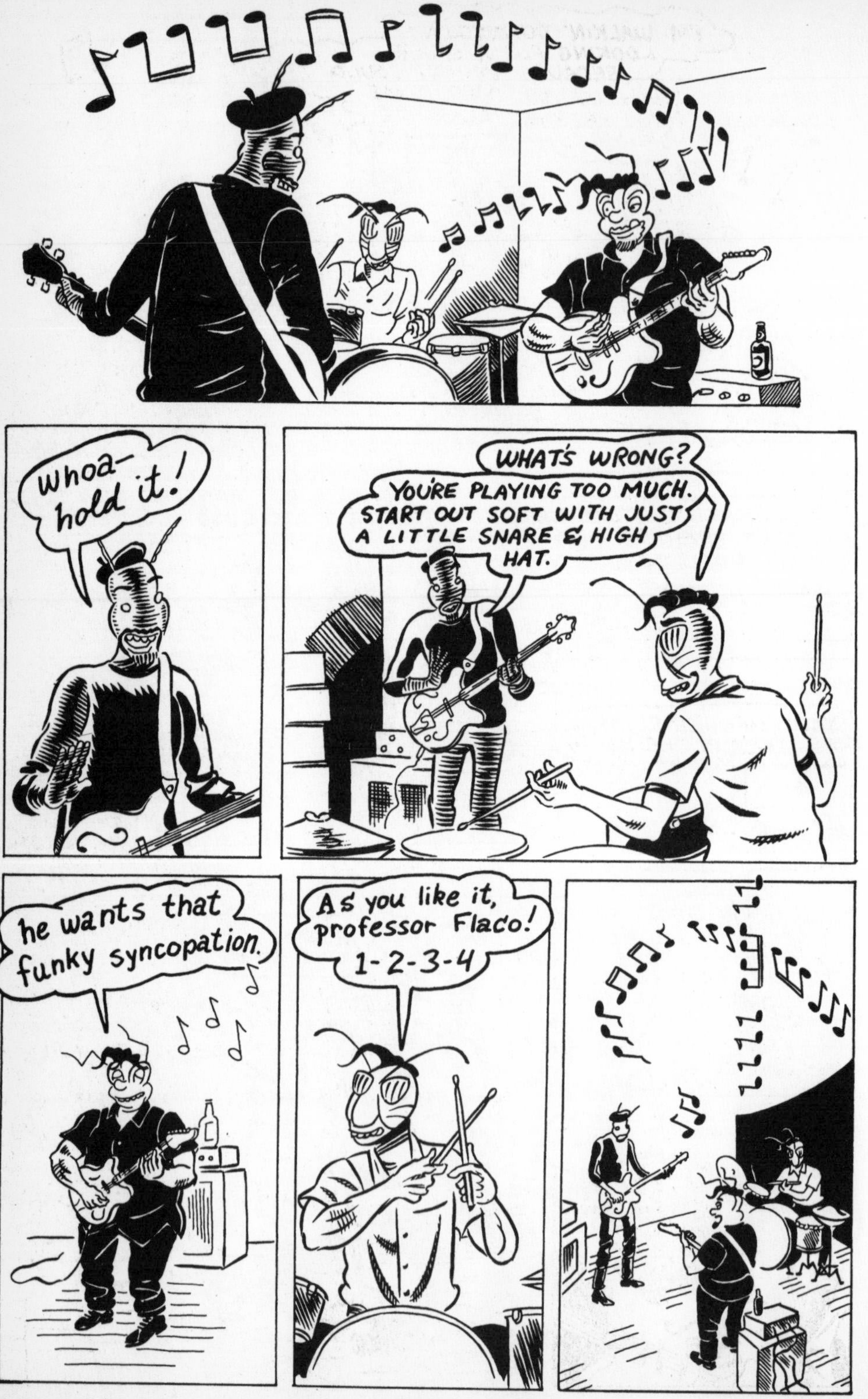
whoa-
hold it!
WHAT'S WRONG?
YOU'RE PLAYING TOO MUCH. START OUT SOFT WITH JUST A LITTLE SNARE & HIGH HAT.
he wants that funky syncopation.
As you like it, professor Flaco!
1-2-3-4

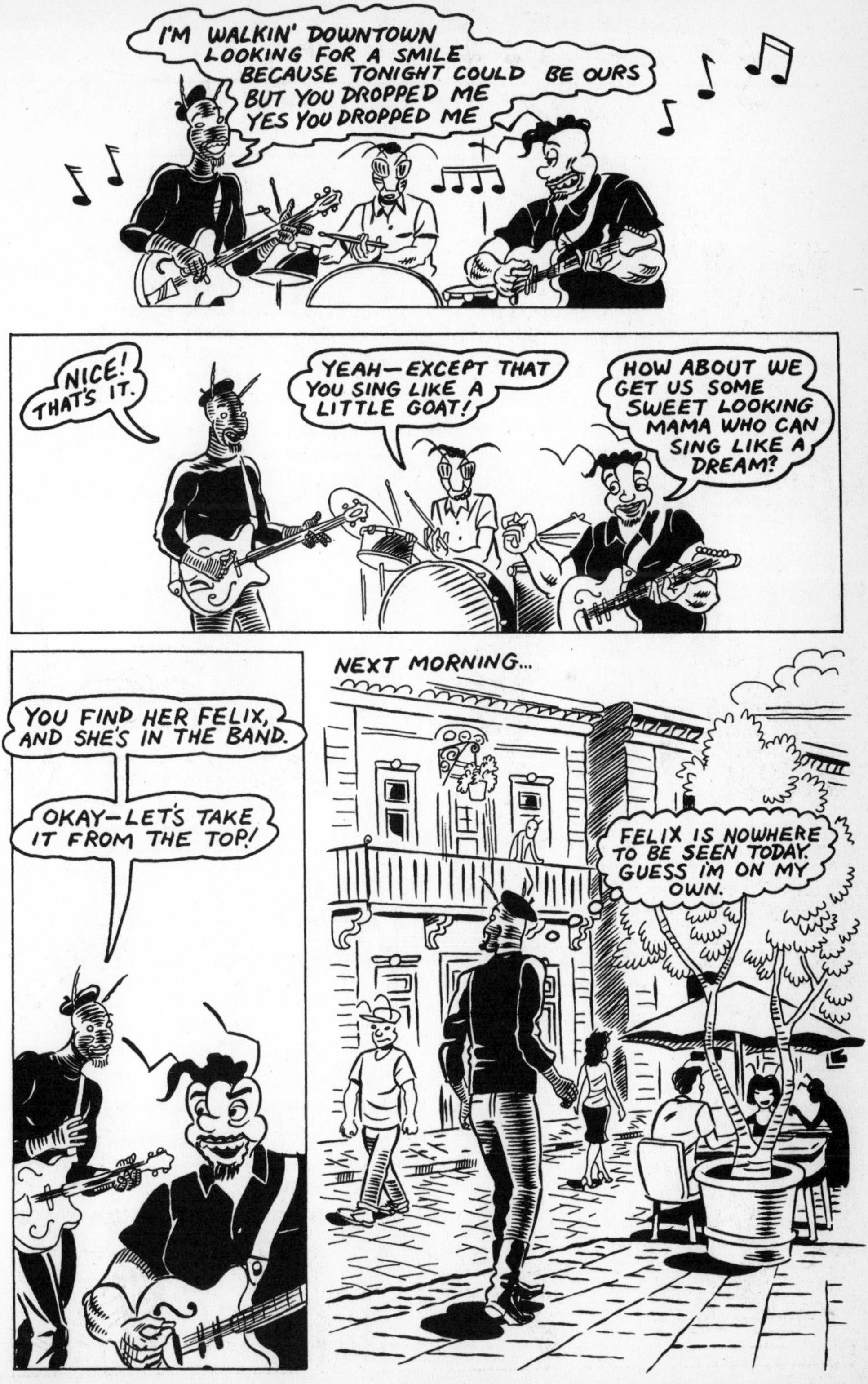

I'M WALKIN' DOWNTOWN
LOOKING FOR A SMILE
BECAUSE TONIGHT COULD BE OURS
BUT YOU DROPPED ME
YES YOU DROPPED ME
NICE! THAT'S IT.
YEAH—EXCEPT THAT YOU SING LIKE A LITTLE GOAT!
HOW ABOUT WE GET US SOME SWEET LOOKING MAMA WHO CAN SING LIKE A DREAM?
YOU FIND HER FELIX, AND SHE'S IN THE BAND.
OKAY—LET'S TAKE IT FROM THE TOP!
NEXT MORNING...
FELIX IS NOWHERE TO BE SEEN TODAY. GUESS I'M ON MY OWN.

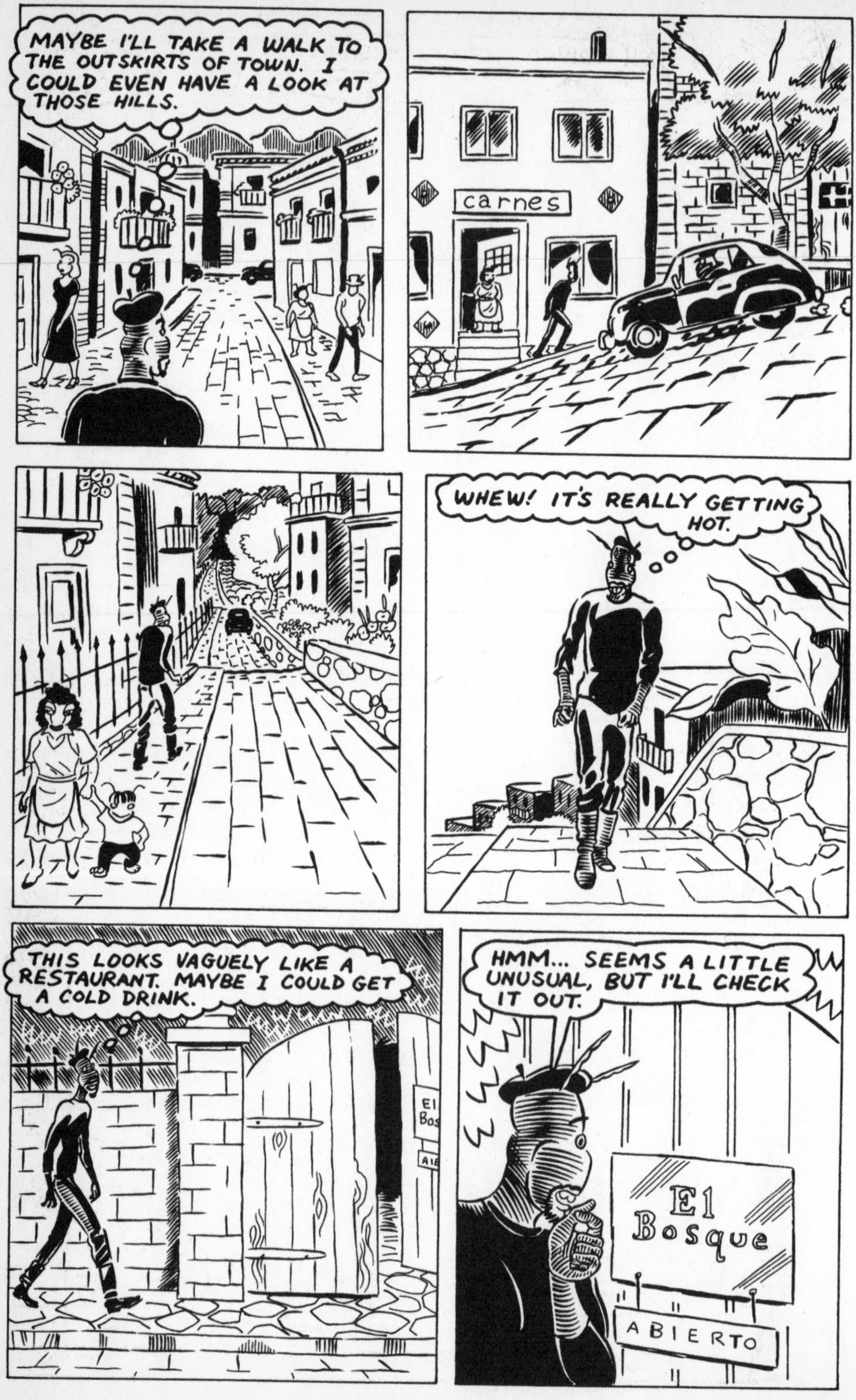
MAYBE I'LL TAKE A WALK TO THE OUTSKIRTS OF TOWN. I COULD EVEN HAVE A LOOK AT THOSE HILLS.
carnes
WHEW! IT'S REALLY GETTING HOT.
THIS LOOKS VAGUELY LIKE A RESTAURANT. MAYBE I COULD GET A COLD DRINK.
HMM... SEEMS A LITTLE UNUSUAL, BUT I'LL CHECK IT OUT.
El Bosque
ABIERTO

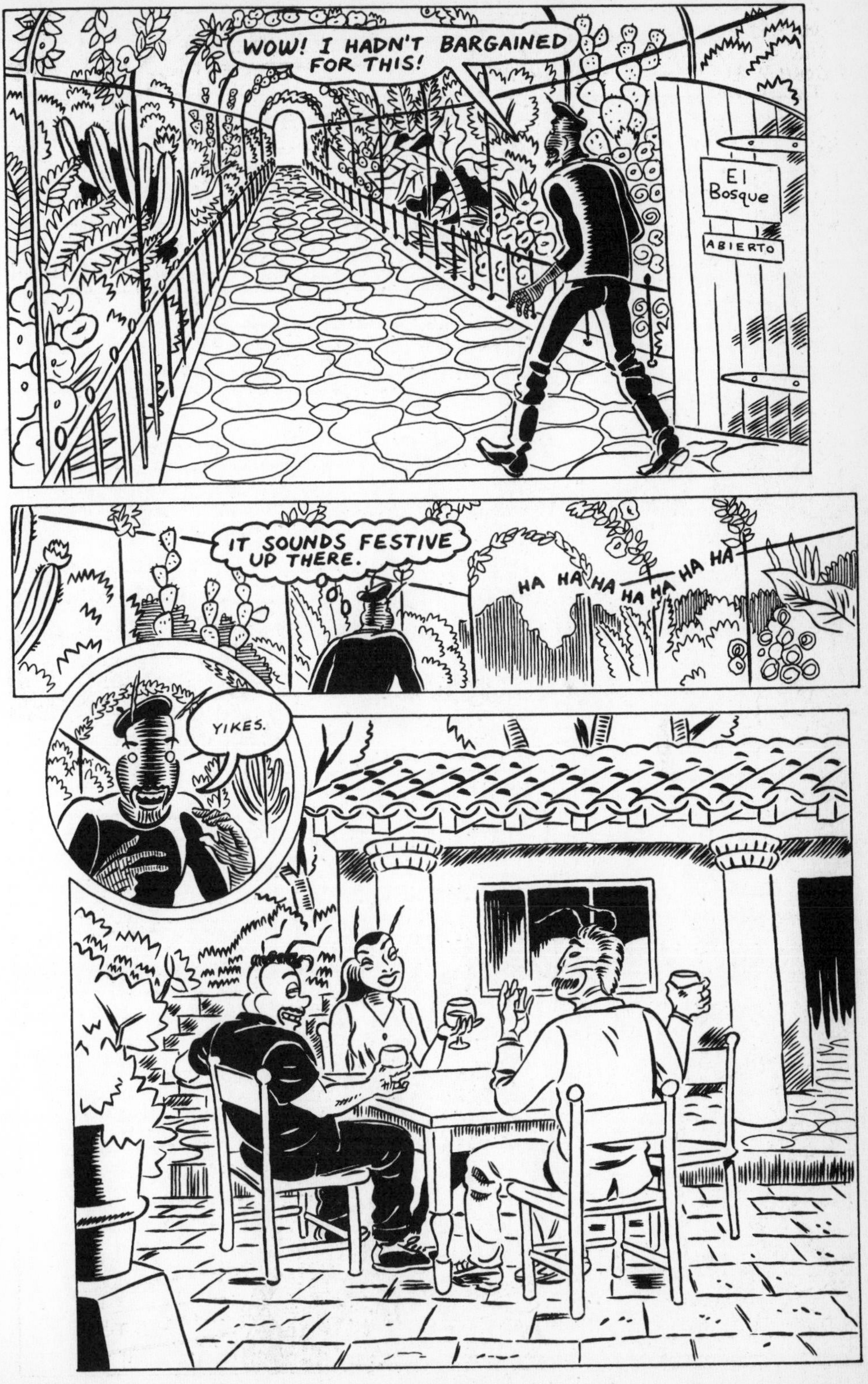
WOW! I HADN'T BARGAINED FOR THIS!
El Bosque
ABIERTO
IT SOUNDS FESTIVE UP THERE.
HA HA HA HA HA HA HA HA
YIKES.

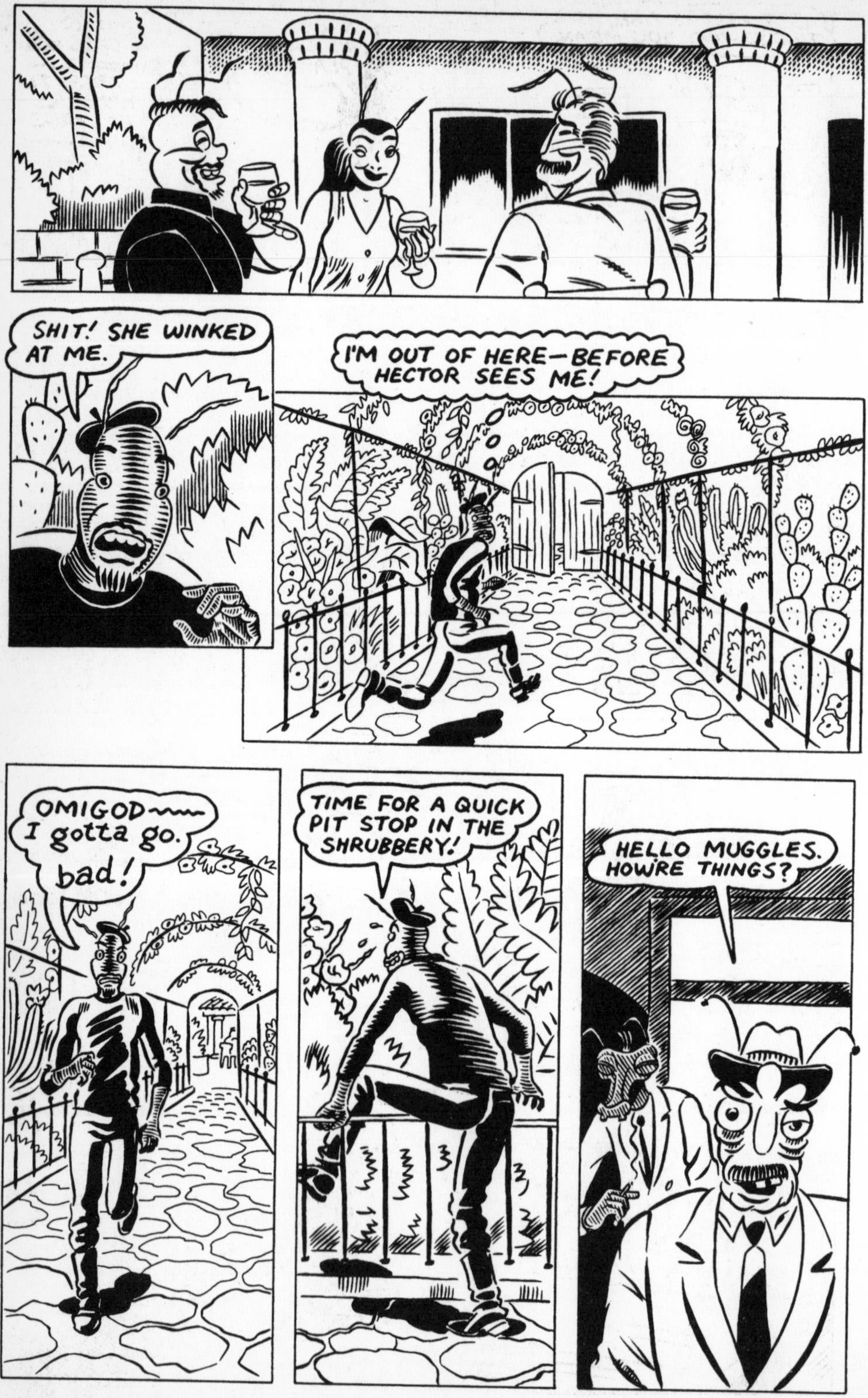
SHIT! SHE WINKED AT ME.
I'M OUT OF HERE—BEFORE HECTOR SEES ME!
OMIGOD~~~ I gotta go. bad!
TIME FOR A QUICK PIT STOP IN THE SHRUBBERY!
HELLO MUGGLES. HOW'RE THINGS?

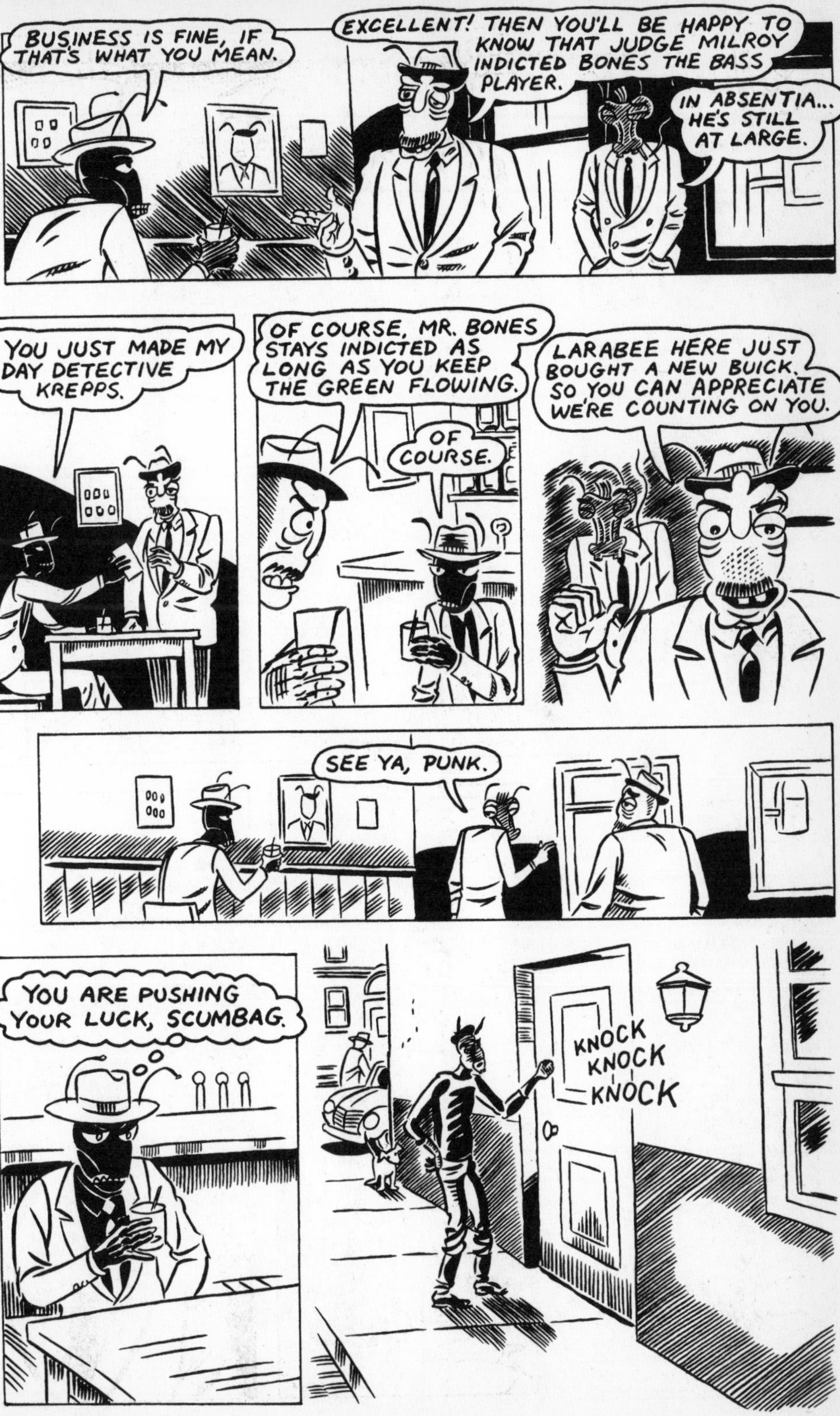
BUSINESS IS FINE, IF THAT'S WHAT YOU MEAN.
EXCELLENT! THEN YOU'LL BE HAPPY TO KNOW THAT JUDGE MILROY INDICTED BONES THE BASS PLAYER.
IN ABSENTIA... HE'S STILL AT LARGE.
YOU JUST MADE MY DAY DETECTIVE KREPPS.
OF COURSE, MR. BONES STAYS INDICTED AS LONG AS YOU KEEP THE GREEN FLOWING.
OF COURSE.
LARABEE HERE JUST BOUGHT A NEW BUICK. SO YOU CAN APPRECIATE WE'RE COUNTING ON YOU.
SEE YA, PUNK.
YOU ARE PUSHING YOUR LUCK, SCUMBAG.
KNOCK
KNOCK
KNOCK

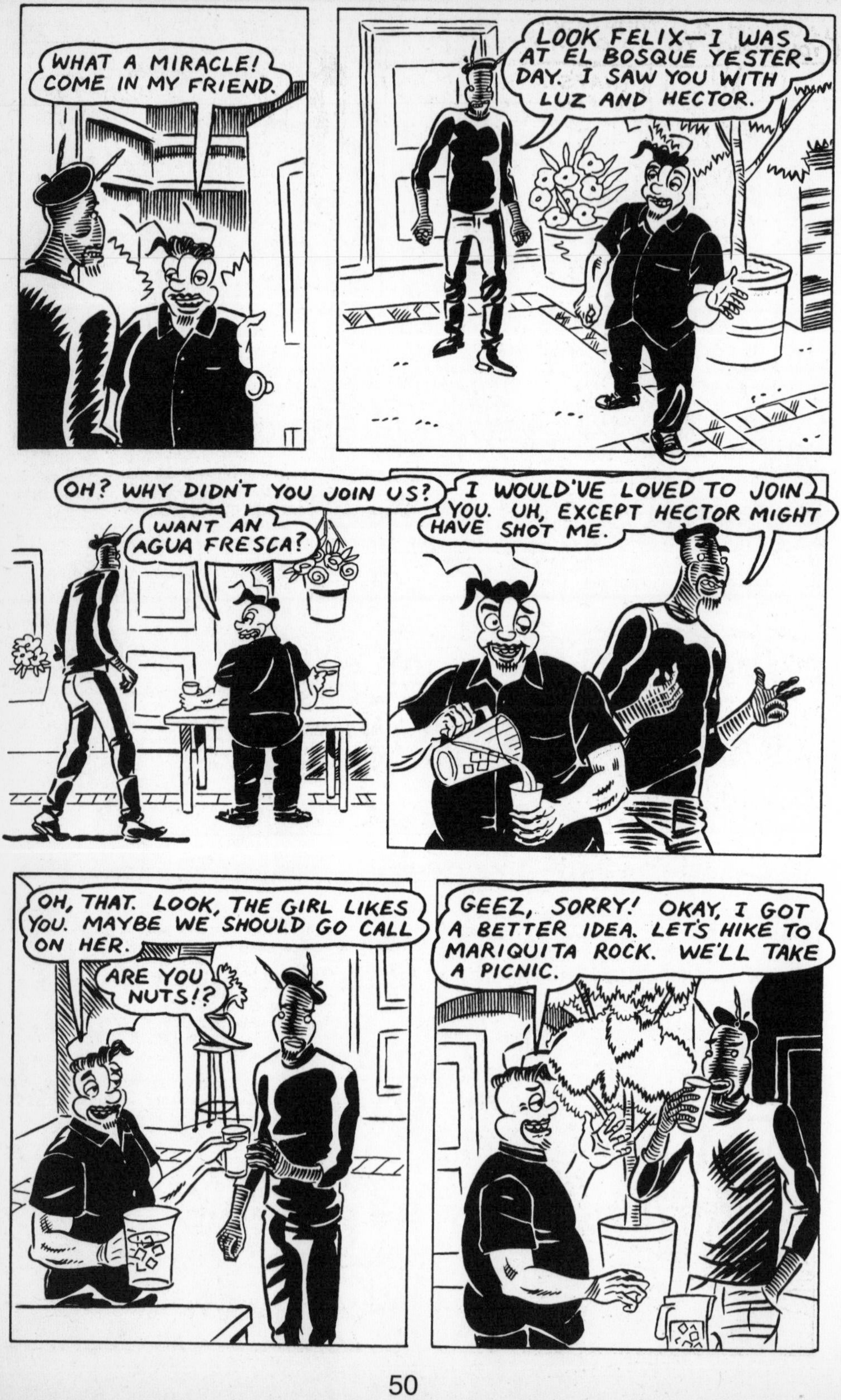
WHAT A MIRACLE! COME IN MY FRIEND.
LOOK FELIX—I WAS AT EL BOSQUE YESTERDAY. I SAW YOU WITH LUZ AND HECTOR.
OH? WHY DIDN'T YOU JOIN US?
WANT AN AGUA FRESCA?
I WOULD'VE LOVED TO JOIN YOU. UH, EXCEPT HECTOR MIGHT HAVE SHOT ME.
OH, THAT. LOOK, THE GIRL LIKES YOU. MAYBE WE SHOULD GO CALL ON HER.
ARE YOU NUTS!?
GEEZ, SORRY! OKAY, I GOT A BETTER IDEA. LET'S HIKE TO MARIQUITA ROCK. WE'LL TAKE A PICNIC.

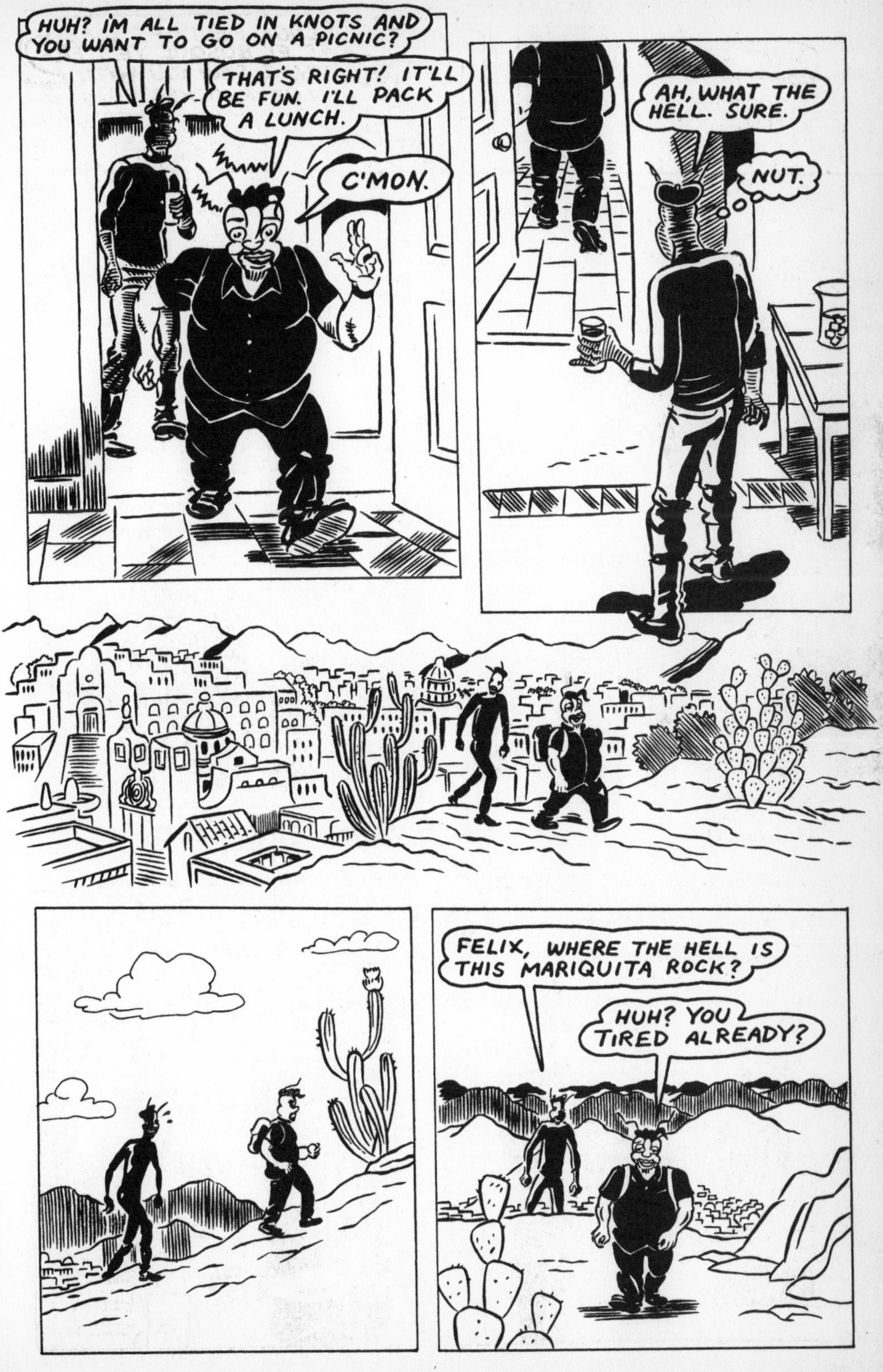
HUH? I'M ALL TIED IN KNOTS AND YOU WANT TO GO ON A PICNIC?
THAT'S RIGHT! IT'LL BE FUN. I'LL PACK A LUNCH.
C'MON.
AH, WHAT THE HELL. SURE.
NUT.
FELIX, WHERE THE HELL IS THIS MARIQUITA ROCK?
HUH? YOU TIRED ALREADY?

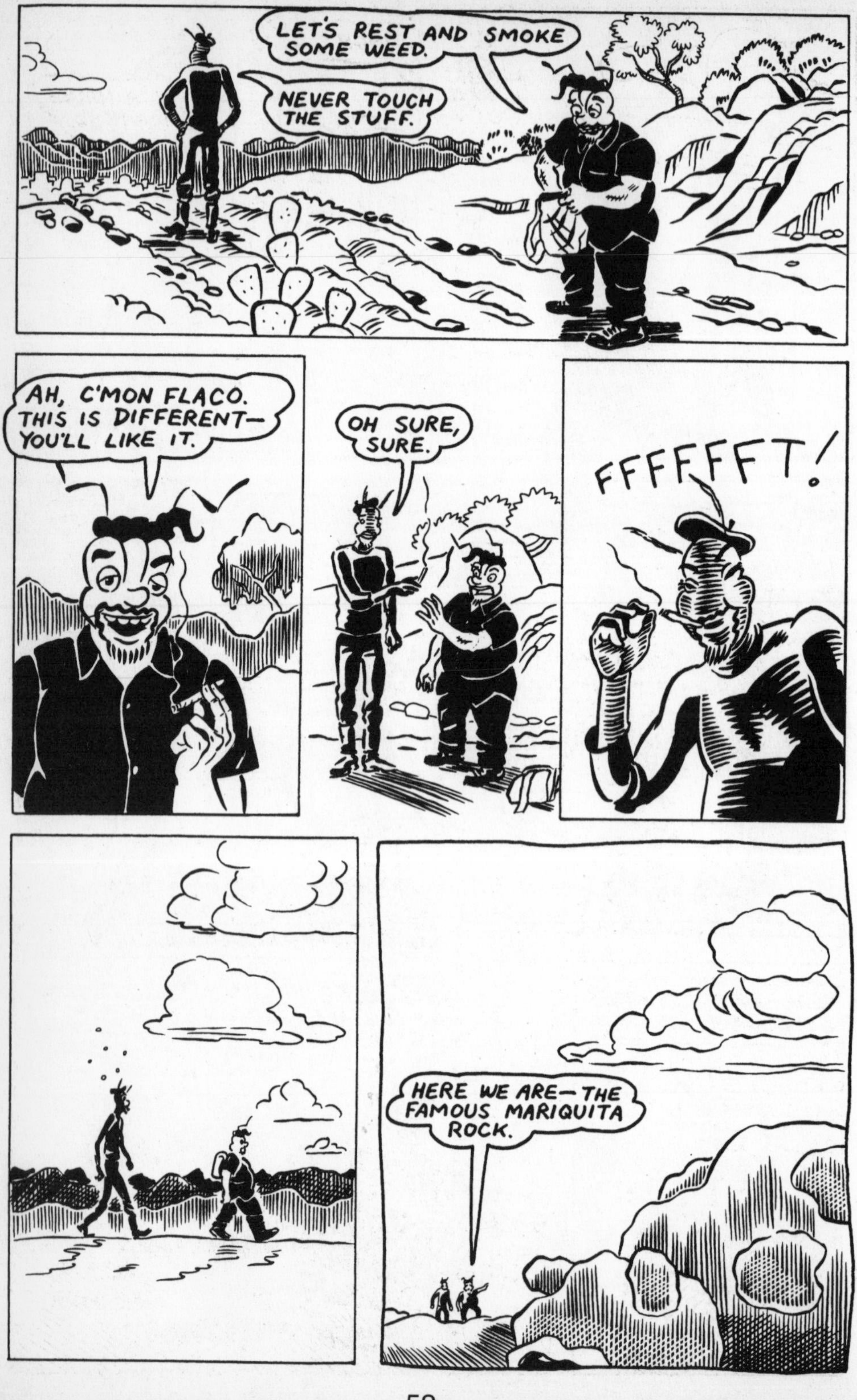
LET'S REST AND SMOKE SOME WEED.
NEVER TOUCH THE STUFF.
AH, C'MON FLACO. THIS IS DIFFERENT— YOU'LL LIKE IT.
OH SURE, SURE.
FFFFFFT!
HERE WE ARE—THE FAMOUS MARIQUITA ROCK.

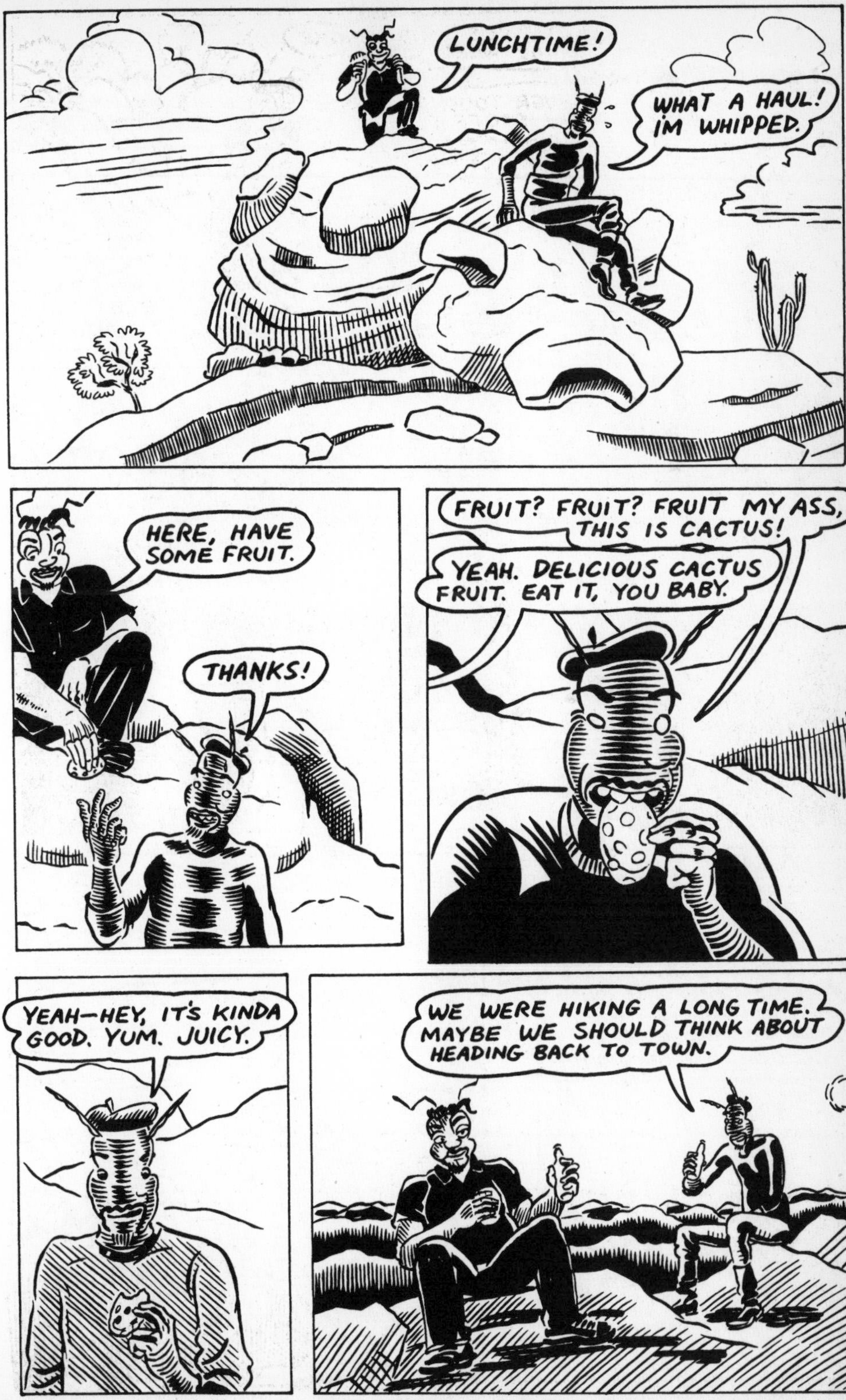
LUNCHTIME!
WHAT A HAUL! I'M WHIPPED.
HERE, HAVE SOME FRUIT.
THANKS!
FRUIT? FRUIT? FRUIT MY ASS, THIS IS CACTUS!
YEAH. DELICIOUS CACTUS FRUIT. EAT IT, YOU BABY.
YEAH—HEY, IT'S KINDA GOOD. YUM. JUICY.
WE WERE HIKING A LONG TIME. MAYBE WE SHOULD THINK ABOUT HEADING BACK TO TOWN.

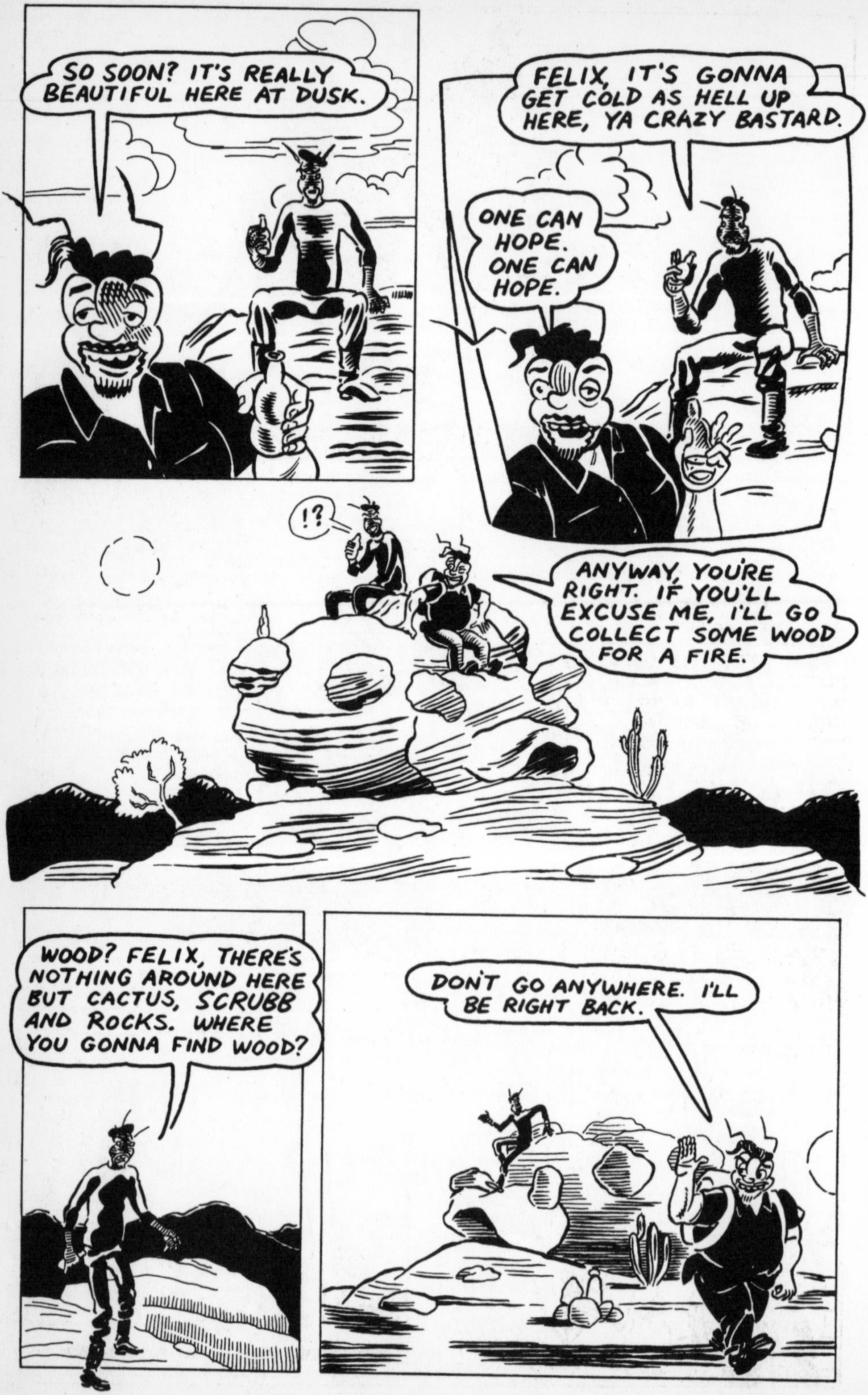
SO SOON? IT'S REALLY BEAUTIFUL HERE AT DUSK.
FELIX, IT'S GONNA GET COLD AS HELL UP HERE, YA CRAZY BASTARD.
ONE CAN HOPE. ONE CAN HOPE.
!?
ANYWAY, YOU'RE RIGHT. IF YOU'LL EXCUSE ME, I'LL GO COLLECT SOME WOOD FOR A FIRE.
WOOD? FELIX, THERE'S NOTHING AROUND HERE BUT CACTUS, SCRUBB AND ROCKS. WHERE YOU GONNA FIND WOOD?
DON'T GO ANYWHERE. I'LL BE RIGHT BACK.

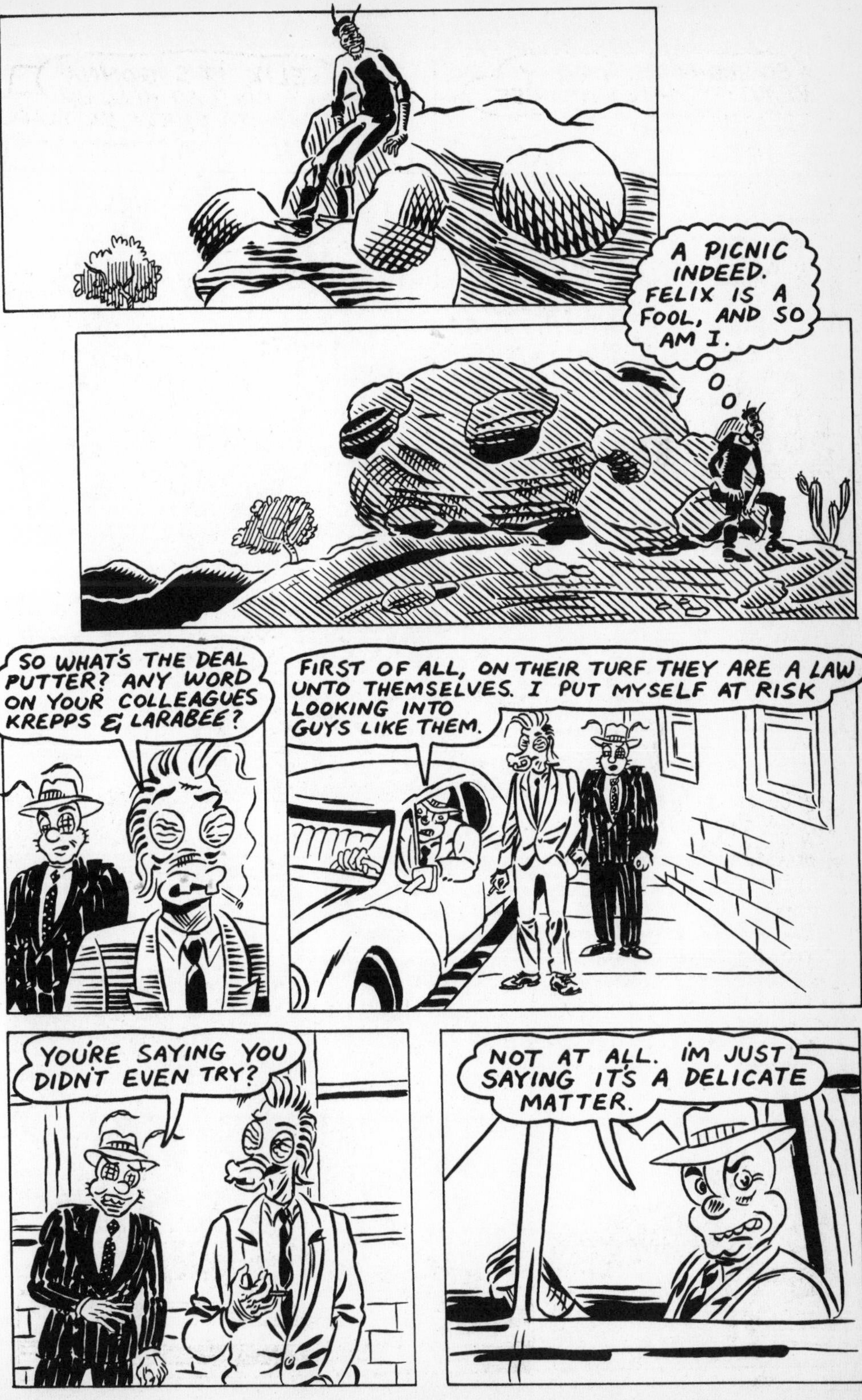
A PICNIC INDEED. FELIX IS A FOOL, AND SO AM I.
SO WHAT'S THE DEAL PUTTER? ANY WORD ON YOUR COLLEAGUES KREPPS & LARABEE?
FIRST OF ALL, ON THEIR TURF THEY ARE A LAW UNTO THEMSELVES. I PUT MYSELF AT RISK LOOKING INTO GUYS LIKE THEM.
YOU'RE SAYING YOU DIDN'T EVEN TRY?
NOT AT ALL. I'M JUST SAYING IT'S A DELICATE MATTER.

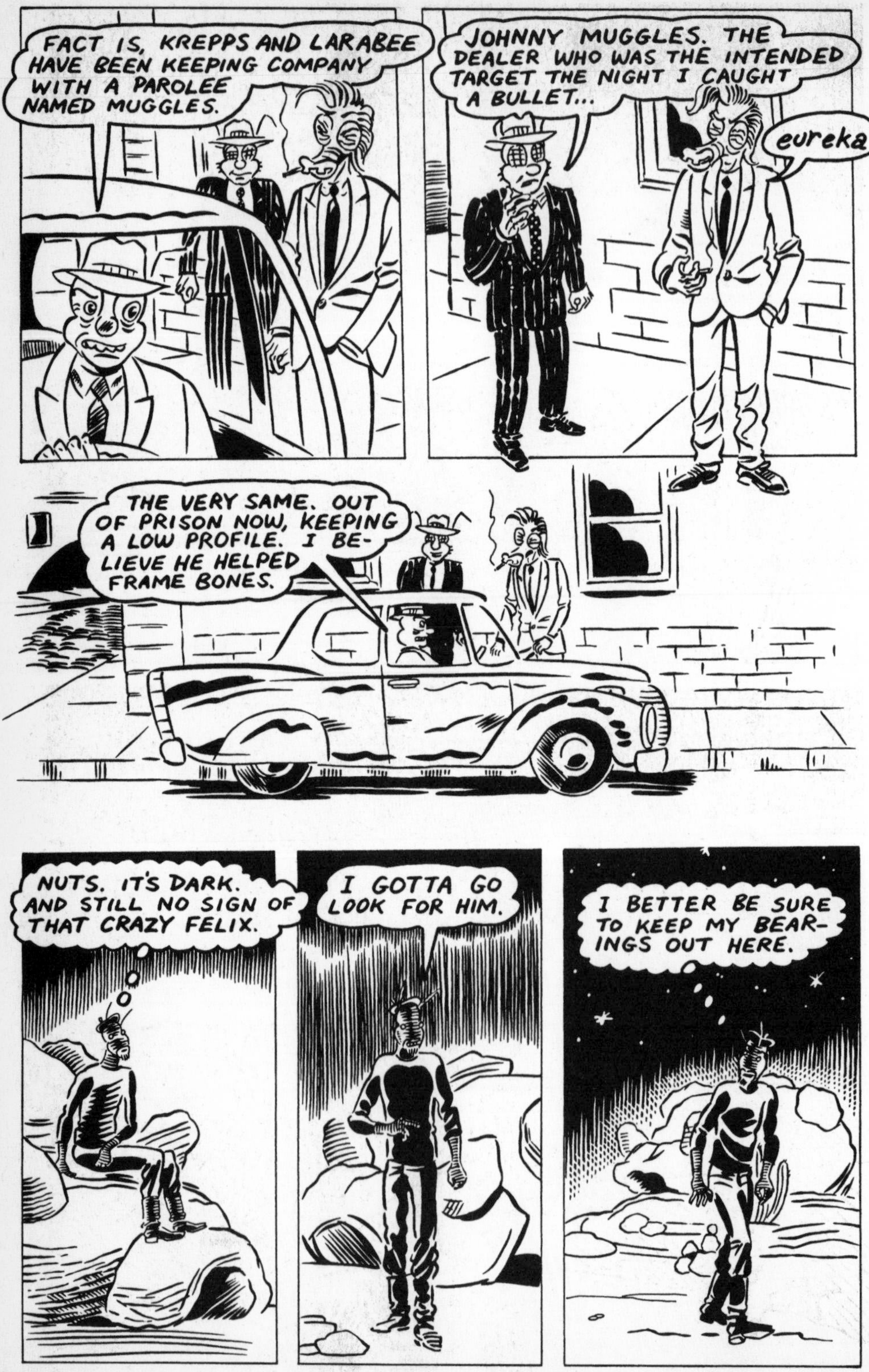

FACT IS, KREPPS AND LARABEE HAVE BEEN KEEPING COMPANY WITH A PAROLEE NAMED MUGGLES.
JOHNNY MUGGLES. THE DEALER WHO WAS THE INTENDED TARGET THE NIGHT I CAUGHT A BULLET...
eureka
THE VERY SAME. OUT OF PRISON NOW, KEEPING A LOW PROFILE. I BE-LIEVE HE HELPED FRAME BONES.
NUTS. IT'S DARK. AND STILL NO SIGN OF THAT CRAZY FELIX.
I GOTTA GO LOOK FOR HIM.
I BETTER BE SURE TO KEEP MY BEAR-INGS OUT HERE.

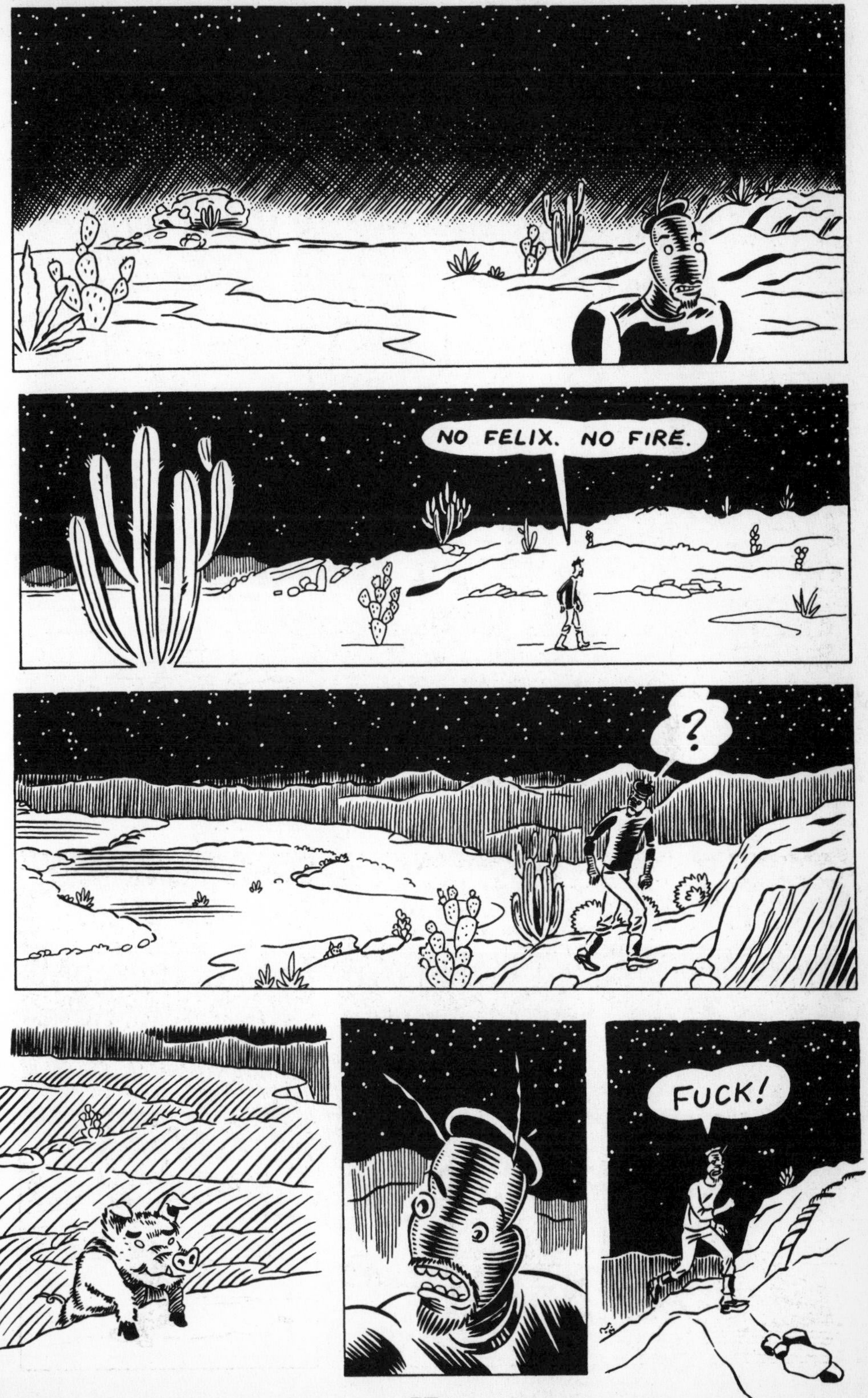
NO FELIX. NO FIRE.
?
FUCK!

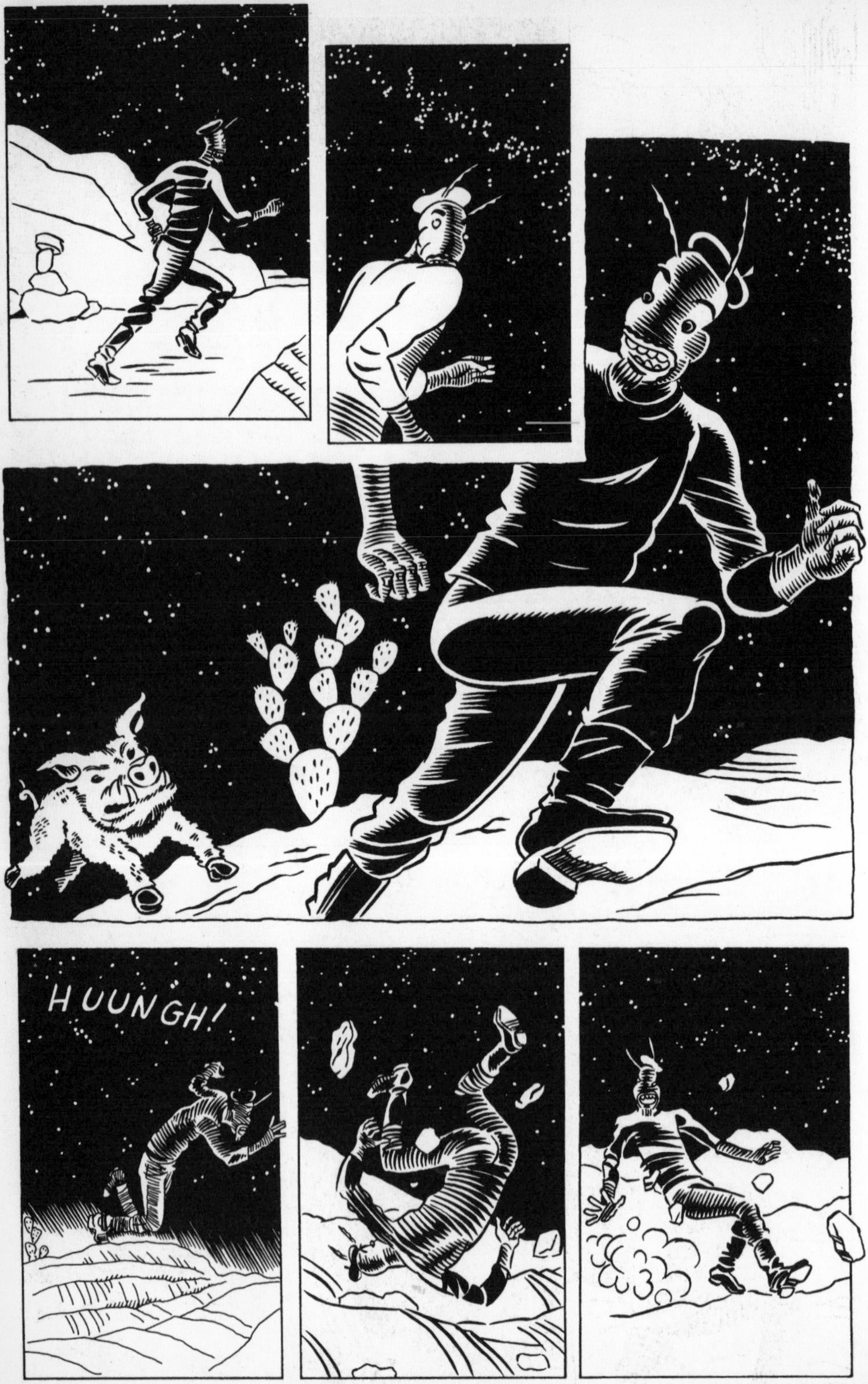
HUUNGH!

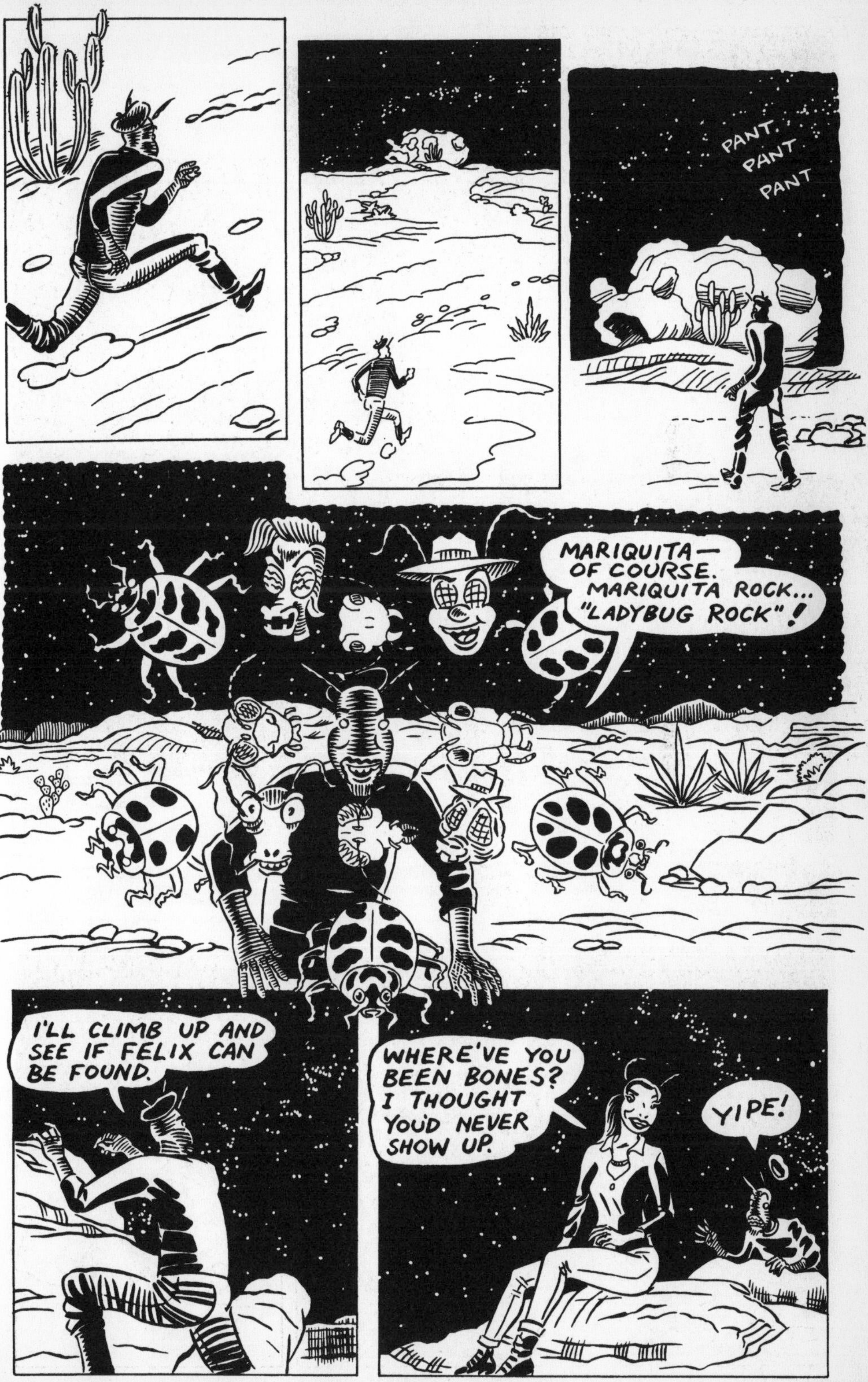
PANT. PANT PANT
MARIQUITA— OF COURSE. MARIQUITA ROCK... "LADYBUG ROCK"!
I'LL CLIMB UP AND SEE IF FELIX CAN BE FOUND.
WHERE'VE YOU BEEN BONES? I THOUGHT YOU'D NEVER SHOW UP.
YIPE!

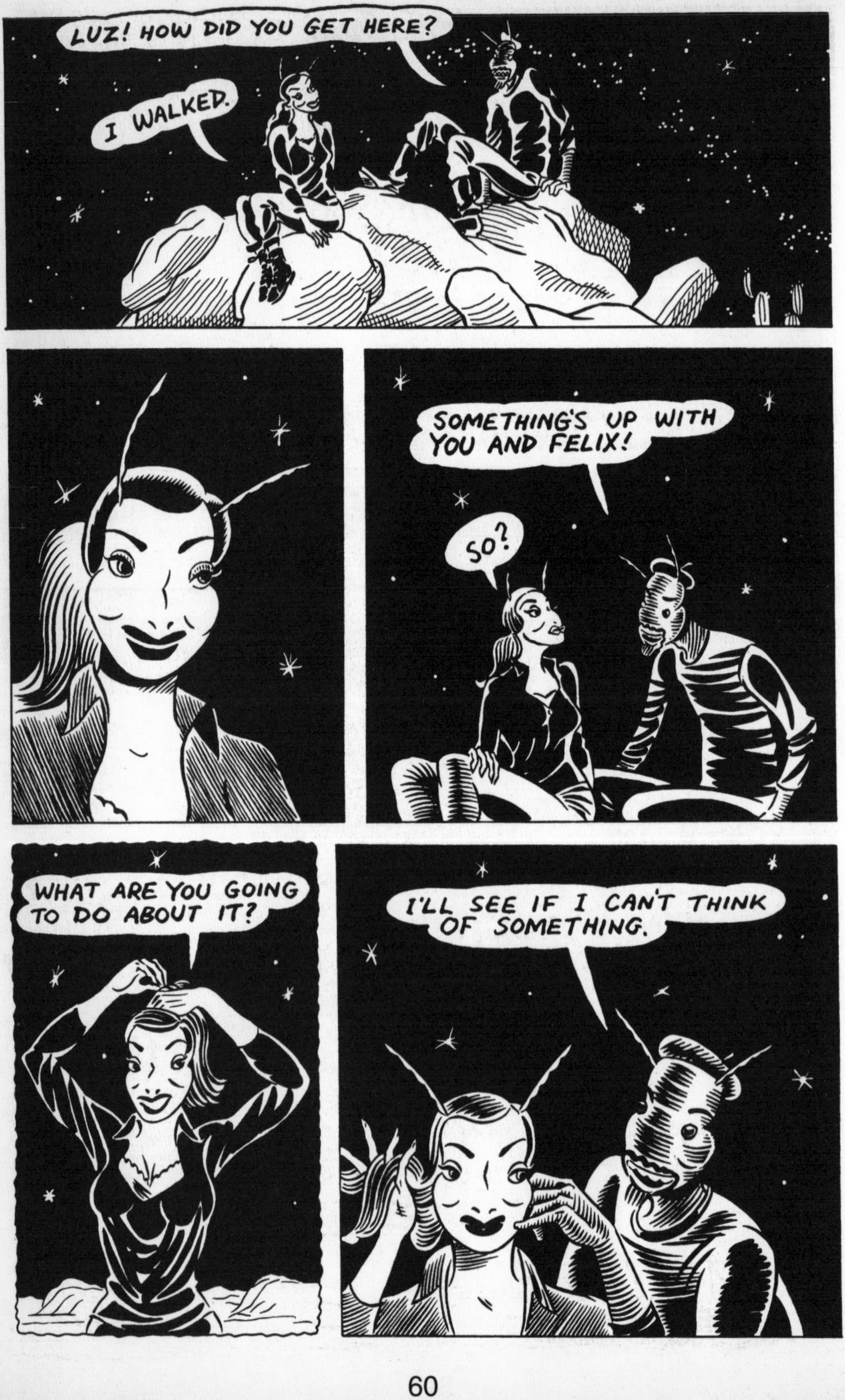
LUZ! HOW DID YOU GET HERE?
I WALKED.
SOMETHING'S UP WITH YOU AND FELIX!
SO?
WHAT ARE YOU GOING TO DO ABOUT IT?
I'LL SEE IF I CAN'T THINK OF SOMETHING.

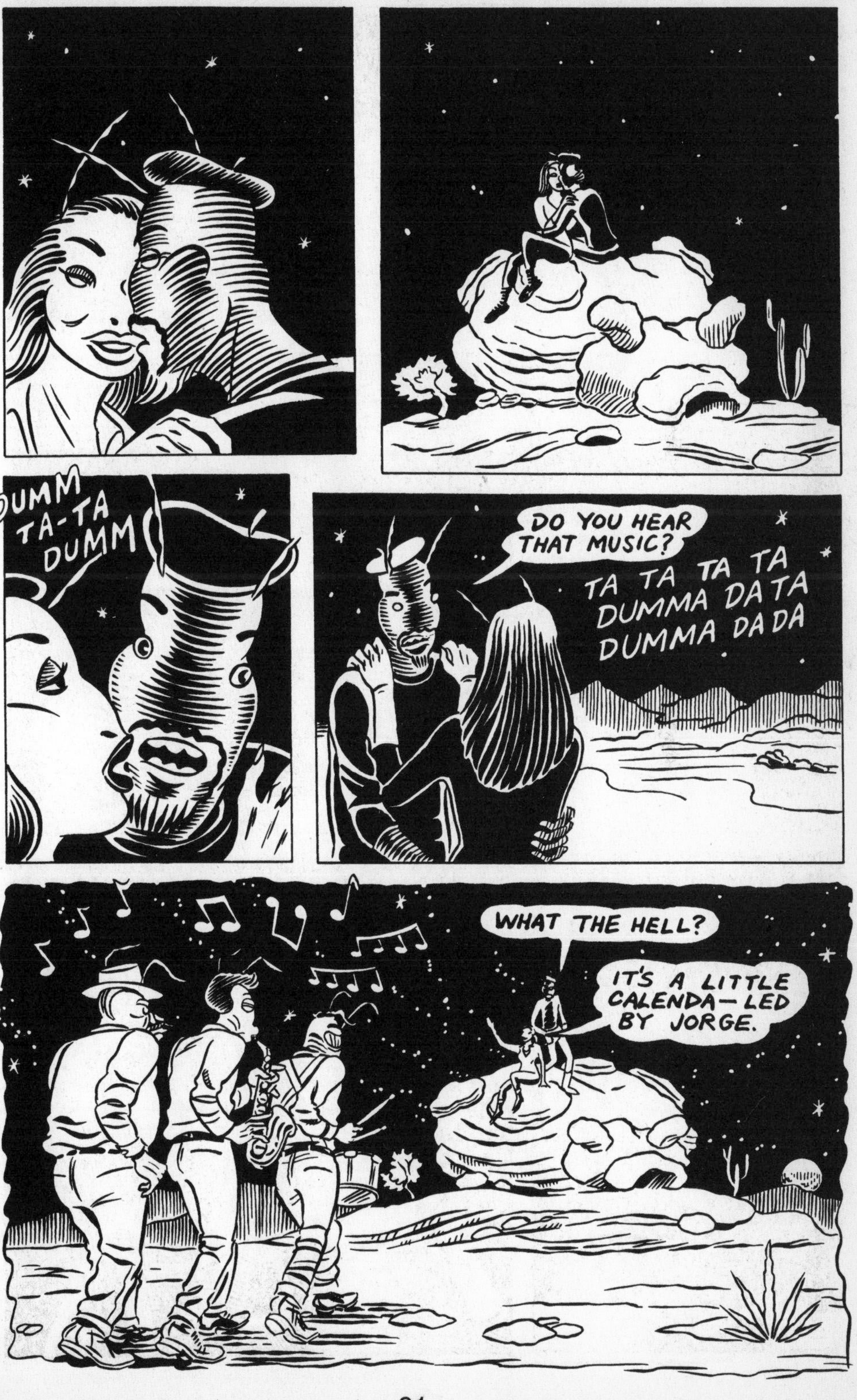
DUMM TA-TA DUMM
DO YOU HEAR THAT MUSIC?
TA TA TA TA DUMMA DA TA DUMMA DA DA
WHAT THE HELL?
IT'S A LITTLE CALENDA—LED BY JORGE.

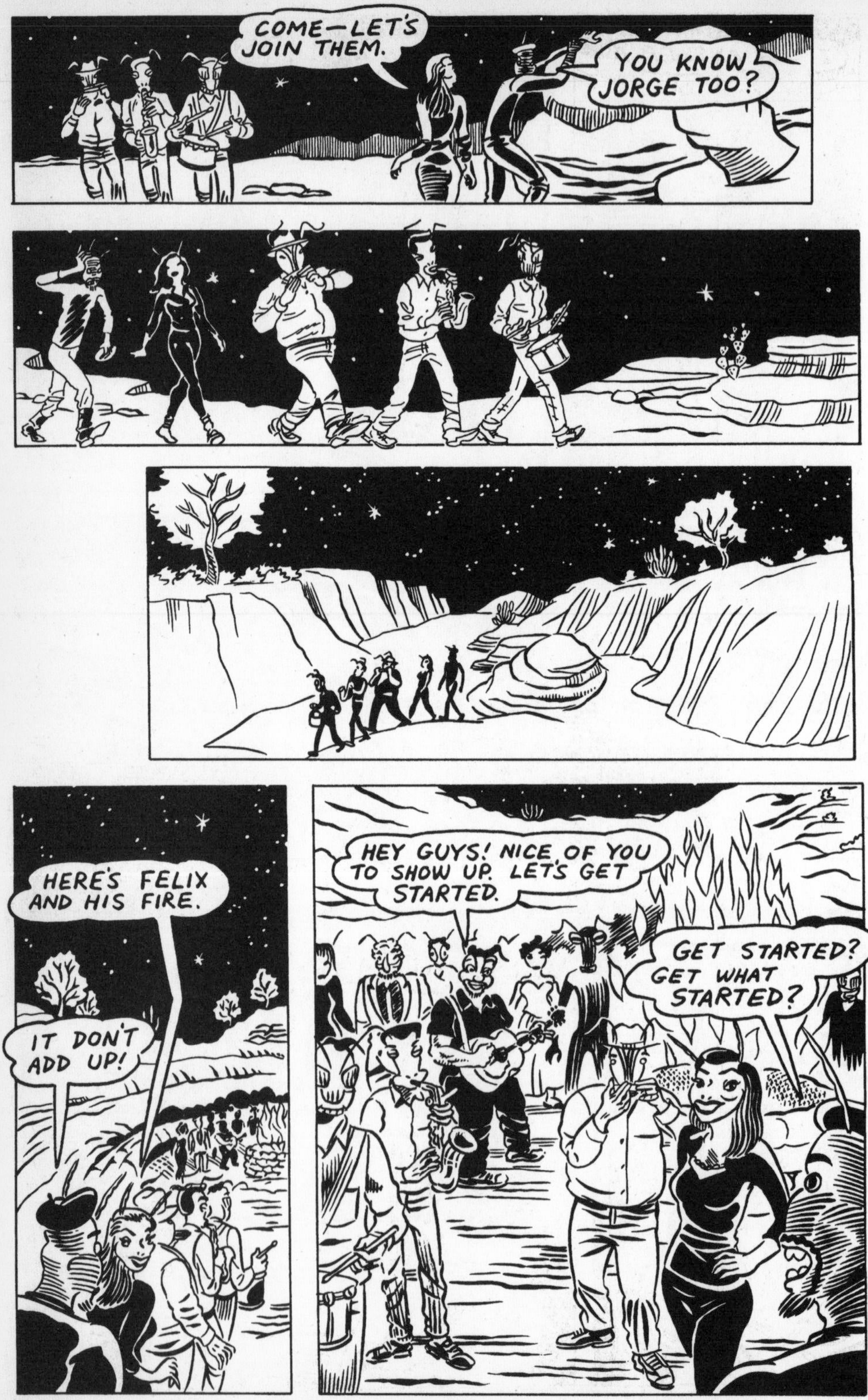
COME—LET'S JOIN THEM.
YOU KNOW JORGE TOO?
HERE'S FELIX AND HIS FIRE.
IT DON'T ADD UP!
HEY GUYS! NICE OF YOU TO SHOW UP. LET'S GET STARTED.
GET STARTED? GET WHAT STARTED?

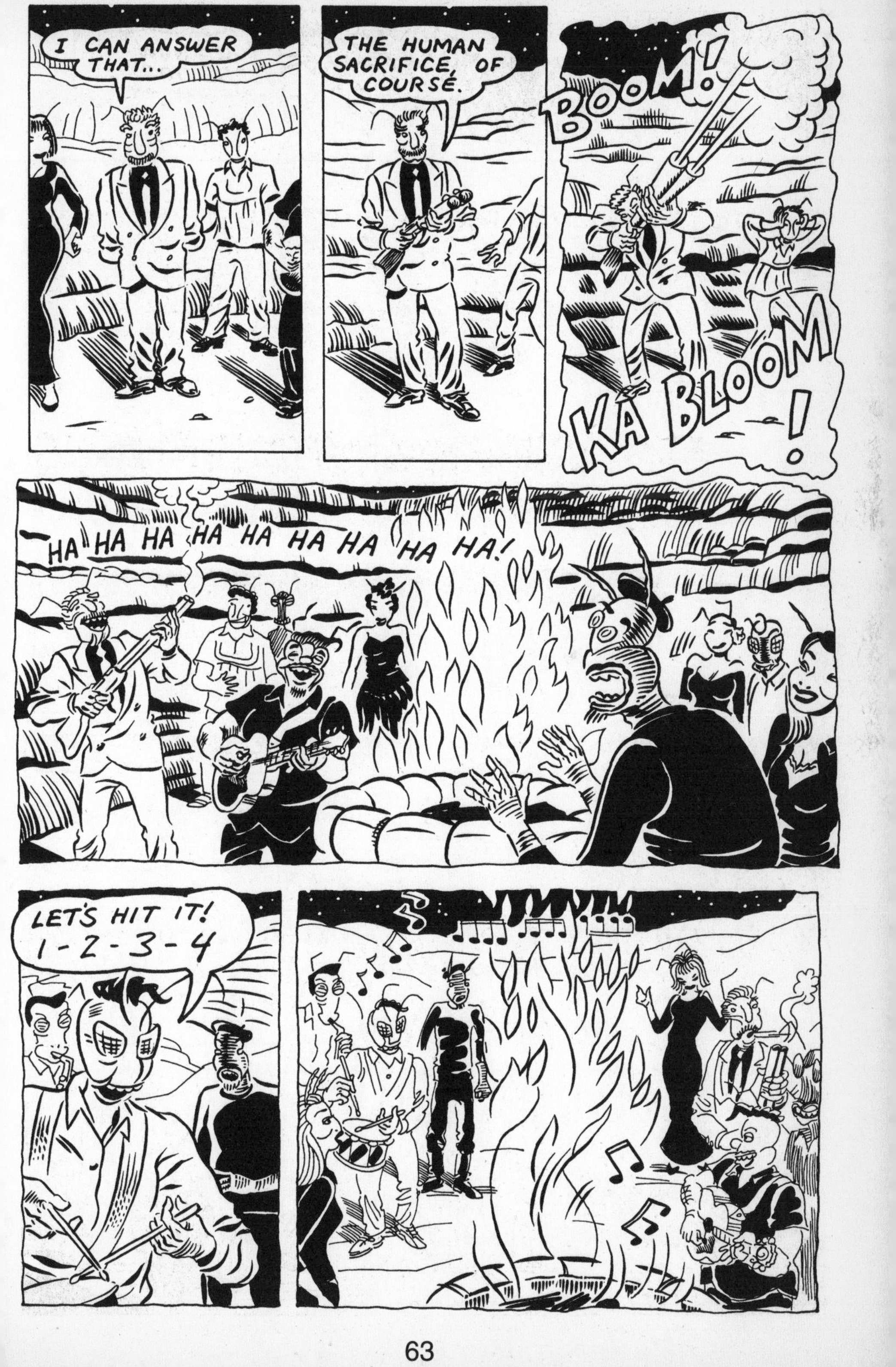
I CAN ANSWER THAT...
THE HUMAN SACRIFICE, OF COURSÉ.
BOOM!
KA BLOOM!
HA HA HA HA HA HA HA HA HA!
LET'S HIT IT! 1-2-3-4

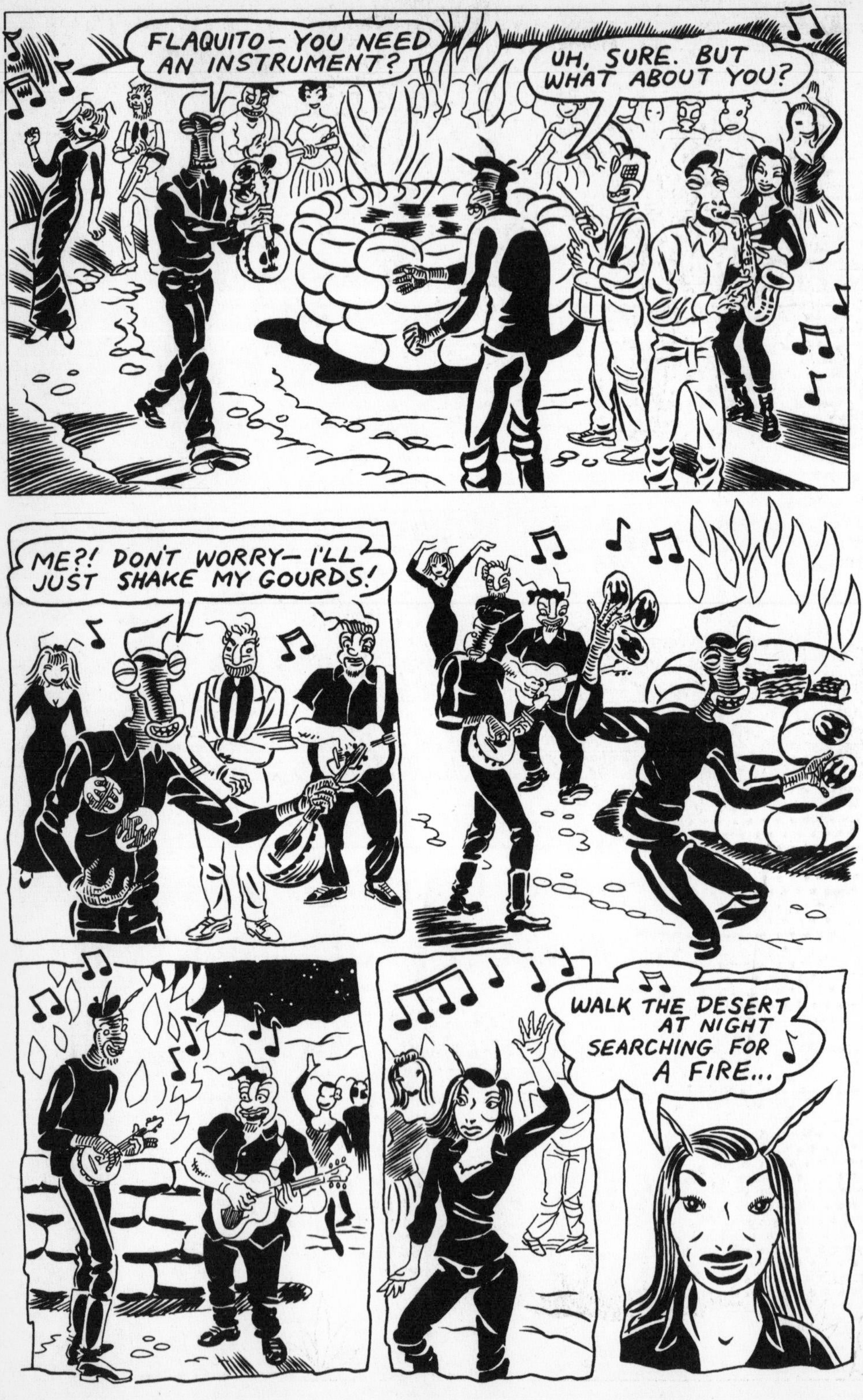
FLAQUITO— YOU NEED AN INSTRUMENT?
UH, SURE. BUT WHAT ABOUT YOU?
ME?! DON'T WORRY— I'LL JUST SHAKE MY GOURDS!
WALK THE DESERT AT NIGHT SEARCHING FOR A FIRE...

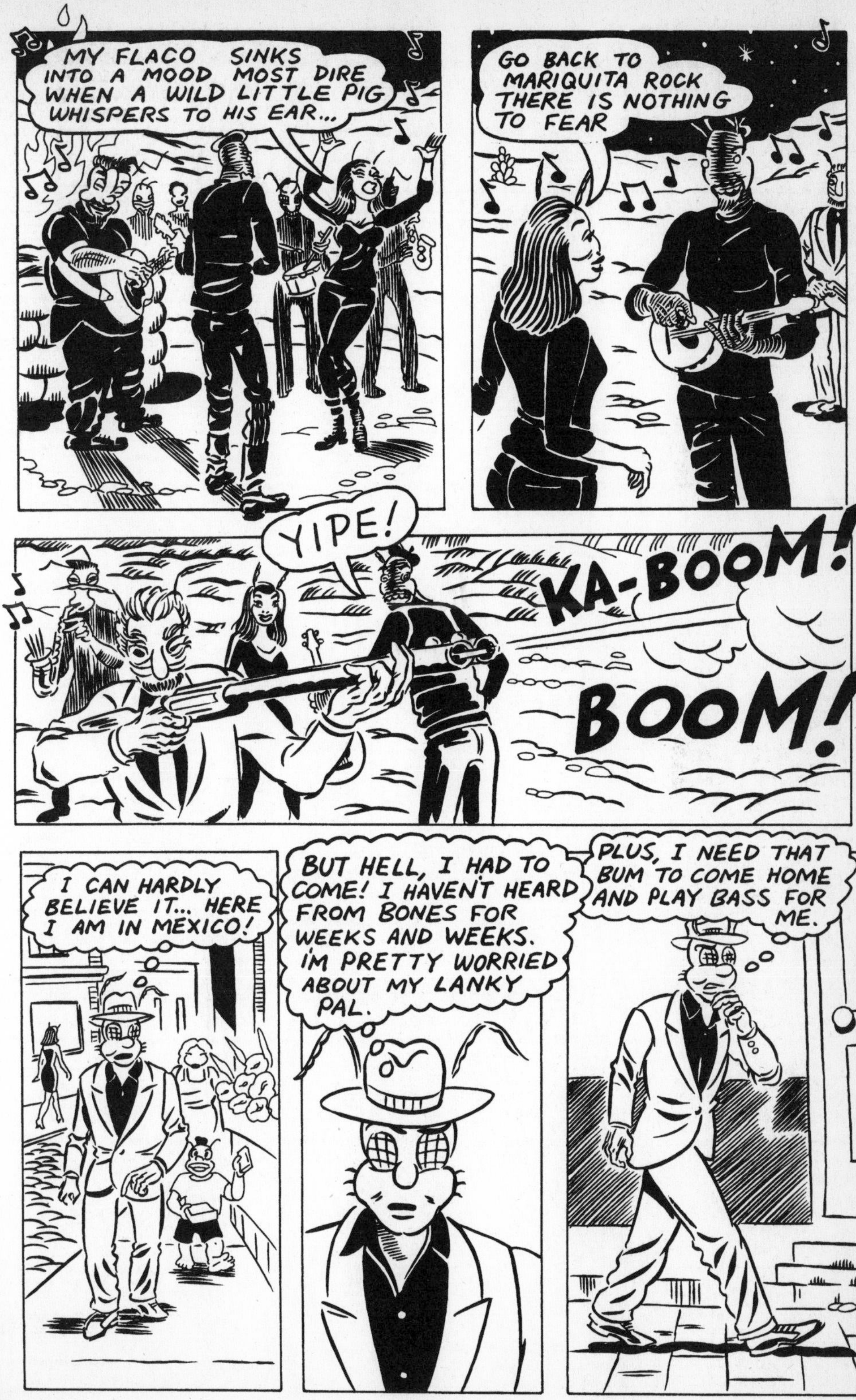
MY FLACO SINKS INTO A MOOD MOST DIRE WHEN A WILD LITTLE PIG WHISPERS TO HIS EAR...
GO BACK TO MARIQUITA ROCK THERE IS NOTHING TO FEAR
YIPE!
KA-BOOM!
BOOM!
I CAN HARDLY BELIEVE IT... HERE I AM IN MEXICO!
BUT HELL, I HAD TO COME! I HAVEN'T HEARD FROM BONES FOR WEEKS AND WEEKS. I'M PRETTY WORRIED ABOUT MY LANKY PAL.
PLUS, I NEED THAT BUM TO COME HOME AND PLAY BASS FOR ME.

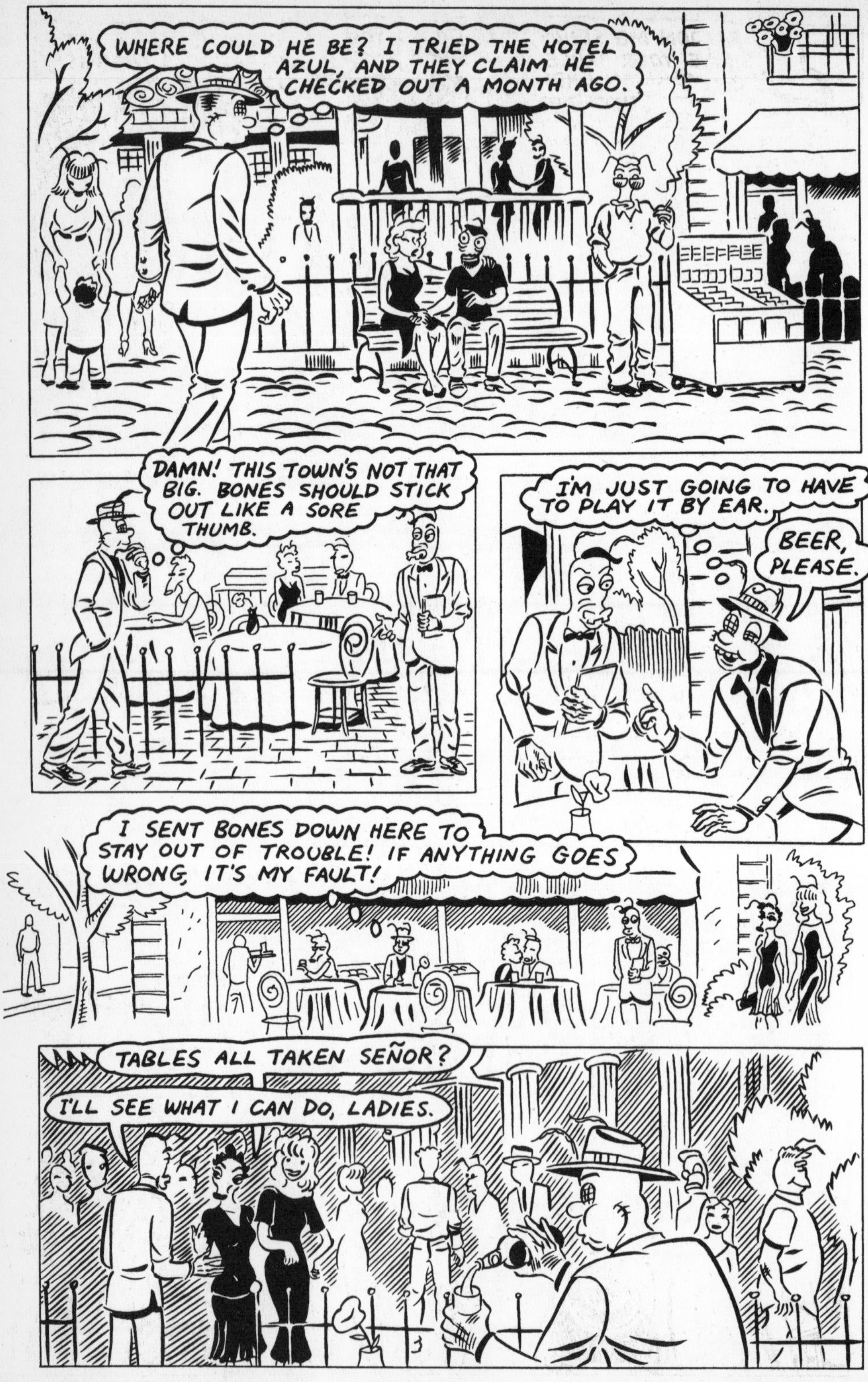
WHERE COULD HE BE? I TRIED THE HOTEL AZUL, AND THEY CLAIM HE CHECKED OUT A MONTH AGO.
DAMN! THIS TOWN'S NOT THAT BIG. BONES SHOULD STICK OUT LIKE A SORE THUMB.
I'M JUST GOING TO HAVE TO PLAY IT BY EAR.
BEER, PLEASE.
I SENT BONES DOWN HERE TO STAY OUT OF TROUBLE! IF ANYTHING GOES WRONG, IT'S MY FAULT!
TABLES ALL TAKEN SEÑOR?
I'LL SEE WHAT I CAN DO, LADIES.

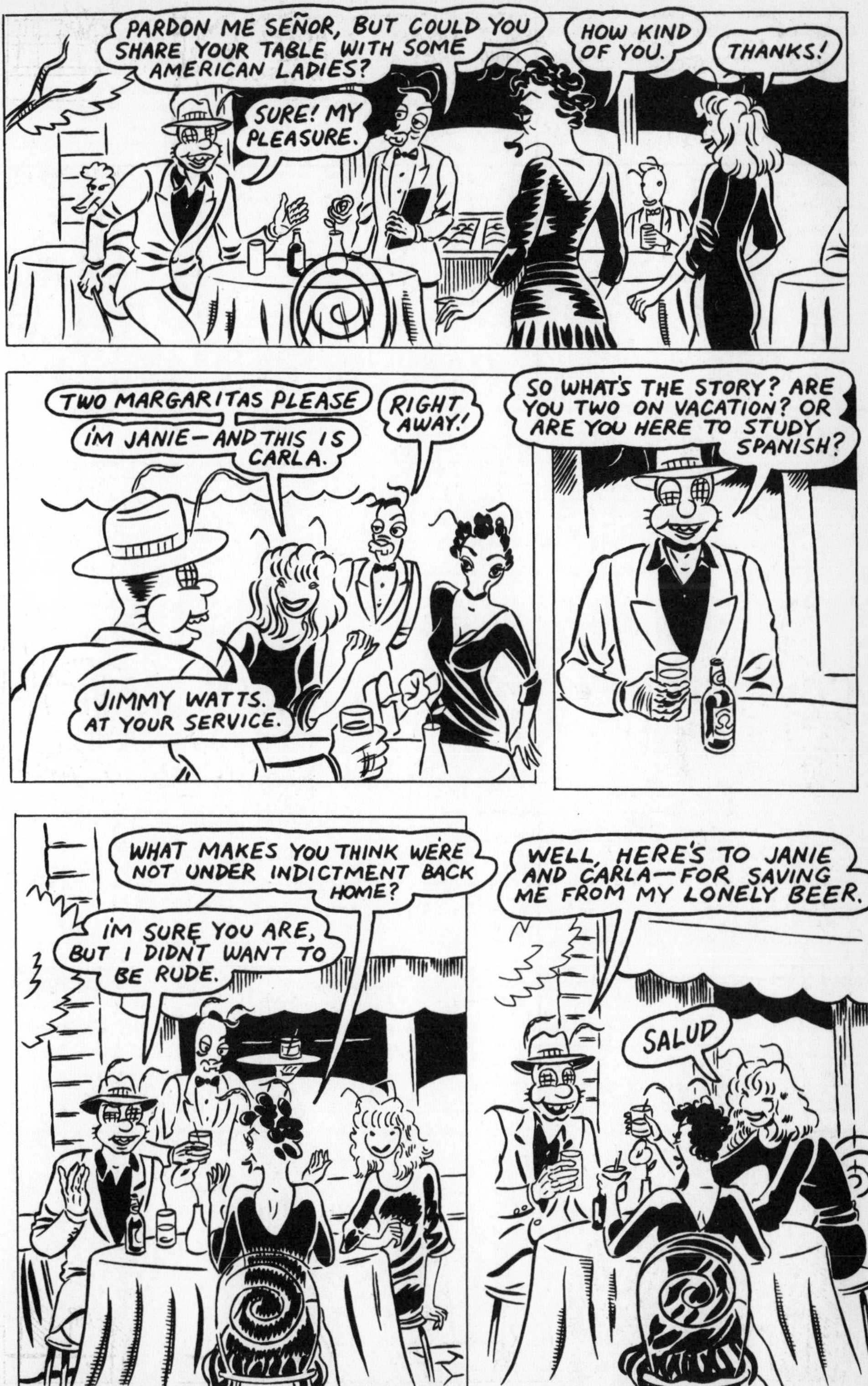
PARDON ME SEÑOR, BUT COULD YOU SHARE YOUR TABLE WITH SOME AMERICAN LADIES?
SURE! MY PLEASURE.
HOW KIND OF YOU.
THANKS!
TWO MARGARITAS PLEASE
I'M JANIE—AND THIS IS CARLA.
RIGHT AWAY!
JIMMY WATTS. AT YOUR SERVICE.
SO WHAT'S THE STORY? ARE YOU TWO ON VACATION? OR ARE YOU HERE TO STUDY SPANISH?
WHAT MAKES YOU THINK WE'RE NOT UNDER INDICTMENT BACK HOME?
I'M SURE YOU ARE, BUT I DIDN'T WANT TO BE RUDE.
WELL, HERE'S TO JANIE AND CARLA—FOR SAVING ME FROM MY LONELY BEER.
SALUD

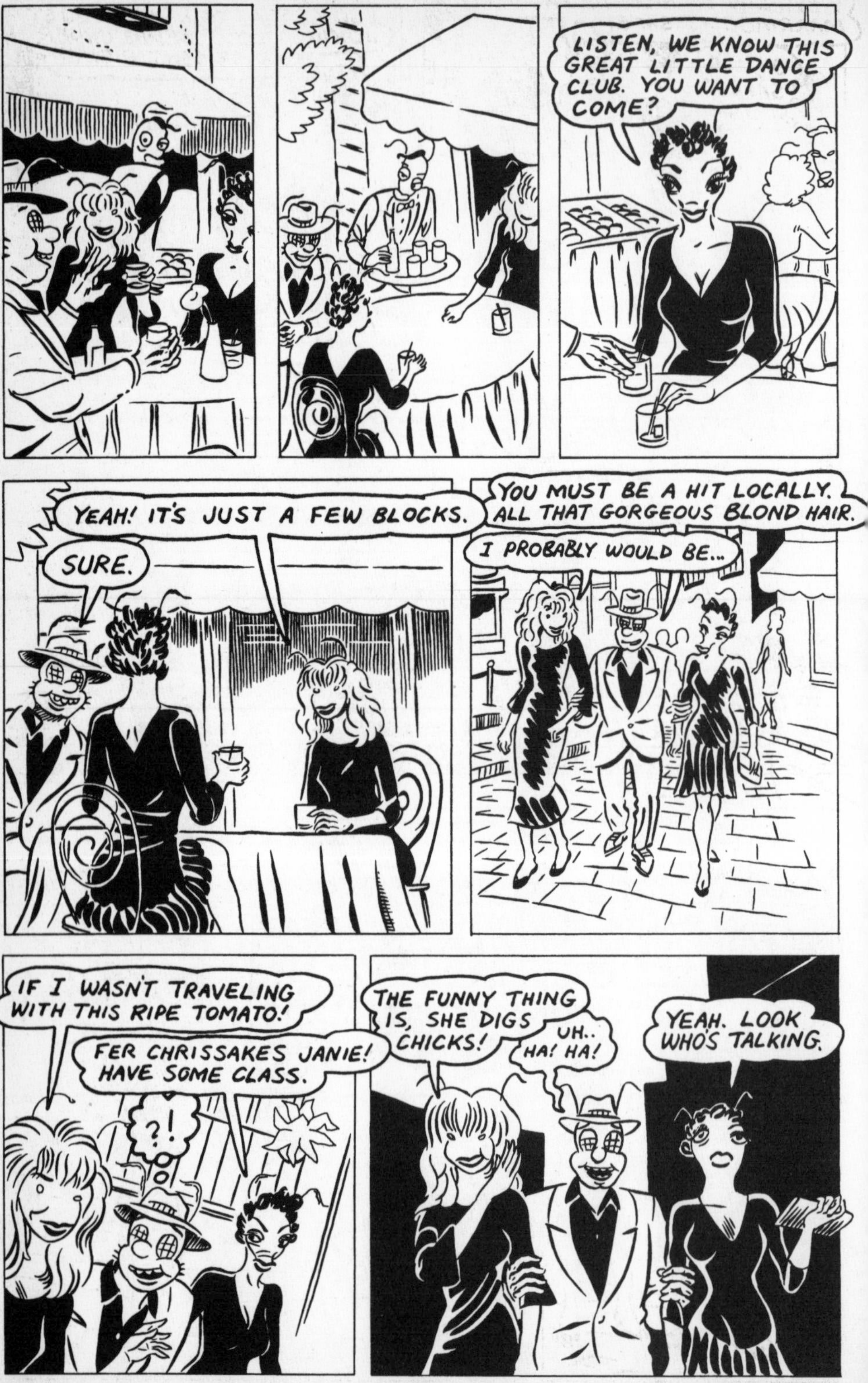
LISTEN, WE KNOW THIS GREAT LITTLE DANCE CLUB. YOU WANT TO COME?
YEAH! IT'S JUST A FEW BLOCKS.
SURE.
YOU MUST BE A HIT LOCALLY. ALL THAT GORGEOUS BLOND HAIR.
I PROBABLY WOULD BE...
IF I WASN'T TRAVELING WITH THIS RIPE TOMATO!
FER CHRISSAKES JANIE! HAVE SOME CLASS.
?!
THE FUNNY THING IS, SHE DIGS CHICKS!
UH.. HA! HA!
YEAH. LOOK WHO'S TALKING.

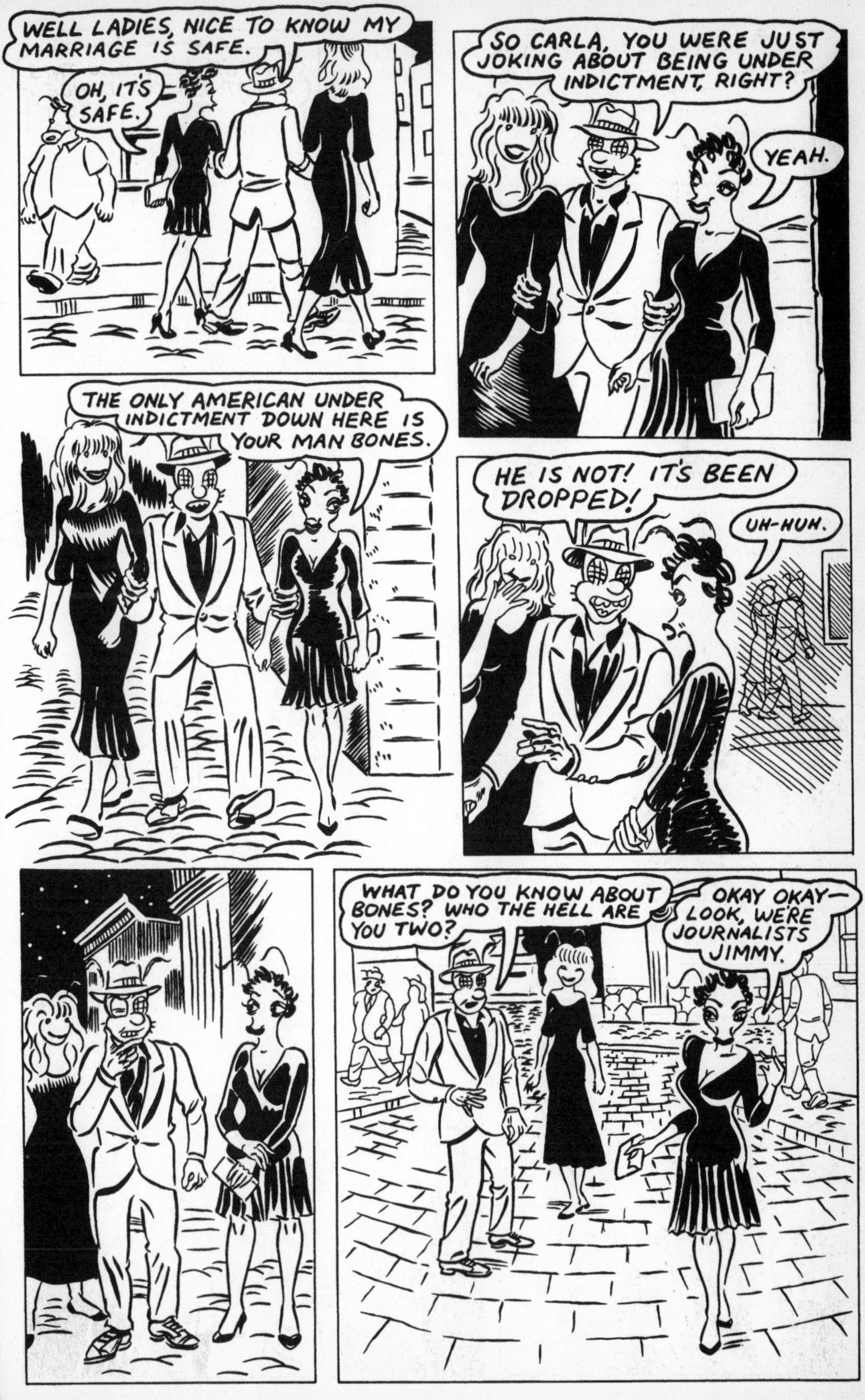
WELL LADIES, NICE TO KNOW MY MARRIAGE IS SAFE.
OH, IT'S SAFE.
SO CARLA, YOU WERE JUST JOKING ABOUT BEING UNDER INDICTMENT, RIGHT?
YEAH.
THE ONLY AMERICAN UNDER INDICTMENT DOWN HERE IS YOUR MAN BONES.
HE IS NOT! IT'S BEEN DROPPED!
UH-HUH.
WHAT DO YOU KNOW ABOUT BONES? WHO THE HELL ARE YOU TWO?
OKAY OKAY— LOOK, WE'RE JOURNALISTS JIMMY.

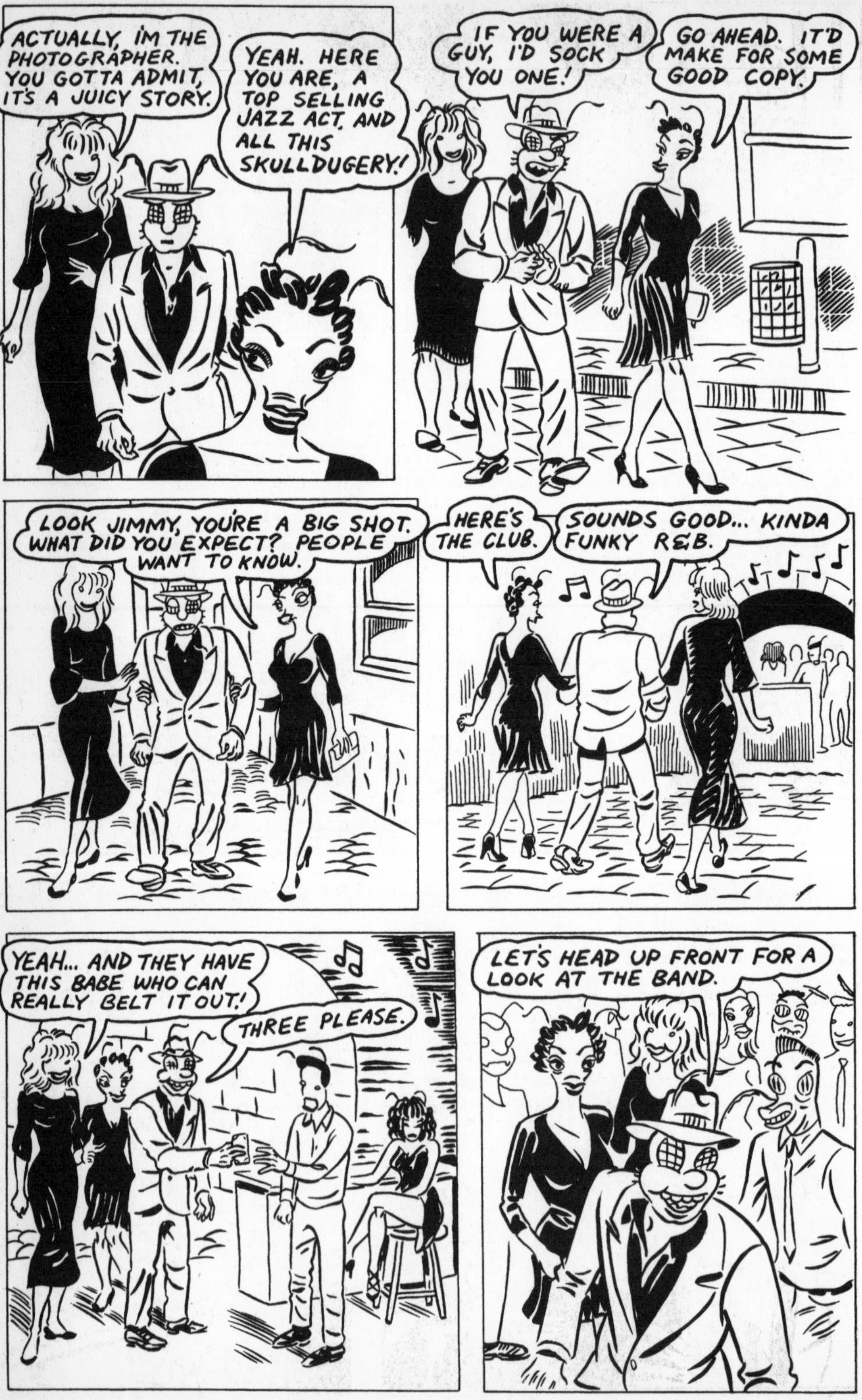
ACTUALLY, I'M THE PHOTOGRAPHER. YOU GOTTA ADMIT, IT'S A JUICY STORY.
YEAH. HERE YOU ARE, A TOP SELLING JAZZ ACT, AND ALL THIS SKULLDUGERY!
IF YOU WERE A GUY, I'D SOCK YOU ONE!
GO AHEAD. IT'D MAKE FOR SOME GOOD COPY.
LOOK JIMMY, YOU'RE A BIG SHOT. WHAT DID YOU EXPECT? PEOPLE WANT TO KNOW.
HERE'S THE CLUB.
SOUNDS GOOD... KINDA FUNKY R&B.
YEAH... AND THEY HAVE THIS BABE WHO CAN REALLY BELT IT OUT!
THREE PLEASE.
LET'S HEAD UP FRONT FOR A LOOK AT THE BAND.

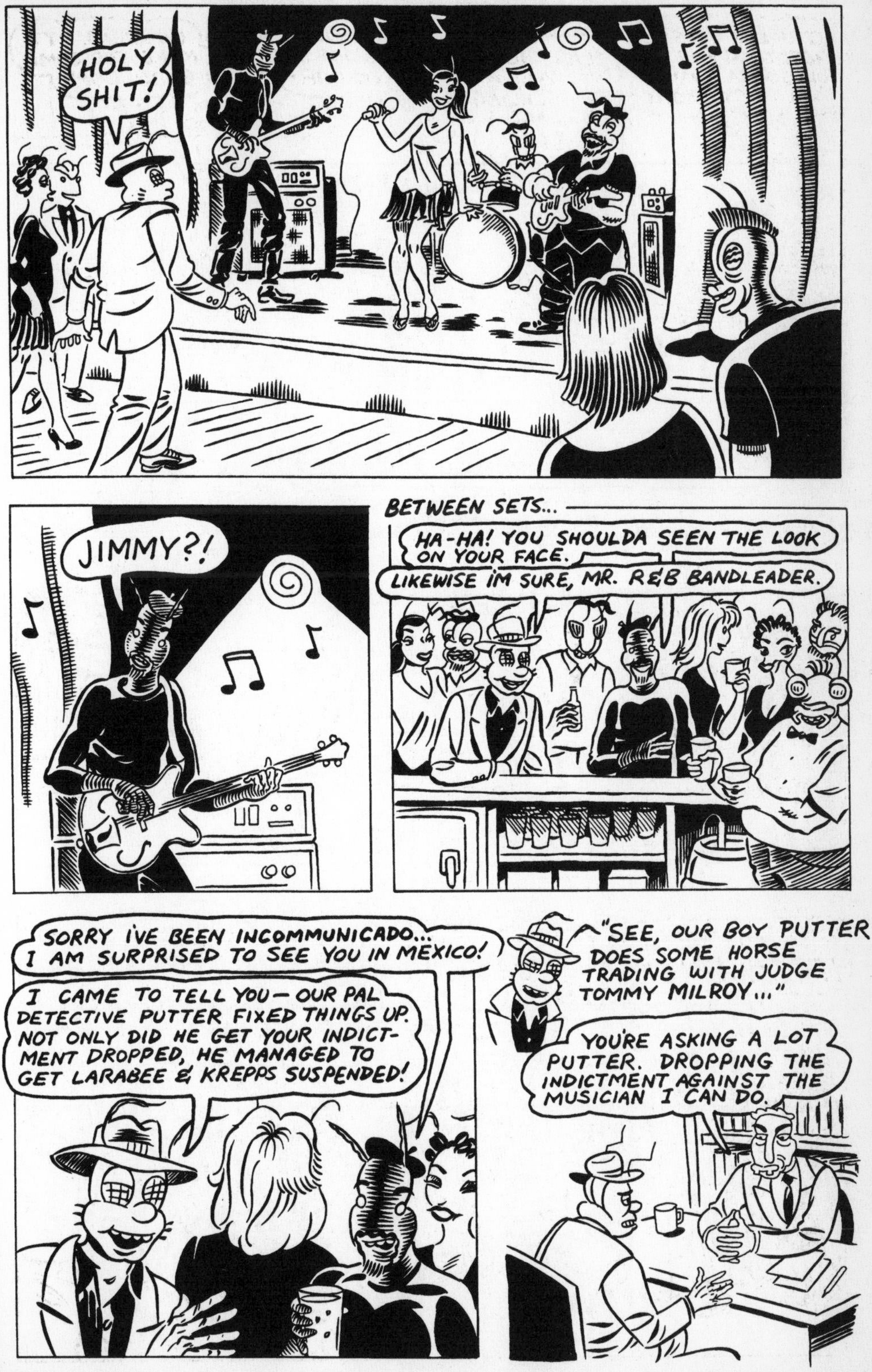
HOLY SHIT!
JIMMY?!
BETWEEN SETS...
HA-HA! YOU SHOULDA SEEN THE LOOK ON YOUR FACE.
LIKEWISE I'M SURE, MR. R&B BANDLEADER.
SORRY I'VE BEEN INCOMMUNICADO... I AM SURPRISED TO SEE YOU IN MEXICO!
I CAME TO TELL YOU— OUR PAL DETECTIVE PUTTER FIXED THINGS UP. NOT ONLY DID HE GET YOUR INDICTMENT DROPPED, HE MANAGED TO GET LARABEE & KREPPS SUSPENDED!
"SEE, OUR BOY PUTTER DOES SOME HORSE TRADING WITH JUDGE TOMMY MILROY..."
YOU'RE ASKING A LOT PUTTER. DROPPING THE INDICTMENT AGAINST THE MUSICIAN I CAN DO.

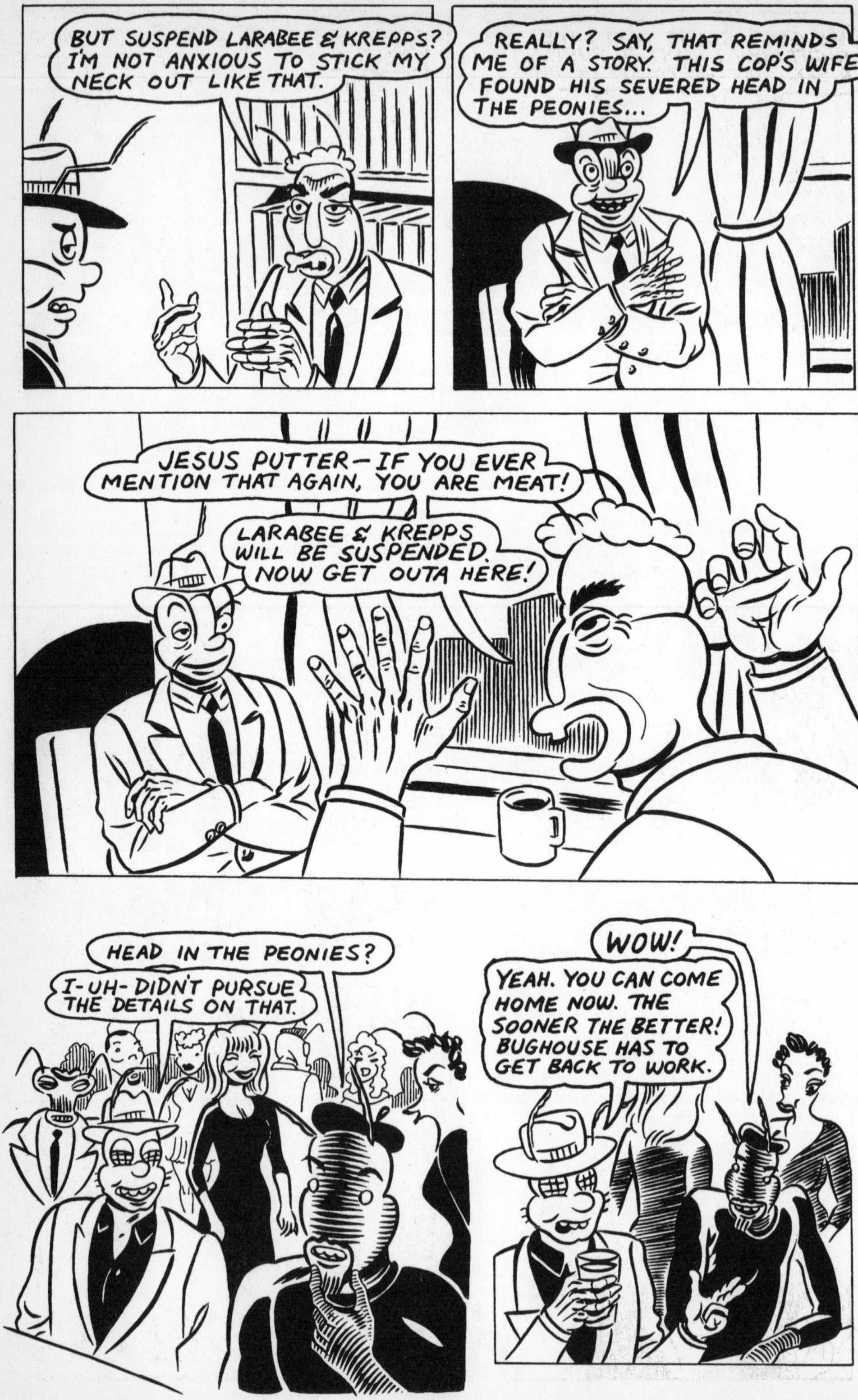
BUT SUSPEND LARABEE & KREPPS? I'M NOT ANXIOUS TO STICK MY NECK OUT LIKE THAT.
REALLY? SAY, THAT REMINDS ME OF A STORY. THIS COP'S WIFE FOUND HIS SEVERED HEAD IN THE PEONIES...
JESUS PUTTER— IF YOU EVER MENTION THAT AGAIN, YOU ARE MEAT!
LARABEE & KREPPS WILL BE SUSPENDED. NOW GET OUTA HERE!
HEAD IN THE PEONIES?
I-UH- DIDN'T PURSUE THE DETAILS ON THAT.
WOW!
YEAH. YOU CAN COME HOME NOW. THE SOONER THE BETTER! BUGHOUSE HAS TO GET BACK TO WORK.

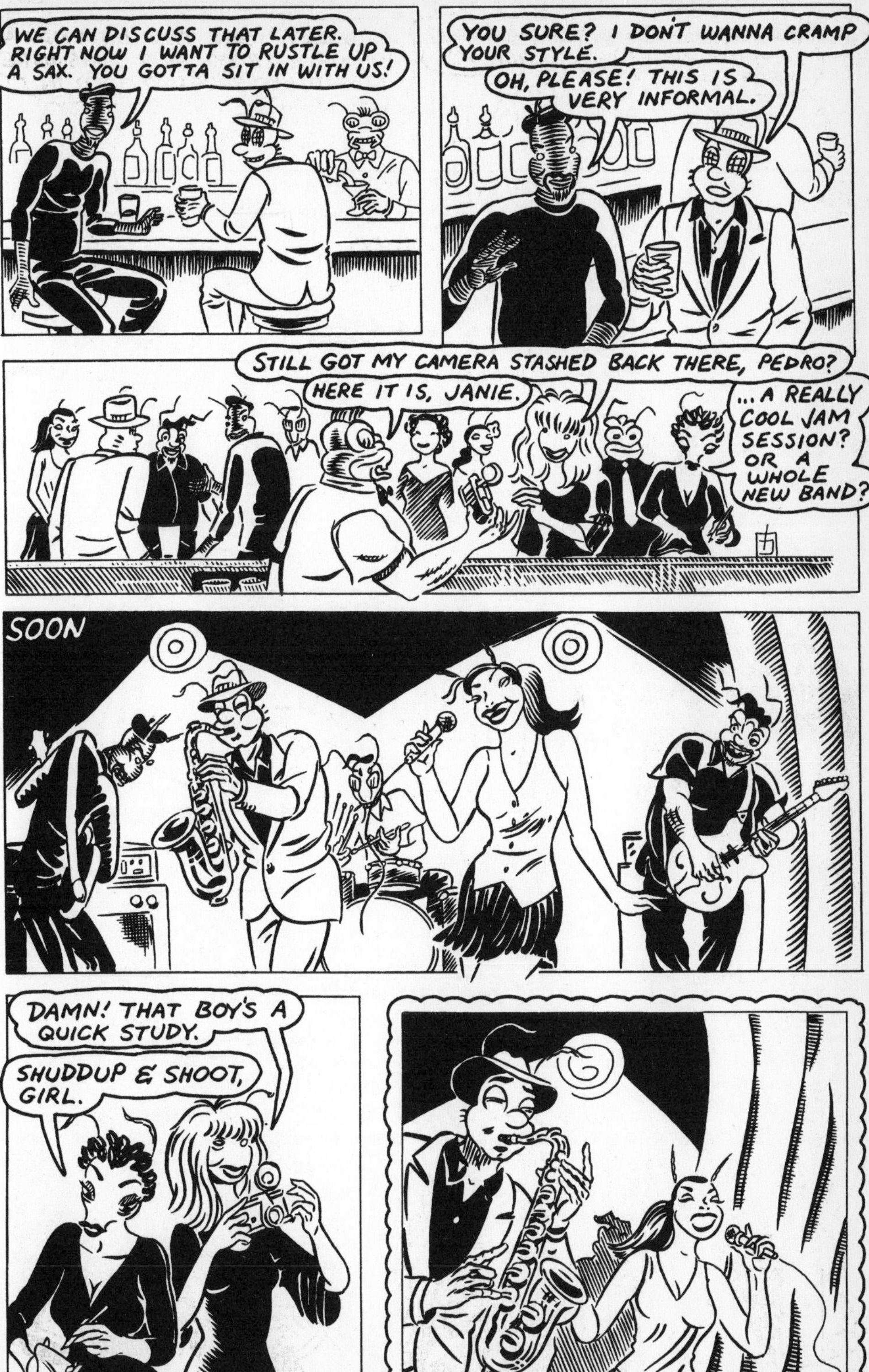
WE CAN DISCUSS THAT LATER. RIGHT NOW I WANT TO RUSTLE UP A SAX. YOU GOTTA SIT IN WITH US!
YOU SURE? I DON'T WANNA CRAMP YOUR STYLE.
OH, PLEASE! THIS IS VERY INFORMAL.
STILL GOT MY CAMERA STASHED BACK THERE, PEDRO?
HERE IT IS, JANIE.
...A REALLY COOL JAM SESSION? OR A WHOLE NEW BAND?
SOON
DAMN! THAT BOY'S A QUICK STUDY.
SHUDDUP & SHOOT, GIRL.

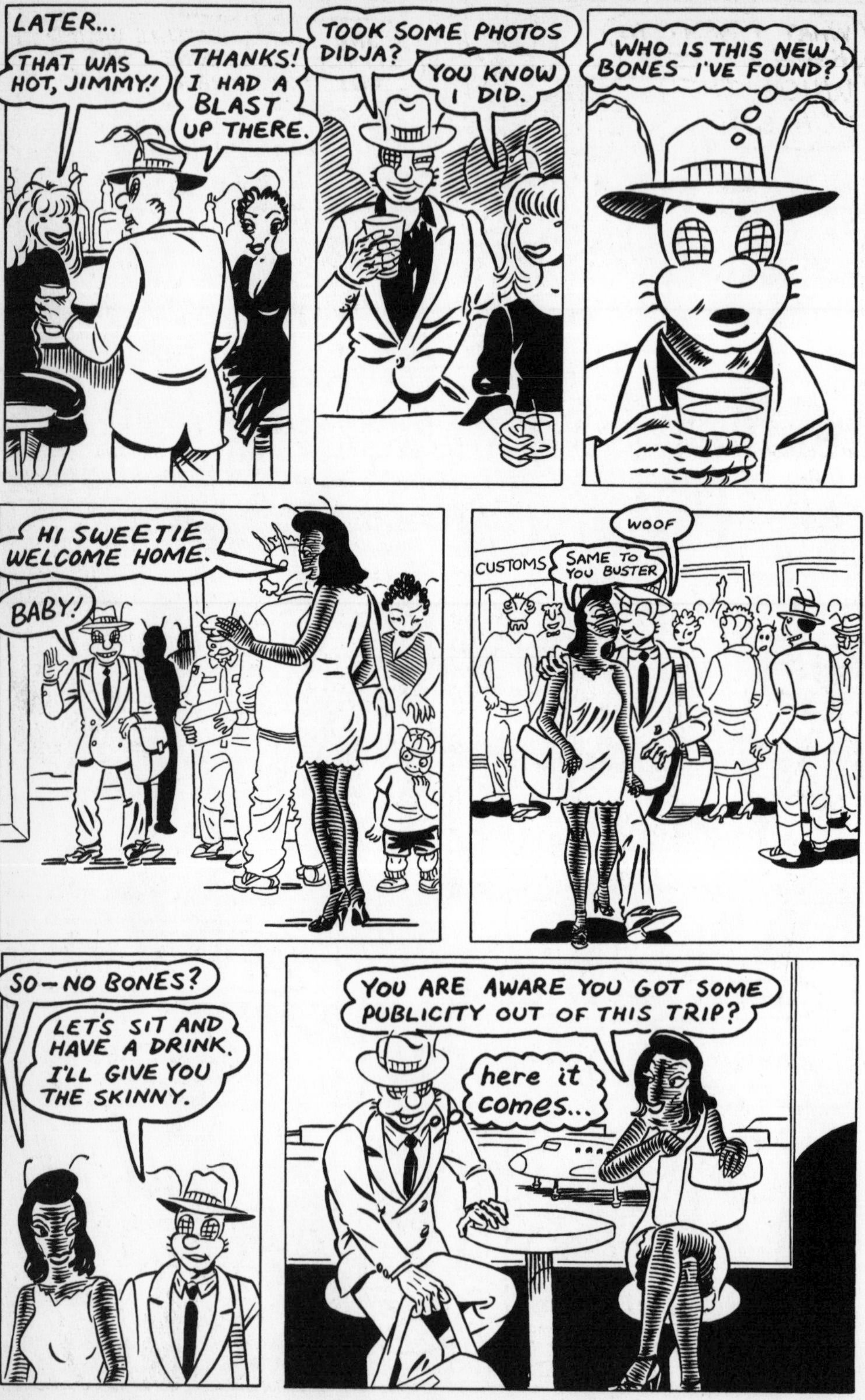
LATER...
THAT WAS HOT, JIMMY!
THANKS! I HAD A BLAST UP THERE.
TOOK SOME PHOTOS DIDJA?
YOU KNOW I DID.
WHO IS THIS NEW BONES I'VE FOUND?
HI SWEETIE WELCOME HOME.
BABY!
CUSTOMS
SAME TO YOU BUSTER
WOOF
SO—NO BONES?
LET'S SIT AND HAVE A DRINK. I'LL GIVE YOU THE SKINNY.
YOU ARE AWARE YOU GOT SOME PUBLICITY OUT OF THIS TRIP?
here it comes...

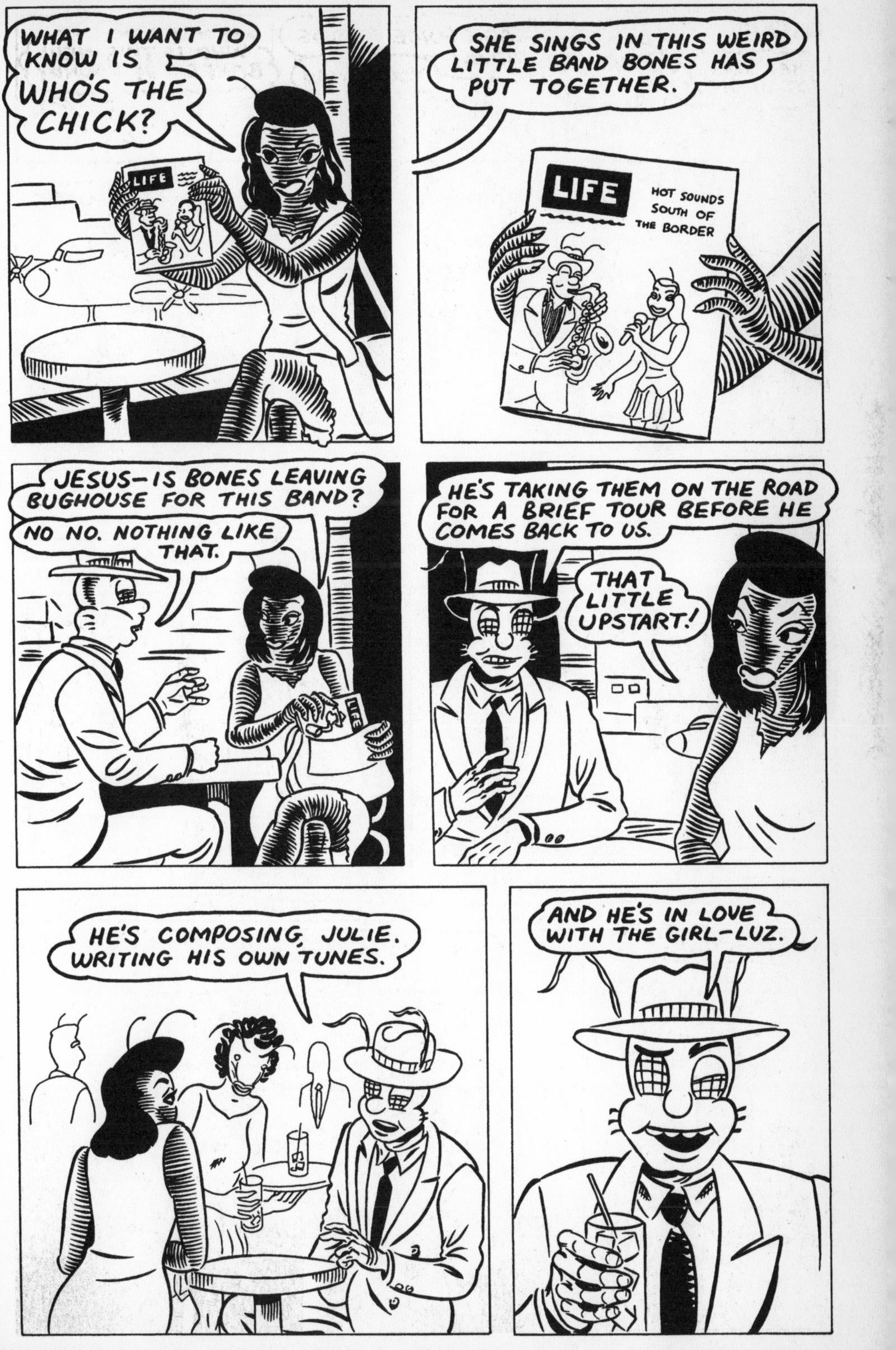

WHAT I WANT TO KNOW IS WHO'S THE CHICK?
LIFE
SHE SINGS IN THIS WEIRD LITTLE BAND BONES HAS PUT TOGETHER.
LIFE
HOT SOUNDS SOUTH OF THE BORDER
JESUS–IS BONES LEAVING BUGHOUSE FOR THIS BAND?
NO NO. NOTHING LIKE THAT.
LIFE
HE'S TAKING THEM ON THE ROAD FOR A BRIEF TOUR BEFORE HE COMES BACK TO US.
THAT LITTLE UPSTART!
HE'S COMPOSING, JULIE. WRITING HIS OWN TUNES.
AND HE'S IN LOVE WITH THE GIRL–LUZ.

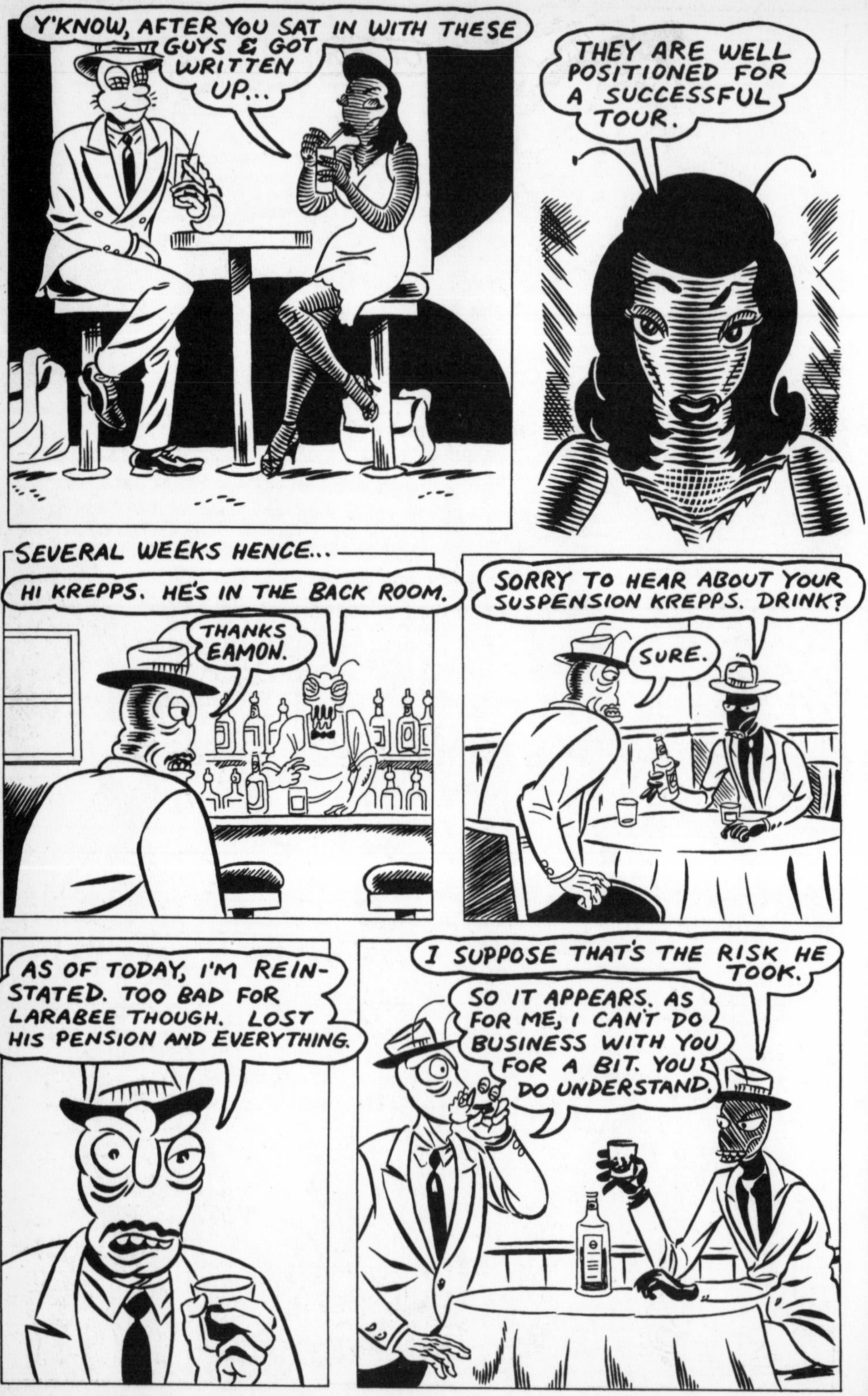
Y'KNOW, AFTER YOU SAT IN WITH THESE GUYS & GOT WRITTEN UP...
THEY ARE WELL POSITIONED FOR A SUCCESSFUL TOUR.
SEVERAL WEEKS HENCE...
HI KREPPS. HE'S IN THE BACK ROOM.
THANKS EAMON.
SORRY TO HEAR ABOUT YOUR SUSPENSION KREPPS. DRINK?
SURE.
AS OF TODAY, I'M REIN-STATED. TOO BAD FOR LARABEE THOUGH. LOST HIS PENSION AND EVERYTHING.
I SUPPOSE THAT'S THE RISK HE TOOK.
SO IT APPEARS. AS FOR ME, I CAN'T DO BUSINESS WITH YOU FOR A BIT. YOU DO UNDERSTAND.

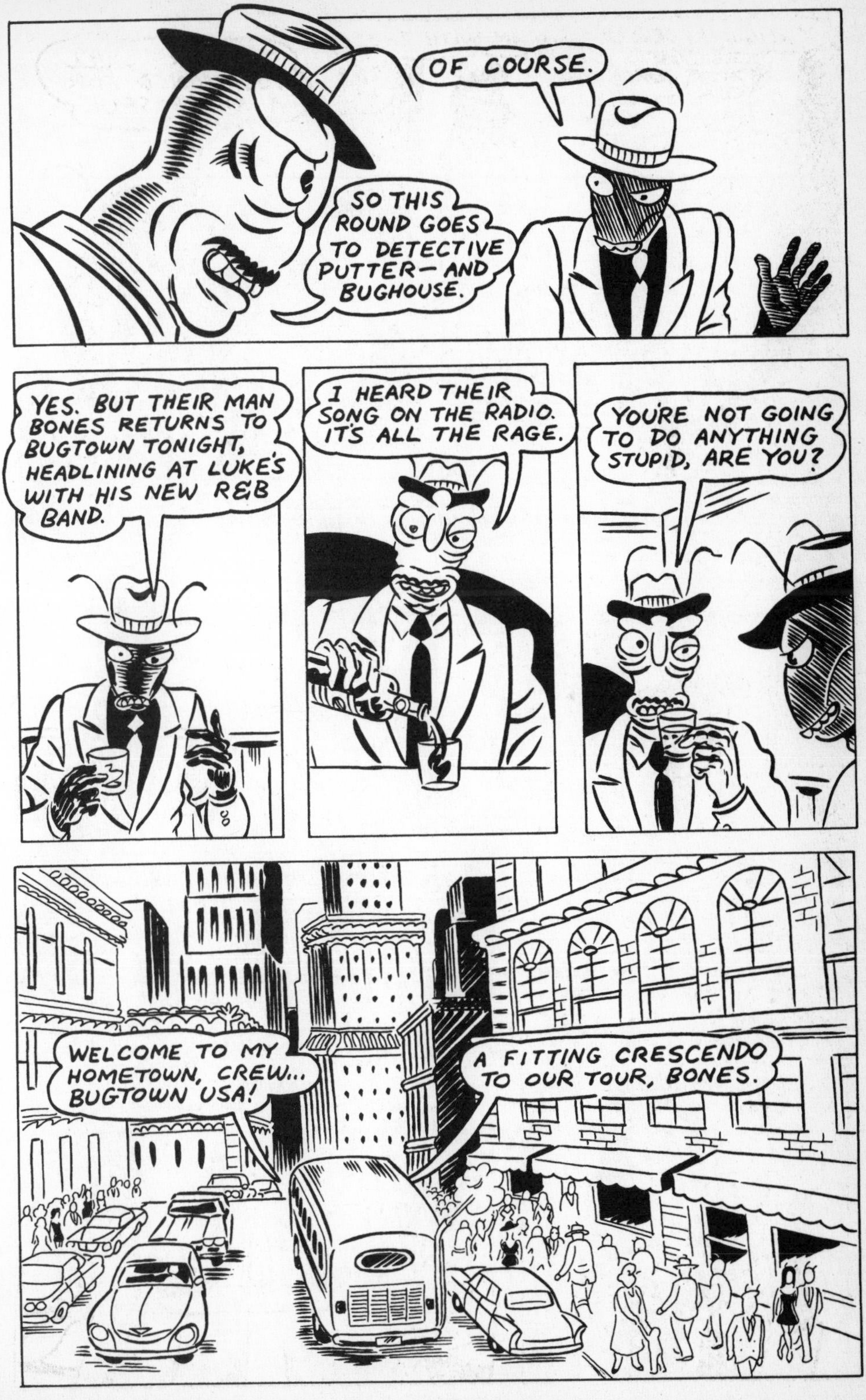
OF COURSE.
SO THIS ROUND GOES TO DETECTIVE PUTTER— AND BUGHOUSE.
YES. BUT THEIR MAN BONES RETURNS TO BUGTOWN TONIGHT, HEADLINING AT LUKE'S WITH HIS NEW R&B BAND.
I HEARD THEIR SONG ON THE RADIO. IT'S ALL THE RAGE.
YOU'RE NOT GOING TO DO ANYTHING STUPID, ARE YOU?
WELCOME TO MY HOMETOWN, CREW... BUGTOWN USA!
A FITTING CRESCENDO TO OUR TOUR, BONES.

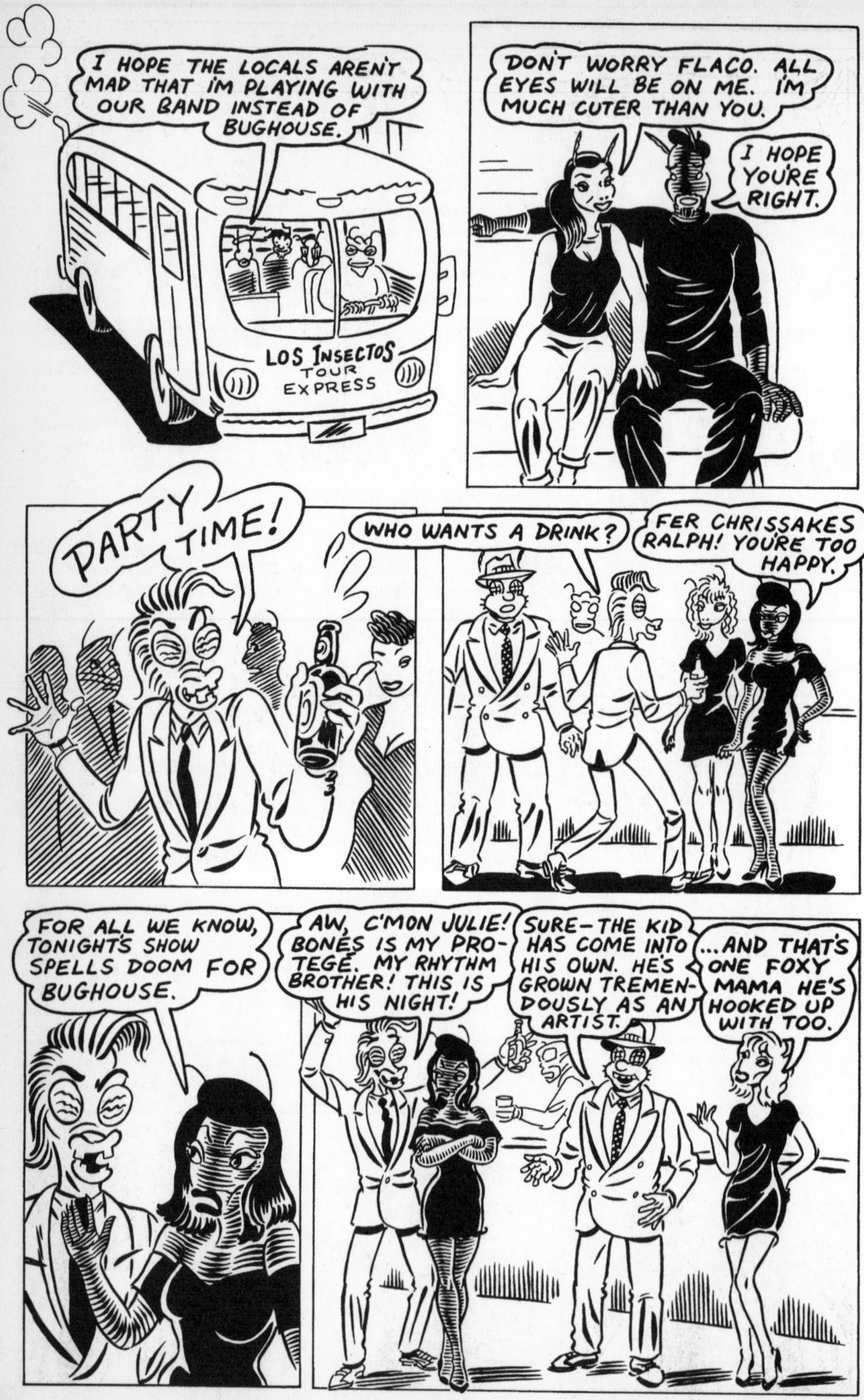
I HOPE THE LOCALS AREN'T MAD THAT I'M PLAYING WITH OUR BAND INSTEAD OF BUGHOUSE.
LOS INSECTOS TOUR EXPRESS
DON'T WORRY FLACO. ALL EYES WILL BE ON ME. I'M MUCH CUTER THAN YOU.
I HOPE YOU'RE RIGHT.
PARTY TIME!
WHO WANTS A DRINK?
FER CHRISSAKES RALPH! YOU'RE TOO HAPPY.
FOR ALL WE KNOW, TONIGHT'S SHOW SPELLS DOOM FOR BUGHOUSE.
AW, C'MON JULIE! BONES IS MY PROTEGÉ. MY RHYTHM BROTHER! THIS IS HIS NIGHT!
SURE—THE KID HAS COME INTO HIS OWN. HE'S GROWN TREMENDOUSLY AS AN ARTIST.
...AND THAT'S ONE FOXY MAMA HE'S HOOKED UP WITH TOO.

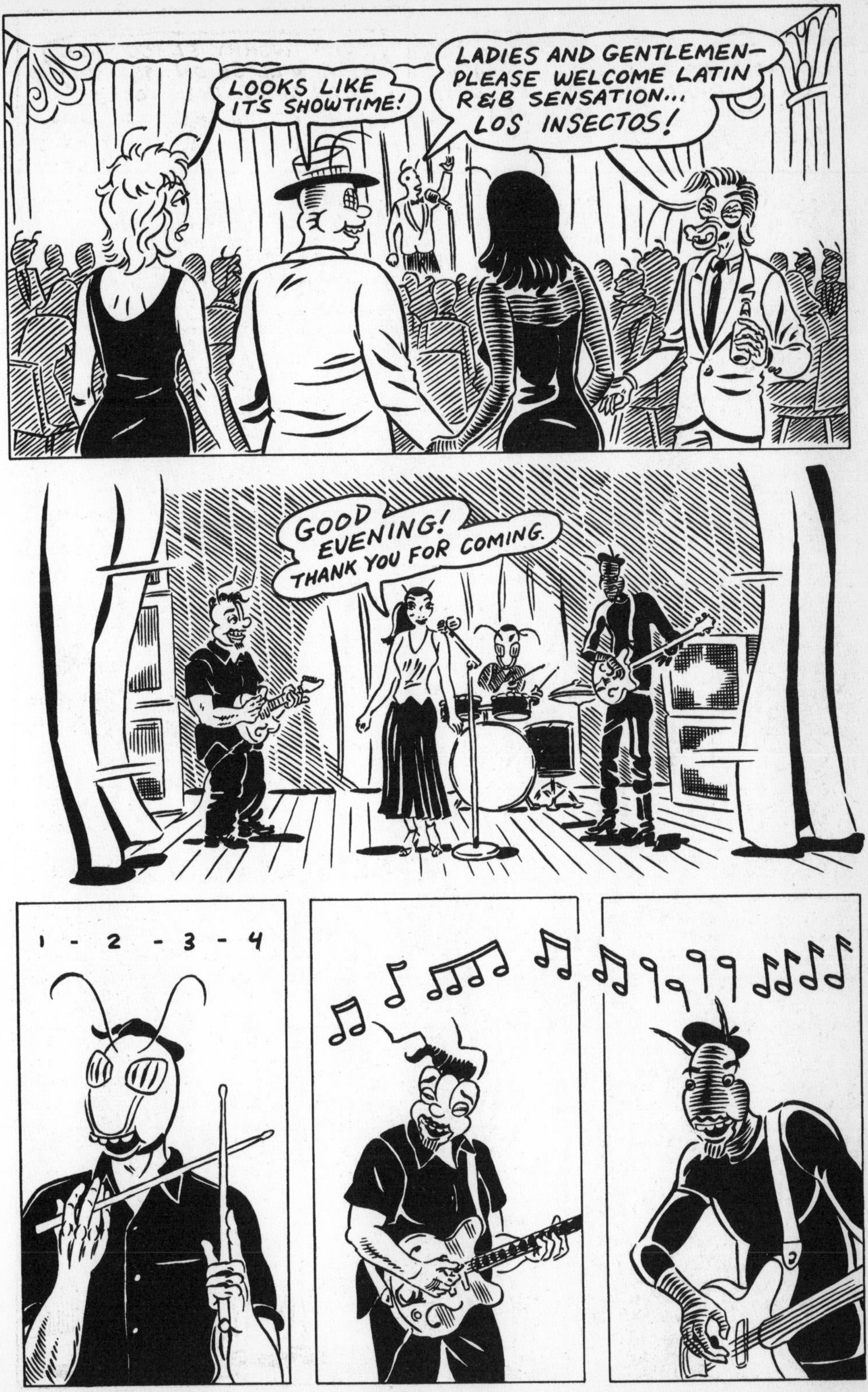
LOOKS LIKE IT'S SHOWTIME!
LADIES AND GENTLEMEN- PLEASE WELCOME LATIN R&B SENSATION... LOS INSECTOS!
GOOD EVENING! THANK YOU FOR COMING.
1 - 2 - 3 - 4

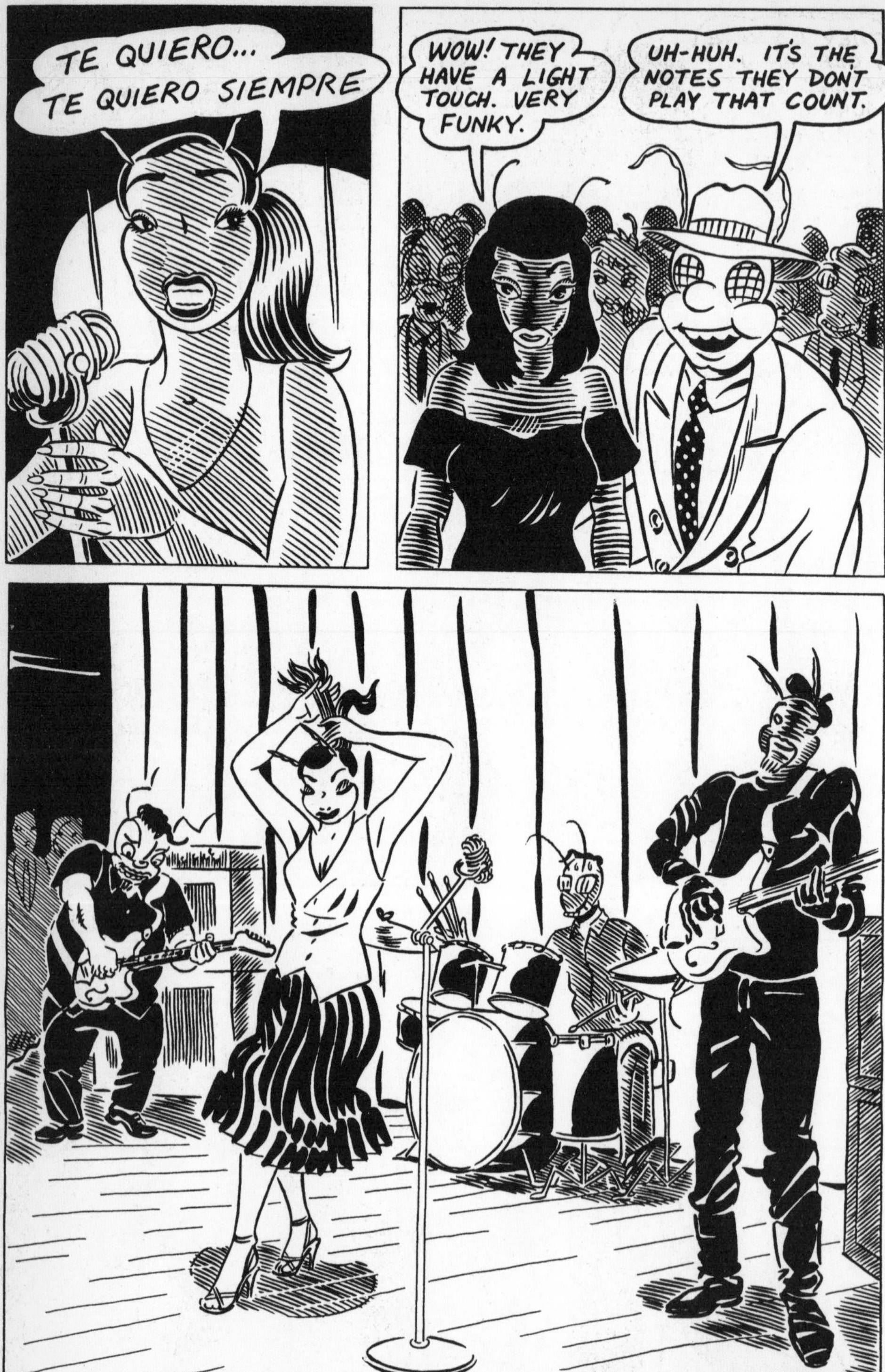
TE QUIERO...
TE QUIERO SIEMPRE
WOW! THEY HAVE A LIGHT TOUCH. VERY FUNKY.
UH-HUH. IT'S THE NOTES THEY DON'T PLAY THAT COUNT.

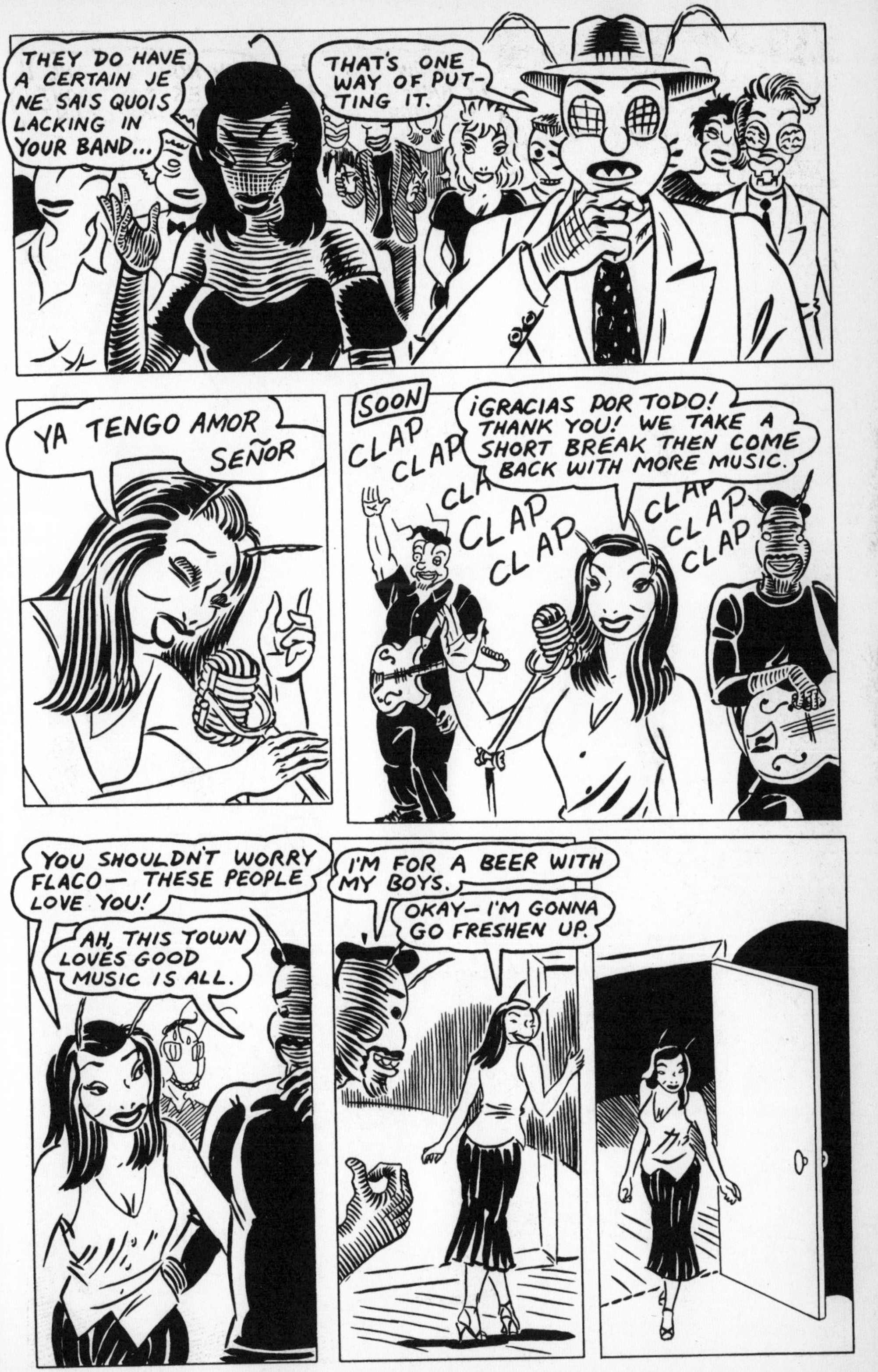
THEY DO HAVE A CERTAIN JE NE SAIS QUOIS LACKING IN YOUR BAND...
THAT'S ONE WAY OF PUTTING IT.
YA TENGO AMOR SEÑOR
SOON
CLAP CLAP CLA CLAP CLAP
¡GRACIAS POR TODO! THANK YOU! WE TAKE A SHORT BREAK THEN COME BACK WITH MORE MUSIC.
CLAP CLAP CLAP
YOU SHOULDN'T WORRY FLACO— THESE PEOPLE LOVE YOU!
AH, THIS TOWN LOVES GOOD MUSIC IS ALL.
I'M FOR A BEER WITH MY BOYS.
OKAY— I'M GONNA GO FRESHEN UP.

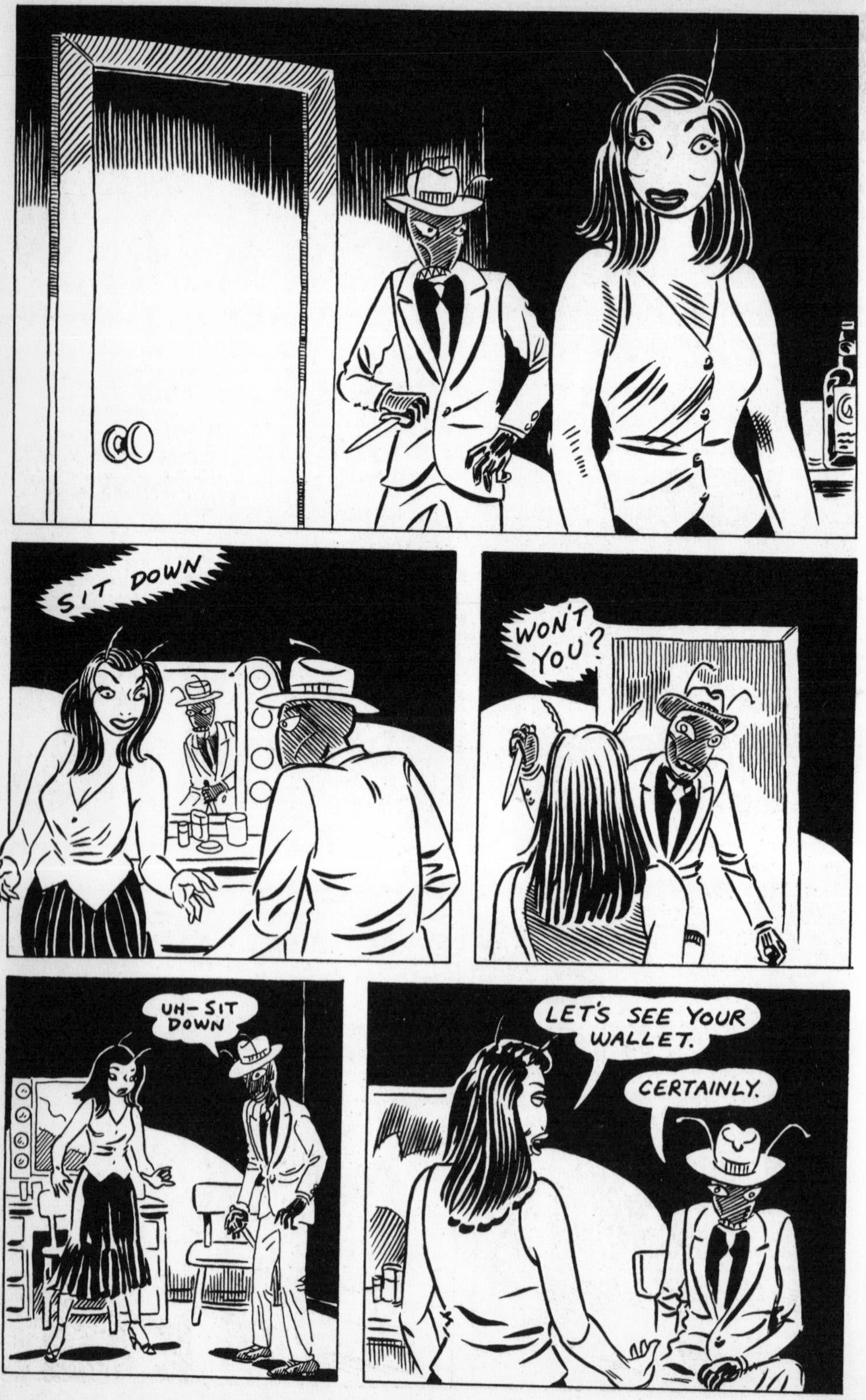
SIT DOWN
WON'T YOU?
UH-SIT DOWN
LET'S SEE YOUR WALLET.
CERTAINLY.

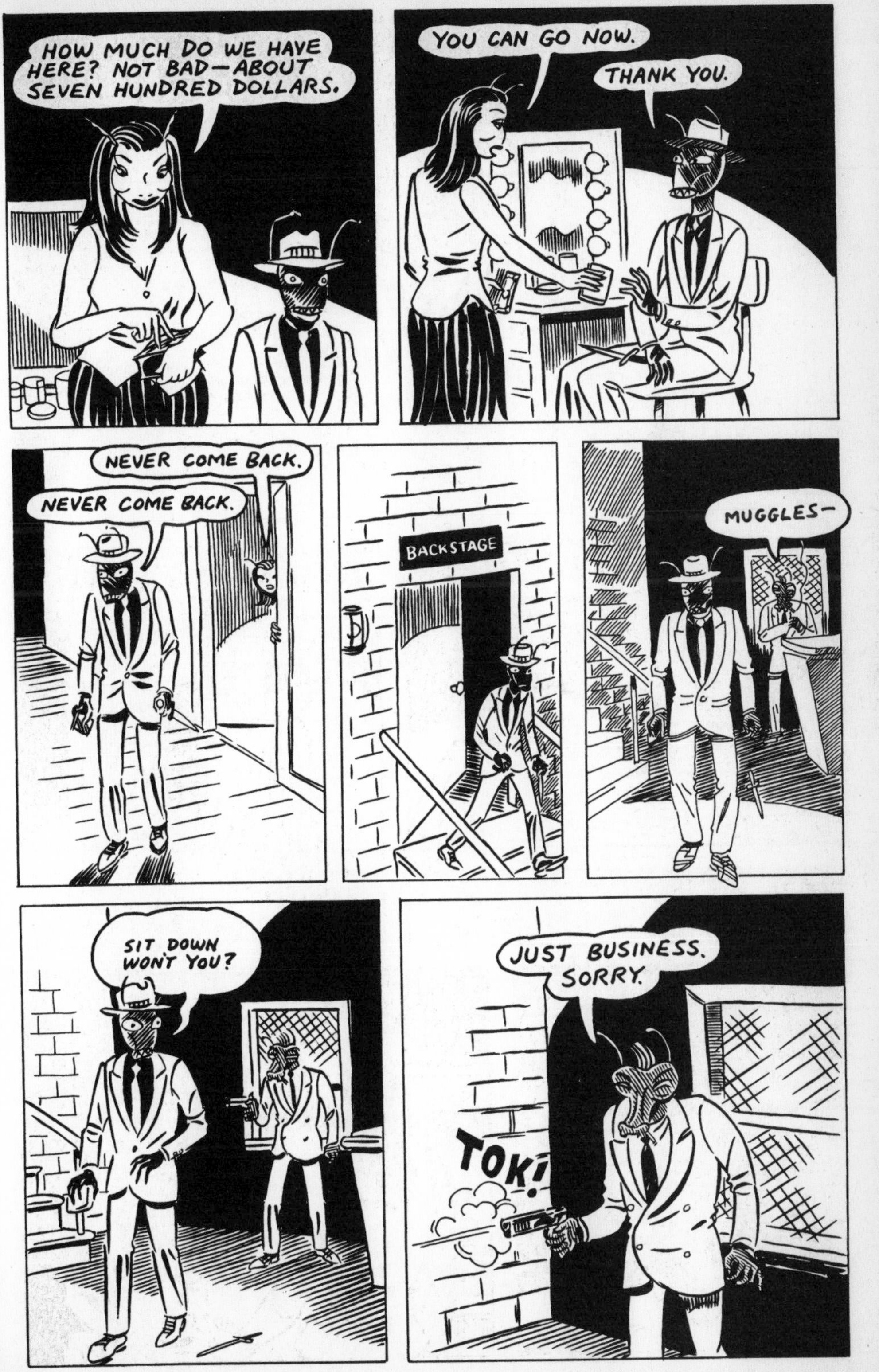
HOW MUCH DO WE HAVE HERE? NOT BAD—ABOUT SEVEN HUNDRED DOLLARS.
YOU CAN GO NOW.
THANK YOU.
NEVER COME BACK.
NEVER COME BACK.
BACKSTAGE
MUGGLES—
SIT DOWN WON'T YOU?
JUST BUSINESS. SORRY.
TOK!

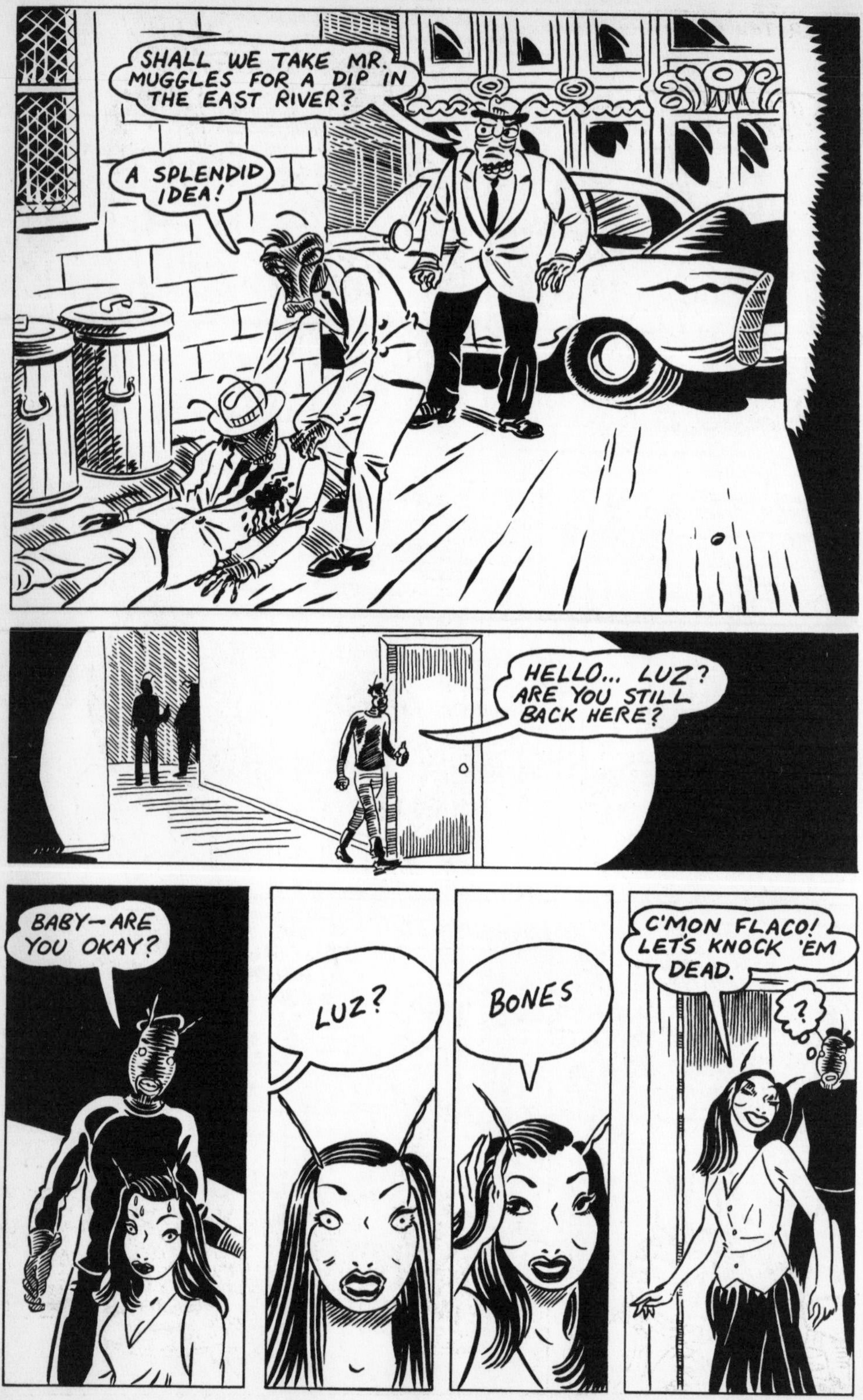
SHALL WE TAKE MR. MUGGLES FOR A DIP IN THE EAST RIVER?
A SPLENDID IDEA!
HELLO... LUZ? ARE YOU STILL BACK HERE?
BABY—ARE YOU OKAY?
LUZ?
BONES
C'MON FLACO! LET'S KNOCK 'EM DEAD.
?

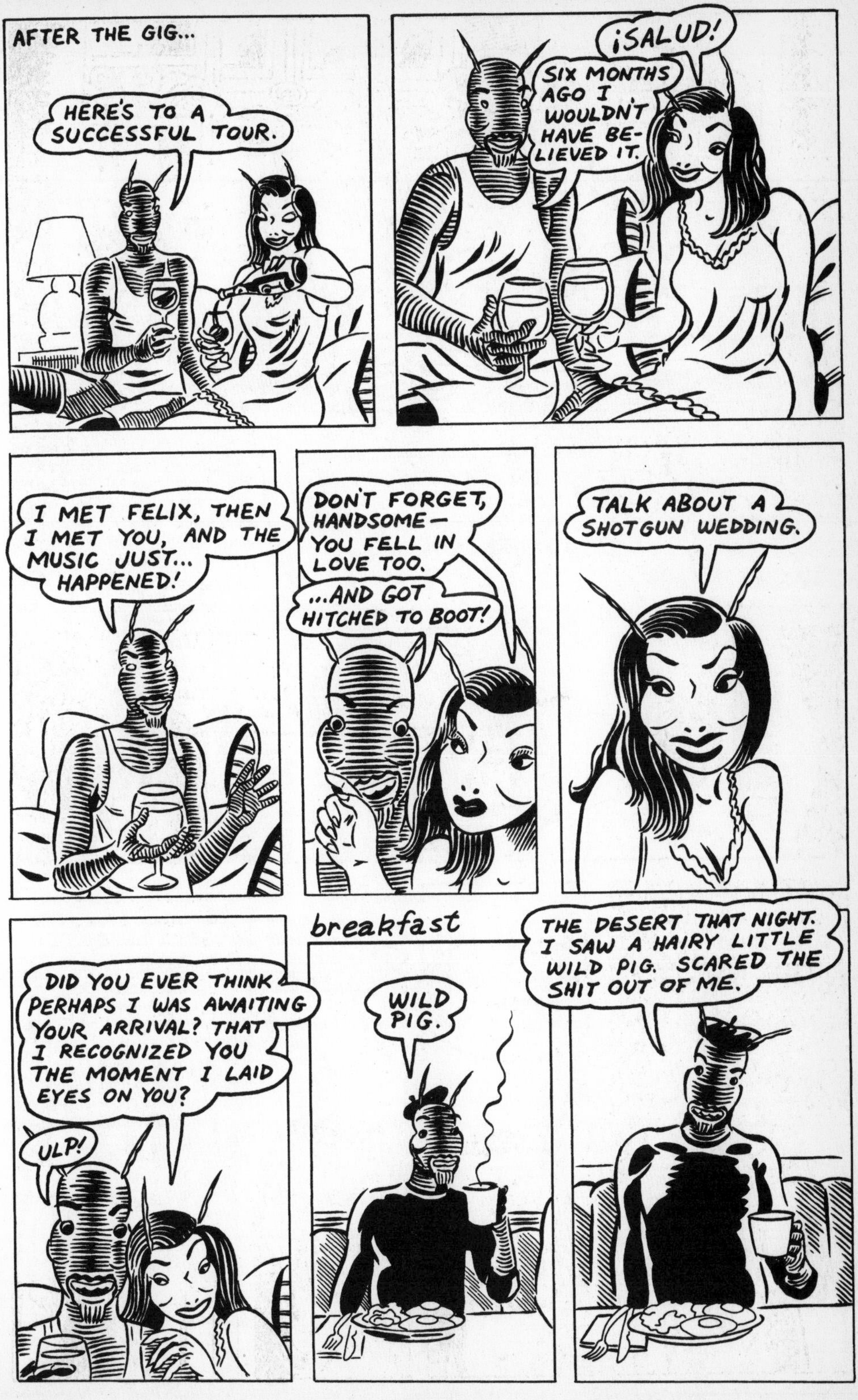

AFTER THE GIG...
HERE'S TO A SUCCESSFUL TOUR.
¡SALUD!
SIX MONTHS AGO I WOULDN'T HAVE BE-LIEVED IT.
I MET FELIX, THEN I MET YOU, AND THE MUSIC JUST... HAPPENED!
DON'T FORGET, HANDSOME— YOU FELL IN LOVE TOO.
...AND GOT HITCHED TO BOOT!
TALK ABOUT A SHOTGUN WEDDING.
DID YOU EVER THINK PERHAPS I WAS AWAITING YOUR ARRIVAL? THAT I RECOGNIZED YOU THE MOMENT I LAID EYES ON YOU?
ULP!
breakfast
WILD PIG.
THE DESERT THAT NIGHT. I SAW A HAIRY LITTLE WILD PIG. SCARED THE SHIT OUT OF ME.

WAS THE LITTLE PIG FRIENDLY? MAYBE HE JUST WANTED TO PLAY.

...OR PERHAPS PIGLET KNOWS SOMETHING YOU DON'T

I'D SAY FURRY PIG HAS A PLAN FOR YOU.

ACCORDING TO LEGEND, BOAR IS THE TOTEM OF THE SHAPE SHIFTER. AND YOU JUST TRANSFORMED FROM A JAZZ MAN INTO THE ECLECTIC R&B AVATAR.

THAT LITTLE PIGGY CHASED YOU RIGHT INTO MY CLUTCHES.

mmm hmm

MEXICO

SO—YOUR BONES WILL BE GONE FOR A MONTH?

JUST LONG ENOUGH TO RECORD AND PLAY SEVERAL DATES WITH BUGHOUSE.

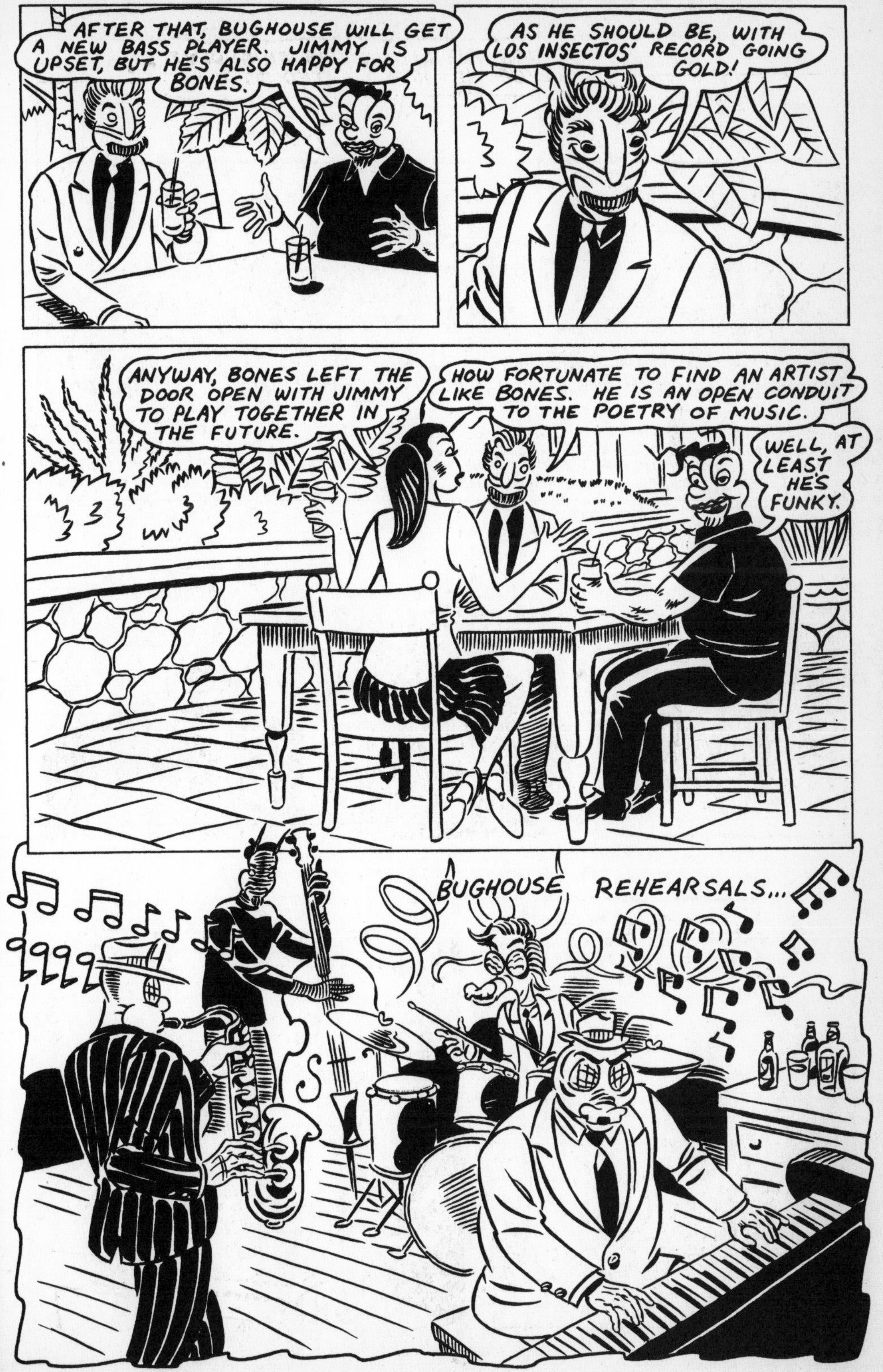
AFTER THAT, BUGHOUSE WILL GET A NEW BASS PLAYER. JIMMY IS UPSET, BUT HE'S ALSO HAPPY FOR BONES.
AS HE SHOULD BE, WITH LOS INSECTOS' RECORD GOING GOLD!
ANYWAY, BONES LEFT THE DOOR OPEN WITH JIMMY TO PLAY TOGETHER IN THE FUTURE.
HOW FORTUNATE TO FIND AN ARTIST LIKE BONES. HE IS AN OPEN CONDUIT TO THE POETRY OF MUSIC.
WELL, AT LEAST HE'S FUNKY.
BUGHOUSE REHEARSALS...

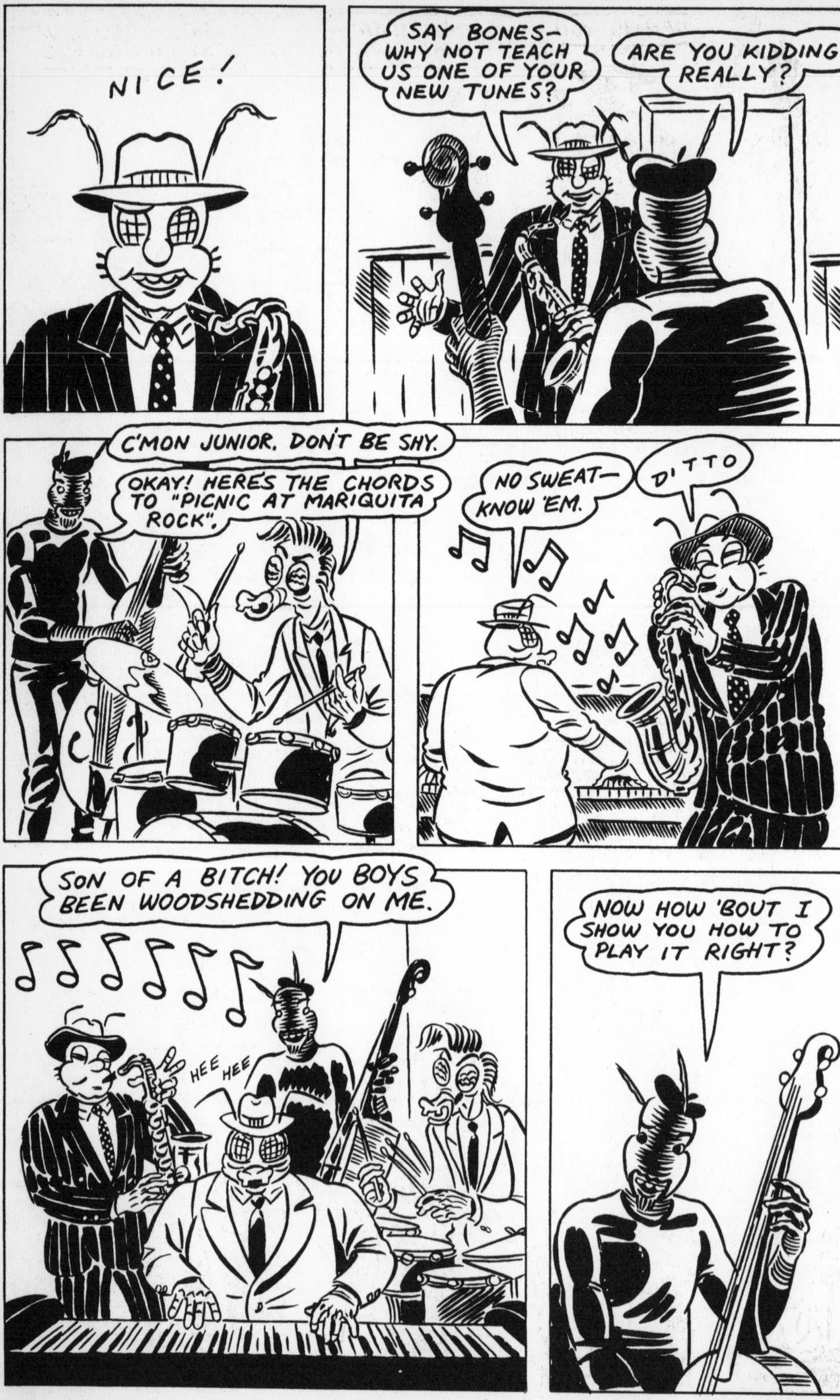
NICE!
SAY BONES— WHY NOT TEACH US ONE OF YOUR NEW TUNES?
ARE YOU KIDDING? REALLY?
C'MON JUNIOR. DON'T BE SHY.
OKAY! HERE'S THE CHORDS TO "PICNIC AT MARIQUITA ROCK".
NO SWEAT— KNOW 'EM.
DITTO
SON OF A BITCH! YOU BOYS BEEN WOODSHEDDING ON ME.
HEE HEE
NOW HOW 'BOUT I SHOW YOU HOW TO PLAY IT RIGHT?

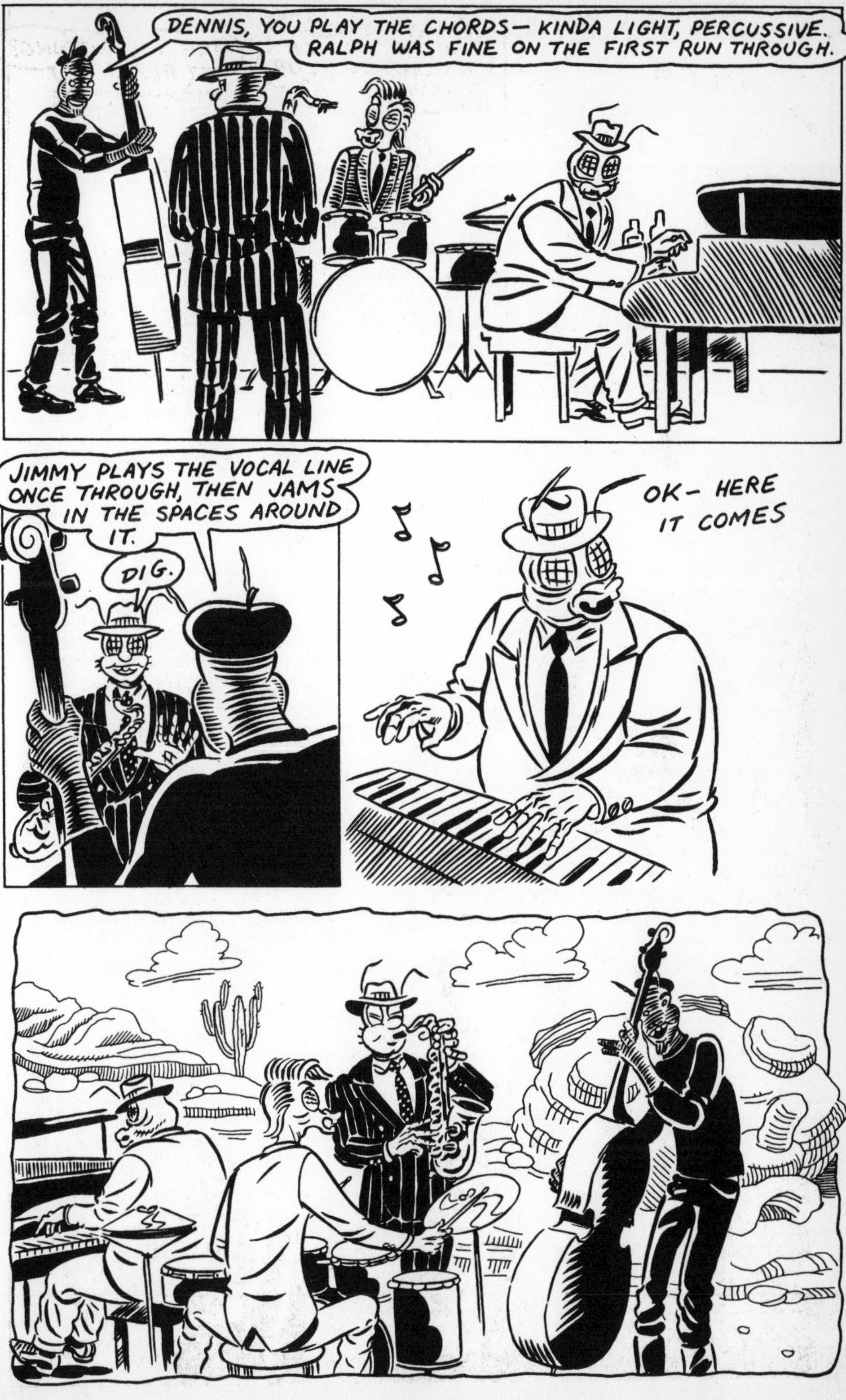
DENNIS, YOU PLAY THE CHORDS— KINDA LIGHT, PERCUSSIVE. RALPH WAS FINE ON THE FIRST RUN THROUGH.
JIMMY PLAYS THE VOCAL LINE ONCE THROUGH, THEN JAMS IN THE SPACES AROUND IT.
DIG.
OK- HERE IT COMES

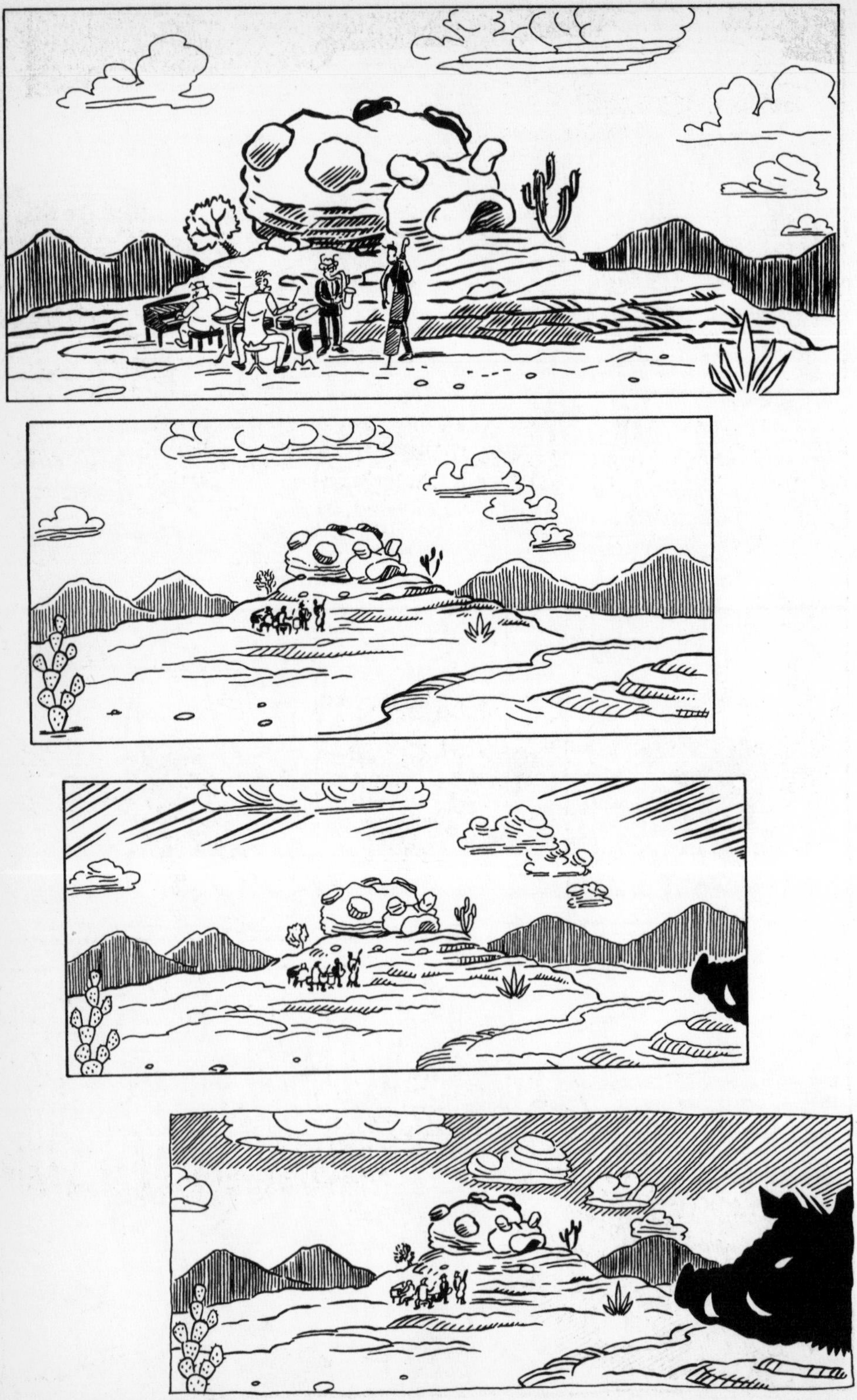

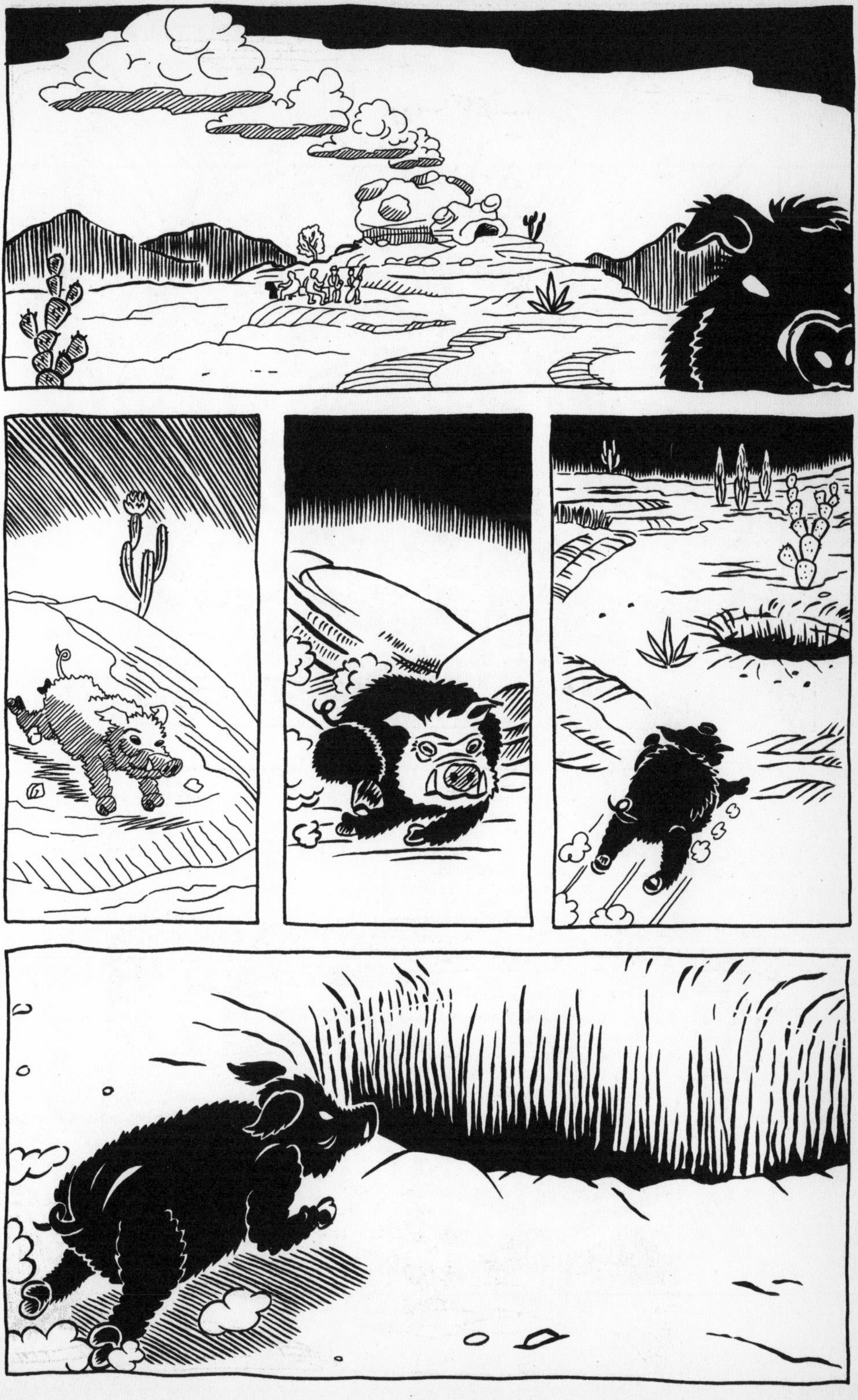

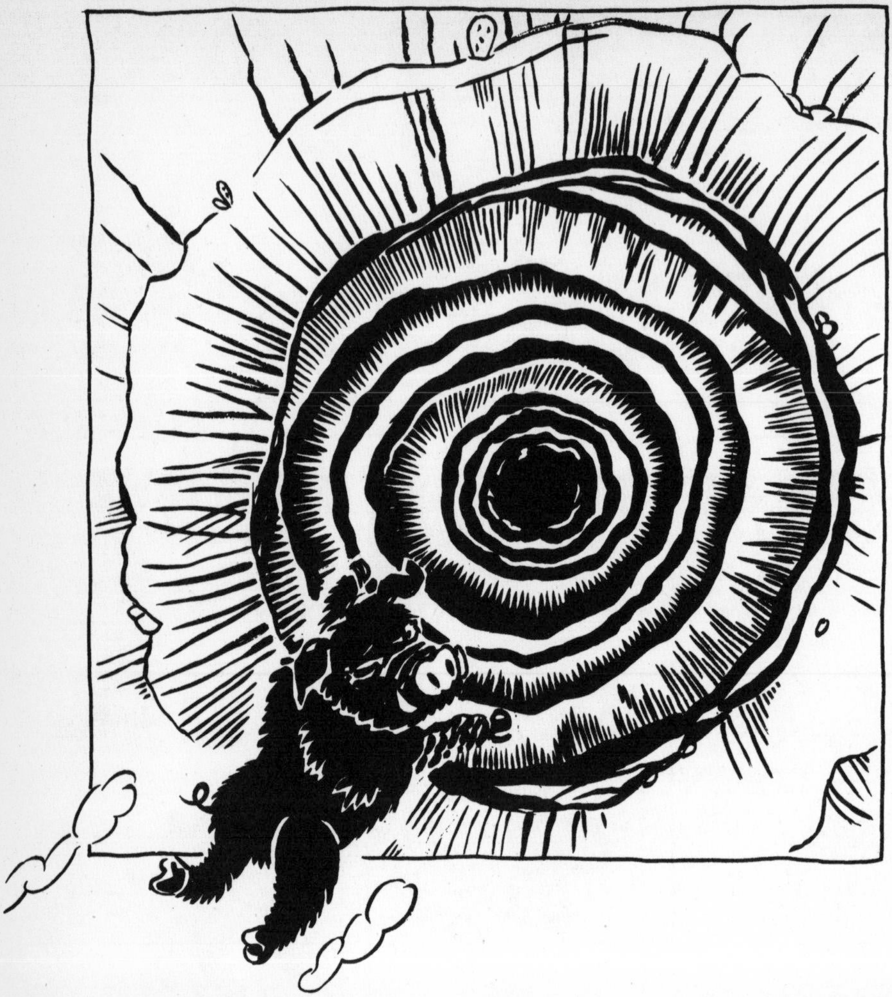

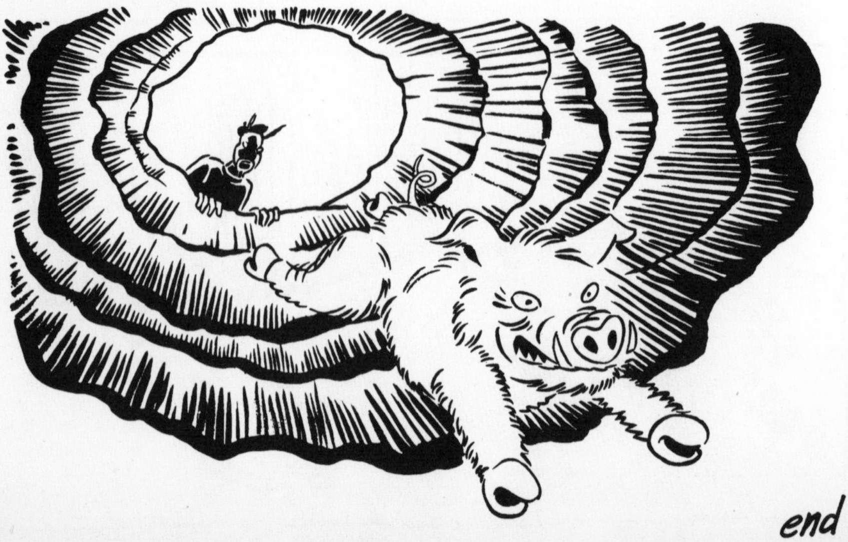
end

author's note

Bones the bass player has come of age—on the surface, this is the subject matter at hand. The youngest member of the be-bop jazz band Bughouse, Bones could already be considered an accomplished individual, yet here in *Baja*, he is transformed into an avatar of an exciting new hybrid music. Oh, and he falls in love. But hold on, let's scratch below the surface. Is Bones really the main character of *Baja*? Or is it some other person—or place?

This work grows out of my love and fascination for the people, landscape, culture and language of Mexico. My wife Serena and I have visited south of the border several times, notably for a six month trek in '97. While the look and feel of *Baja* is heavily influenced by these travels, it is by no means an accurate depiction of what I found there. In fact, I beg the indulgence of the people of Mexico for my presumption to set a fiction in your sublime land. While my enthusiasm is obvious, it's a fair bet that I've barely scratched the surface of a true Mexico. My visual reference for the look of the *Baja* would be the jewel-like city of Guanajuato (and to a lesser degree, the southern city of Oaxaca).

Baja was written and drawn over an almost two year period from August '99, when I wrote the first draft over a leisurely breakfast at the Café Galeria in Guanajuato, to earlier this afternoon, the final day of June 2001 when I inked the last page here in good old Oaktown, California.

I'd like to thank Serena Makofsky for soulful support and crackerjack proofreading, Chris Staros for his brilliant editorial direction, Brett Warnock for his impeccable graphic eye and wonderful enthusiasm, and Jenny Makofsky and Jeff Roysdon for friendship and moral support. Thanks to the Graphic Artist's Guild for jump starting my awareness of the issues and challenges facing professional artists (gag.org). If you put burritos on the table with your cartoons (or graphic art), you owe it to yourself to join the Guild. Finally, I'd like to encourage a visit to my website, bugcomix.com, where among other things, the reader will find information about purchasing the original art for *Baja*.

Steve Lafler
Oakland, California

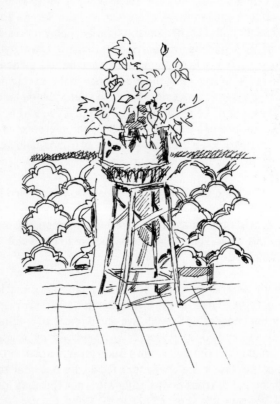